LESSONS IN LOVE

A Study Abroad Novel

JESSICA PETERSON

ALSO BY JESSICA PETERSON

FOLLOW ME, Y'ALL!

- Join my Facebook reader group, The City Girls, and hang out in one of the coolest spots on the internet. I'm biased, but I'm also pretty thrilled by how awesome the people in my group are.
- Follow my not-so-glamorous life as a romance author on Instagram @JessicaPAuthor
- Follow me on Goodreads
- Follow me on Bookbub
- Like my Facebook Author Page

CHAPTER ONE

August
Madrid, Spain

I clutch the scrap of paper with trembling fingers. The address I've scrawled on it in purple felt-tip pen is smeared with sweat; the paper feels fuzzy, worried by my hands as I've stumbled through Barajas International Airport.

The taxi driver, a nice-looking dude with stringy blond locks that stream from a receding hairline, glances at me in the rearview mirror.

"Um," I say, tears stinging the backs of my eyes. Years of Spanish go out the open window as I struggle to remember how to say *fourteen* and *street* and *I'm so sorry I'm an idiot*. I've practiced saying my señora's address a hundred times on the plane. I've even coached myself on the proper Spanish accent, perfecting the soft hiss of *c* and *s*.

Sweat trickles down the gutter of my spine. Spanish words and phrases dart through my head like blinking fireflies, going dark just when I think I've caught one.

For the first time, I wonder what the hell I was thinking

1

when I decided to study abroad for a semester in Spain. I am not ready for this. While I've managed to slip through high school and college classes on the strength of my written Spanish, it's obvious my speaking skills are gringo-level—and that is being generous.

I've always wanted to study in Madrid, mostly because I'm a huge art history nerd and the museums here are some of the best in the world. Seeing, in the flesh, the masterpieces of my favorite artists—Goya, Dalí, Picasso—along with the country that inspired them is going to be the coolest thing ever.

But even though art history is my jam, I have yet to discover any *real* jobs you can land with a major like that. Considering Mom and Dad kindly but firmly told me I'm off the payroll the day I get my diploma, I needed a more practical major with good job prospects.

So like most Meryton University students, I am an economics major. Along with a solid GPA, it will help me nab internships that will lead to a well-paying job after I graduate —consulting, maybe, or investment banking. I also chose it because, let's be honest, peer pressure is a bitch, and I don't want to be left behind by my super smart, and super competitive, classmates.

Unlike most Meryton students, however, I'm not very good at econ. In fact, my GPA tanked ever since I declared it as my major last year. Which is why I plan on getting a tutor through the Meryton in Madrid program this semester. I'm hoping they can help me slay the business classes I'm taking, and maybe the one or two art history classes I'll sneak in before I settle into my I-banking track for good.

But if I can barely mumble a coherent word in Spanish, how the hell am I going to pass, much less slay, classes that cover sophisticated economic theory— classes taught in one hundred percent Spanish? I doubt even the best, most dedicated tutor can teach me to speak an entire language in a handful of months.

The taxi driver is waiting.

"Um," I say again, my voice wavering. "Por favor, voy a . . . um . . . quatro, no, no, catorce . . ."

The driver turns around and offers a small smile of sympathy. He nods at the scrap in my hand, and with a sigh of relief I pass it to him.

"Gracias," I say. "Muchisimas, muchisimas gracias."

He turns back, looks down at the address. "Ah, vale. Veinte, veinticinco minutos con el trafico."

That I understand. Twenty, twenty-five minutes with the traffic.

Okay.

I settle back in my seat, let out a breath. *Okay*. I look forward to twenty-five minutes of relative peace before I face the second trial of my study abroad adventure: meeting my señora. I have been warned she speaks "little to no English."

Just the thought of it makes my stomach clench. Social situations can stress me out—I'm an introvert—and I know interacting with my substitute mom who can only communicate in Spanish is going to take my anxiety to a whole new level. I want to be gracious and kind; I want her to like me. None of those things will happen if I can't speak her language.

The driver fights our sputtering taxi into gear. We lurch into traffic, the driver zipping between cars and mopeds with stupid speed. A tiny blue lighter slides across the dashboard. He snatches it, tucking it into his shirtfront pocket, the pack of cigarettes he keeps there crinkles as he does it.

He does not put on his seatbelt. I take that as a sign that I should definitely put on mine.

My first sight of Madrid is disappointing. We pass through dreary suburbs at lightning speed, faceless building after faceless building whizzing past, a blurry weave of grey and beige. Between buildings, I catch glimpses of the countryside. It is arid, desert-like with pops of intense, eucalyptus green—exactly how I imagined it when I read *Don Quixote*. The sky is hazy with heat.

The warm wind blares through the window. It feels good. Growing up in the South, I'm used to hot weather. But I didn't realize how much I took air conditioning— sweet, sweet air conditioning—for granted.

Looking out the window, I notice everything is a little different here. The cars, for one thing, are tiny, dinged up, and dirty; not a shiny SUV in sight. The people driving them have slightly different haircuts, they wear a slightly different style of clothing; their expressions of road rage are startlingly vibrant to my American eyes. The highway itself is clean and orderly, the pavement several shades darker than at home.

The suburbs eventually crowd into a city. My heart pops around in my chest. Mostly because we are getting closer to my señora's apartment, and I'm already stressed about what I'm going to say.

But my heart also works double time because excitement peeks around the great mass of my anxiety. Madrid is huge— and this part is *beautiful*. The taxi slows down as we run into traffic, giving me a chance to gawk as we inch farther toward city center.

It's not gritty like New York, or shiny and new like Atlanta. Madrid is gorgeously old, and I can see its age in the zigzag of its streets, in the mishmash of Gothic and Mediterranean and belle époque architecture. The mid-afternoon light softens corners and gilds trees. Beautifully dressed people stroll along the sidewalks, puffing on cigarettes or chatting on their phones. My eyes move over the trim, broad-shouldered profiles of the guys we pass—Madrileños. They are the "holy shit" variety of gorgeous.

But as delicious as they look, I wouldn't touch these dudes with a ten-foot pole. After suffering through my first real heartbreak last semester, followed by a string of disappointing hookups I hoped would lead to something but never did, I need a win. And falling for a hot Spanish dude who, if he even likes me back, I'll have to leave in six months' time is definitely *not* a win.

I've been so close to romance, to that happily ever after, before. And then I had to let it—let *him*—go after one semester. It hurt like hell.

I definitely don't want to go through that again.

I want a guy who's going to be around for coffee in the morning and dinner dates at night.

I want a guy who's going to be around for a long, long time. Maybe forever. And by virtue of their hotness, their geographical location, and their seriously superior Spanish skills, these Madrileños are definitely not forever material.

It's intimidating, Madrid, but already I'm picking up on its easy energy, the sense of promise that hangs in the air. If I can ever manage to utter a complete sentence in grammatically correct Spanish, I think I'll like it here.

After weaving in and out of traffic, we make a turn and zoom up a smaller street. I strain my neck to look up at the stately white apartment buildings we pass. The neighborhood looks nice. Very nice. The bustle and noise of the city recedes the farther we move up the street, until at last the driver darts into an open parking spot in front of a blue paneled door.

I brace my hand on the back of his seat to keep from lurching forward.

"Aqui." The driver points out the window. "Calle de Villanueva, numero catorce."

Oh God.

I'm here.

My home for the next six months. Whether I'm a gringo or not, I'm here, four thousand miles from home. There is no turning back.

The driver motions to the meter, and I dig my monopoly-sized Euro bills out of my wallet. My mind races as I try to calculate the tip. *Shit*, there are no single bills, I'd forgotten the Euro dollar is a coin.

Shit shit shit.

My hands are shaking again, and I end up shoving an enormous tip into the guy's hand because my brain isn't working and I feel like I'm about to burst into tears. He grins and hops out of the car, helping me with my enormous suitcase.

He drops it at the door. I say thanks in halting Spanish, and he speeds away, muffler coughing in protest.

I glance down at the scrap of paper he placed in my palm. *Calle de Villanueva, 14, second floor*. I look up at the door. I am so nervous I feel sick.

But the sun is hot on my head and shoulders, the heat from the pavement radiating up my legs. I probably look like a hot mess, and smell like one too. I can't remember ever being so exhausted; I need a siesta, stat.

I push the door open, dragging my suitcase behind me. Its wheels clack against the marble floor. The air in the small, shadowed foyer is cool, like jumping into a pool after that sweaty cab ride.

There is a quaint, fragile-looking elevator in the middle of the room. I slide back the *Titanic*-esque gate, and barely manage to squeeze into the elevator beside my suitcase. I press the button and after a minute the elevator jerks into motion, moving slowly, *slowly*, to the second floor.

And all of a sudden—three airports, four awful airplane meals, and eighteen hours after I left home—I'm staring down my señora's door.

Swallowing my heart, I knock.

I hear the *rut-tut-tut* of a dog's nails against the floor-boards, a bark, a woman's voice, and then the door opens, revealing a petite blonde woman with kind brown eyes. There's a frazzled look about her, or maybe I think that because she's trying— and failing—to hold back a giant German shepherd by his collar.

"Chiquitin!" she implores. "No, Chiquitin, no!"

But Chiquitin gets the better of her, wrangling from her grasp. He pounces on me, teeth nicking my chin. I let out an embarrassing sound, something between "hola" and a stran-gled cry for help.

No one told me there would be a dog. A mean, employed-by-the-department-of-corrections dog.

My señora starts to holler, and eventually she manages to wrestle Chiquitin away from me. He barks, she slaps. I wonder if I'm going to faint.

Then she turns to me.

"Vivian?" she asks, smiling. It sounds like *Vee-vee-an* when she says it. I kinda like it. I wonder if I can ever hope to live up to this exotic version of myself.

I manage a smile. "Si. Me llama Vivian. Um. I'm. Uh. Encantada, Señora."

I *think* that's how you say "nice to meet you." I think.

I hope.

She manages to wedge back the dog, and steps out into the foyer to give me a hug. A quick *kiss kiss* on each cheek, and she pulls away, introducing herself as Stella. She picks up pretty quickly on the fact that my Spanish isn't so great. She speaks slowly, using hand gestures. I appreciate her kindness.

The following hour is a blur. After locking Chiquitin in a bedroom, Stella shows me around her apartment. It is lovely, dressed-up without being stuffy. The floor, wood parquet lovingly marred by generations of use, creaks as we move through each room: a small kitchen—no oven—a pretty bathroom, a well-worn living room with couches huddled around a TV.

There is no air conditioning in any of the rooms. It's got to be close to one hundred degrees outside.

I try to engage Stella in conversation. I want to let her know how much I love her apartment, how much I appreciate her hospitality. But I'm really feeling the jet lag now, and my brain seems to short-circuit anytime I need to say something. Either I can't think of anything to say at all, or I do but I can't remember how to translate it into Spanish.

I end up using dumbed-down phrases that make me sound like a total tool. "Que bella!" (I'm pretty sure that's Italian, but whatever), "muchas gracias", "es preciosa" ("it is precious" or maybe "it is pretty") Gah!

By the time the tour ends and Stella shows me to my room, I want to die of embarrassment. Exhaustion too. She asks if I'm hungry, if I'd like anything—maybe a glass of wine to celebrate my arrival?

I decline as politely as I am able, which is to say, not well at all. Stella leaves me to unpack, closing the door quietly behind her.

I look around the small guest room. It is spare, but cozy. A pair of huge casement windows are thrown open onto a silent courtyard. It is so damn hot in here I can hardly stand it.

I dig my phone out of my backpack and fall onto the trundle bed. I call my parents, and when my mom answers the phone—she sounds relieved, excited to hear from me—a lump forms in my throat. She asks about my flight, and about Stella. I rush her off the phone, telling her I need to unpack; telling her *yes*, Mom, really, I'm okay, just tired.

I set the phone on the desk beside the bed and fall back onto the pillows. I should unpack, I should set up my computer to proofread my econ take-home before I turn it in tomorrow, I should take Stella up on that glass of wine.

I cry instead. I turn my head away from the heat of the window and let the tears roll down my temples, soaking the pillow.

I let the homesickness roll over me, a great stone weight that settles on my chest. Even though I've been away at college for the past two years, I'm pretty close with my family. I love going home for breaks and holidays, love not having to wear shoes in my own shower, love sleeping in my own bed in my own room. Most of all I love hanging with my mom and my dad and my brother, the four of us slurping Mom's Sunday night spaghetti and meatballs around the well-worn kitchen table. Because home—we live in Charlotte—is less than a two-hour drive from campus, I rarely go more than a month without seeing my family.

But other than Mom and Dad's potential visit to Spain around Thanksgiving, I have no plans to see them the entire six months I'll be here in Madrid.

Six months.

How in the world am I going to make it six months here?

And how am I going to pass my classes if I can't speak the damn language?

CHAPTER TWO

Later That Evening

I crack open an eye. For a minute I forget where I am.

I am sticky with sweat, the heat of the room swelling around me. I take it as a sign I had a good, PTFO-style nap.

Light—less ardent now, more golden—slants through the windows. It is unfamiliar, this kind of light, and so pretty. I can hear the dull whine of a blow dryer through an open window across the courtyard. People getting ready to go out on a Saturday night.

It's Saturday, August 29. The Saturday I've been looking forward to for my entire college career.

The Saturday I land in Madrid.

It comes back to me in a rush—the flight, the fraught cab ride, Stella and *Chiquitin, no!* and the weight of my homesickness. I don't know what to feel first.

My hair rustles against the pillow as I turn my head to look at the mattress set flush against mine. Maddie, my roommate for the semester, is going to laugh when she sees it. Our marital bed. She doesn't land until tomorrow morning; I can't *wait* for her to get here. Not only because she speaks fluent Spanish—she spent a summer in Colombia during high school—but also because she's one of my besties for the resties. We met freshman year, when we lived two doors down from each another in the same dorm. Mads is not only an excellent person, but she's funny as hell too. I have no doubt she'll make me laugh off my homesickness over an enormous jug of Spanish wine.

My phone vibrates on the desk beside the bed. It's a text from my friend, Katie—a sorority sister who is also doing Meryton in Madrid this semester—asking if I'd like to meet up later tonight at a bar. A few people in our program are getting together for our first night out in the city.

A spark of excitement catches in my chest. We've all heard about Spain's ridiculous nightlife. The eight-level discoteca—sounds so seventies, I know—the clubs that stay open until six, seven in the morning, revelers rubbing elbows on the Metro with men in suits headed to the office. Our program director back at Meryton told us our señoras will not only tolerate us stumbling home at 6 a.m., they *expect* it. "It's part of the Spanish cultural experience," she'd said.

A cultural experience I'm all too glad to partake in. Being twenty years old in the States is kind of a bummer, considering I can't even get into a bar. But here? I can get into a bar, and for the first official time I can order an official drink.

Pretty exciting stuff.

Besides. I'm sure seeing some familiar faces will help alleviate my homesickness. I can't help wishing I were back home at my parents' house tonight, grilling out in their backyard.

I suck in a breath at a violent stab of longing. Oh, America, I've barely been gone a day and already I miss you like crazy! I will myself to blink back the tears. There are friends to see, and sangria to be had. No time for more crying.

An hour later, I emerge from my room, dressed to

impress. I have a feeling the clothes I wear for a night out in Durham are a lot different from what people wear to dance in a discoteca in Madrid, but I give it the old college try.

I hear Stella in the kitchen down the hall. Just as I turn in that direction, a *tut-tut-tut* sounds behind me. I simultaneously break out in a sweat and into a run, but Chiquitin, that wily bastard, is already on me. He nips at my bare heels, causing me to teeter on my wedges. My hands scrape at the walls for balance as I make an awkward run for it. I must look like the too-stupid-to-live heroine from a horror movie, but I don't care. The last thing I need right now is a prison dog taking a juicy chunk out of my ass.

Stella must hear my distress, because she comes flying out of the kitchen, hissing admonishments at Chiquitin. He, in turn, merely nips at me harder, until Stella yanks him away and throws him behind a closed door.

Wiping her brow, she turns to me and apologizes for her dog's behavior. She is speaking quickly, and I only catch about half of what she's saying. I focus so hard on translating that when it's my turn to speak, I haven't thought of a response in English, much less in coherent Spanish. So I resort to my doofus-like pantomime of her beautiful language, stuttering something about "un perro" (a dog) and "no te preocupes" (don't worry about it).

It's traumatizing. Somehow I convey to Stella that I'm going out with friends. She smiles, and tells me not to worry about getting home too early, just use the key she gave me; I am free to come and go as I please. And, oh! Here is her cell phone number, in case I need anything or there's an emergency.

The second my feet hit the sidewalk, the hand that's been squeezing my heart relaxes. I hate having nothing to say in a conversation; it's like being caught with my pants down. I *have* to work on my Spanish. Otherwise I'm going to give myself a heart attack trying to say "thanks for this delicious dinner" to my señora.

It's still hot, but the afternoon has faded to a beautiful evening. This is my favorite time of day—these hours just before dark, when the air cools and the light is bruised shades of orange and purple and blue, potent with possibility.

Sometimes I think the anticipation of the night ahead is even sweeter than the night itself.

Maybe it's the way Madrid smells. It just smells . . . different. I can't explain it. It's a combination of scents—the heat of the sidewalk, the yeasty smell of bread, diesel—that permeates everything. It's not unpleasant; it just gives Madrid a very distinct sense of place. It's a constant reminder that I'm in a foreign country, thousands of miles from home. There's something very old-world about the smell, ancient even. Occasionally, when I walk over a grate or manhole, it gets potently medieval.

I try to play it cool and look like I know where I'm going, but I end up glancing at the map on my phone every ten seconds anyway. I grew up in the 'burbs, and Meryton's campus is in the middle of a medium-ish-sized town, so this city thing is new to me; I'm more than a little intimidated by the buzz of traffic and people that surround me. Eventually I manage to hail a cab. It's easier this time around. I merely need to say the name of the bar and we're zooming through the city.

The driver lets me out at the mouth of a long, wide alley. It's throbbing with people and sound. Young, attractive Madrileños, their skin glowing with a fine sheen of sweat, spill out from bars and gather around quaint café tables; I can hear the scrape of metal chairs against the cobblestones. The driver motions to the alley, and says something about a bar on the left.

My heart is pounding as I move through the crowd. The

sting of cigarette smoke hangs in the air, mingled with the sweeter, almost potent smell of sangria. People laugh, they chat in rapid-fire Spanish.

"Vivian!"

I turn at the sound of my name, and a second later Katie is jumping on me like a baby monkey, pulling me into a tight hug. I cannot describe the happiness I feel at the sight of a familiar face. I'm smiling so hard I feel it in my eyeballs.

"Oh my God," I say. "Oh my God, Katie, I am so happy to see you."

Katie pulls back. As usual, she's got her laid-back boho thing going on, a strappy paisley dress hanging off her wiry frame. She's adorable.

"So?" she asks. "How is it?"

"How is what?"

She smiles. "Everything."

"All right," I say, looking around. "A little overwhelming, but all right."

"A little overwhelming?" Katie laughs. "Girl, fifteen minutes ago I was sobbing outside a head shop in the Spanish hood. I took the wrong train on the Metro and got totally lost."

"Oh my God." It seems I've started repeating dumb phrases not only in Spanish, but in English too. "Are you okay?"

"Better, now that you're here." She loops her arm through mine. "C'mon, mujer, let's get our bebida on. We're right over there."

She leads me around the corner to another alley, this one slightly smaller but just as crowded with bars and beautiful people. A few guys check Katie out as we pass. No one looks twice at me, though. I'm used to it; I'm never the girl that gets the guy.

Still, it stings.

I hear snatches of English as we draw up to a long table surrounded mostly by guys. I recognize a few of them from Meryton, others I haven't seen before. Mismatched pitchers of sangria crowd the table, along with a couple pints of half-finished beer.

"Viv Bıngley!" a familiar voice calls out. I turn my head to see Alberto Montoya gesturing to the empty chair beside him. I bite my lip against my smile; it's really starting to hurt.

Al is in a fraternity my sorority mixes with a lot back at Meryton. He is cute, charming, and hella smart; to say he is excellent is an understatement. Considering the fact that *nobody* dates—our campus is very much dominated by a hookup culture—Al is something of a legend for making the very first chick he met at freshman orientation his girlfriend. They've been together ever since.

Al stands to give me a hug, and that's when I see the guy sitting next to him.

For a split second our eyes meet over Al's shoulder. My stomach does a backflip. This guy is *cute*; like, one-look-and-I-feel-my-face-go-up-in-flames cute. His eyes are slate blue, and warm with laughter; they are a handsome foil to the freckles that dot his nose and cheeks. He's got a movie star jaw and deep, shapely smile lines that frame his nose and mouth.

I don't know, but there's something about him—the wild licks of his dark hair, maybe, or his crisply pressed white button-down shirt, undone at the neck—that makes me think he's Madrileño. Guys at Meryton don't dress like Prince Harry.

And they sure as hell don't look at girls like this. Like they want to say hello and make you laugh.

A slow, tingling wave of awareness moves up my spine, trailing goose bumps in its wake. It's strange, this feeling, and new. The physical sensation echoes in my head, causing my thoughts to scatter in a starry rush.

"Viv," Al says, turning to the Madrileño beside him. "Meet my cousin, Rafael. He's from Madrid, so he's going to show us all the good spots tonight. Rafael, this is my friend Vivian. We're in the study abroad program together."

I swallow, hard, and venture another glance in Rafael's direction. I can't think of anything else to do, so like an idiot I wave. "Hi, Rafael."

Rafael stands—oh, dear Lord, he's tall, a head taller than I am—and before I can so much as blink he's leaning over the table and pressing a kiss onto both my cheeks.

I blink, my body ringing with the pleasant shock of such an intimate, unexpected gesture.

The kisses themselves are killer. But it's the way he smells that really gets me. He smells delicious, like just-showered boy, a hint of woodsy aftershave. If it was socially acceptable, I would lick his neck.

"Mucho gusto," he says, his Spanish as crisp and intimidatingly perfect as his shirt. "And please, Vivian, call me Rafa."

Rafa. It's like a Spanish pirate name. A *sexy* Spanish pirate name.

I like pirates.

I feel my stupid smile tugging at the edges of my lips. "Rafa," I say, trying it on for size. I dig it. "Nice to meet you."

A split second of silence settles between us as Rafa looks at me. And keeps looking. I can't tell if it's awkward, the silence, or if I like it. All I know is I feel warm, a little giggly even.

All I know is I got a lot less homesick all of the sudden.

Al glances from me to Rafa and back again, a smirk playing at the corner of his mouth. "Vale." He claps his hands together. "Viv, the sangria is amazing—we're all on our second, so you gotta catch up."

"Thanks," I say, tucking my hair self-consciously behind

my ear. "Make it a heavy pour, if you don't mind."

Al arches a brow as he fills a glass to the brim. "Long day?"

"Very."

He presses the glass into my hand. Pieces of fruit float on the sangria's inky surface. The sweet scent of brandy fills my head. This is going to be good.

I start when Rafa taps his glass against mine. "Salud."

"Salud," I say, meeting his eyes. It's like a sock to the gut. They are so damn pretty.

I surreptitiously check him out as I sip my sangria. His perfect white shirt is tucked into a perfect pair of dark jeans; he's rolled the sleeves up to his elbows, revealing tanned, muscular forearms. One hand is in his pocket, an appropri-ately Prince-Harry-ish frayed bracelet wrapped around his wrist. His understated brown belt doesn't match his shoes—tan suede—but somehow it works.

Oh, how it works.

I look away, my face burning, and catch Katie staring me down from across the table. There's a knowing gleam in her eye.

Talk to him! He is hot! she mouths, fanning herself.

I sip my sangria. It's delicious, not too sweet, not too strong, refreshing in the heat. I sneak a glance at Rafa. He's still standing next to me, the smell of his aftershave tickling my nostrils. My cheeks burn with the memory of his kisses.

I'm usually pretty shy around guys. Which probably explains why I don't have many notches in my belt—and why, at twenty, I am still in possession of my v-card. I was ready to "do it," as Maddie says, with the last guy I was with. A guy I thought I loved, a guy I thought loved me. But when I told him I was ready, he told me about the girlfriend he had back home. You know, the girlfriend he'd been dating the whole time he and I were together.

The girlfriend he was in love with.

Needless to say, the sex didn't happen; apparently he didn't consider oral sex cheating, but *sex* sex was where he drew the line.

After that, along with some seriously unsatisfying hookups, I swore I wouldn't allow myself to get burned again. No more casual dating, no more booty calls. I want respect, I want real, and I want romance—the forever kind.

The kind I definitely can't get with this guy—this ridiculously handsome Spanish pirate. He is way hotter than any guy I've ever been with or talked to. I should be intimidated. I should be crawling back into my shell.

But I don't. He is so far above my pay grade it's laughable. He is some random Madrileño dude, and chances are I'll never see him again. If I do, I can order a bucket of sangria and drown myself in it.

I have nothing—absolutely *nothing*—to lose. Which makes me feel a hell of a lot less shy.

I look back at Katie and lift my shoulder, grinning. *Okay.*

"So, Rafa," I say, turning to him. "You and Al are cousins?"

He nods, swallowing. "You know Alberto's father is Spanish, yes?"

"I do," I say. "But Al was born in New York."

Rafa nods again. "Our fathers are brothers. My uncle moved to the United States to marry a woman he met at university there—those are Al's parents. I went to live with them one summer to take classes at NYU. And now Alberto comes to live with us in Madrid while he studies."

I sip my sangria. "Is that how you learned to speak English so well? Yours is very good. Way better than my Spanish."

He grins, and oh, *God*, it tears a hole in whatever stuff my heart is made of. "Thank you. Students in Europe, we learn a lot of languages. Alberto definitely helped with my English, though. My family goes to New York to visit them—Al and my aunt and uncle—a lot." He drains his glass. "Is your Spanish really so bad?"

I scoff into my sangria. "It's abysmal. I can read it, and I can write it, but I can't speak it. I get, like, flustered, trying to translate everything in my head. And my accent—yack."

Rafa reaches for the pitcher on the table. "Yack?"

"Um," I say, rolling my lips between my teeth. "You know, like. Throw-up? Puke? Just . . . totally gross."

He laughs as he refills his glass. He looks up, his eyes meeting mine, questioning me. I nod and hold out my glass. He fills it.

"Totally gross?" he says, setting the pitcher back on the table. "I think you are exaggerating. But it will help if you practice. All of the time, practice. Don't think so much. And one night, when you have too much sangria, your Spanish will come."

"I didn't know sangria had such magical powers."

Rafa shrugs. He takes a pull from his glass. "If it can make me dance like Justin Timberlake, then it can make you speak perfect Spanish."

I don't know if he mentions JT on purpose, but I appreciate the common cultural reference nonetheless. It helps me get my bearings, helps me feel a little less lost.

I bite my lip. "Justin Timberlake. Really?"

"Really." He meets my eyes. His spark with mischief. "Justin Timberlake. It has been confirmed by people I trust."

I don't think Rafa needs much sangria at all to dance well. He's one of those guys you can tell knows his way around a dance floor.

One of those guys you know is good in bed. Not that I have much practice. But still. There's something so . . . quietly virile, confident about him. He would know what he was doing, and he would do it *well*.

"Well then"—I tip back my glass—"I definitely have some

catching up to do."

"I have a lot of practice with sangria," Rafa says. "I am telling you the truth. I am very confident in this—that you will be speaking perfect Spanish by the end of the semester. Not only that. I think you will dream it too."

"That's a tall order," I say. "You have to be pretty fluent to dream in a different language."

He smiles. The curving lines around his mouth deepen, making him look boyish. Cute. "I think you can do it."

"I think your confidence is misplaced," I say. "But I could use all the motivation I can get, so thanks."

"Vale," he says, using that quintessentially Spanish word with a thousand meanings I have yet to tease out. I've heard it described as "okay" or "cool," but it seems like neither of those words fully capture its nebulous spirit. "You just need a little bit of courage, and you will figure it out."

"Vale," I reply. I'm teasing him now, flirting. Openly. It's fun.

"See?" He nods at the glass in my hand. "Already, the sangria is working."

"Hardly. Words are easy. But sentences?" I shake my head. "I need a lot more liquid courage for those."

Over the rim of my cup, I notice Al is talking to some of the other guys from Meryton, his back angled away from Rafa and me; we're cut off, secluded in our own little corner. The sounds and smells of the alley crowd surround us, but it feels like we're alone, somehow, the space between our bodies vibrates with silent warmth.

At least *I* feel it vibrating. I wonder if Rafa does too, or if my sudden interest is unrequited. My crushes are usually—no, they're *always* unrequited. No one ever looks twice at me. Ever. It's like I'm always the bridesmaid, never the bride; I can make out with a guy, but he never seems to feel the fluttery things I do.

"You came to Spain to learn our language," Rafa says. "But what else will you study while you're here?"

I swallow my sangria. "Last semester I declared Economics for my major, so I'll be taking business classes, mostly. A literature class. And then I'd love to take some Spanish art history, but I don't know if I'll have room on my schedule for such a guilty pleasure. I don't want to take too much on."

"Guilty pleasure?" Rafa arches a brow. "Madrid has some of the best art museums in the world. There is nothing guilty about studying it, especially while you are here."

"Have you?" I ask. "Studied art history, I mean."

"I have. Quite a lot, actually. You too?"

"Some classes. I love it, I do, but you can't really do much with an art history major, so. Yeah." I sip my sangria. "Who are your favorite painters?"

"I like all the Spanish painters. Goya. Velázquez." He says the names in his perfect, succulent Spanish, and never in my life have I heard anything so sexy. I make note of his pronunciation, his accent; *Goy*-ja, Vel*ash*-quez; I will have to practice them later. "El Greco, even though he isn't really Spanish. We still like to take credit for his genius. But my favorite? My favorite is Sorolla."

I blink. Sor-*roya*. "Sorolla? I don't think I've ever heard of him."

Rafa grins. "You must take art history, then, if only to learn of Sorolla. There is a whole museum here just for his work. I think it's the best museum in all of Spain. I'll take you there—even if you don't take the art history class, you must see it."

I don't know if it's the sangria—it's probably the sangria—or the way Rafa is looking at me, but the backs of my knees begin to tingle. It's my first night in Madrid, and here I am, getting my buzz on, talking my favorite thing—art!—with an incredibly good-looking Spaniard. He's probably only offering to take me to this museum because he's drunk and trying to be polite, but I don't care. However fleeting it may be, even if nothing comes of it, I am in love with this moment.

And that's got to count for something.

"The Sorolla Museum," I say. "I'll have to remember that. Thanks for the tip."

"You're welcome," he replies. "I hope you like it here, Vivian. I know coming to a different country can be hard. The language, the food, all the little things—I remember being so homesick in New York when I first got there I called my parents ten times a day."

I look down at my cup—almost empty now—and slowly nod my head. "I admit I've cried a little bit today. And by a little bit, I mean a lot."

"It will get better," he says. "You are here for, what, five months?"

"Almost six."

"That probably feels like a lifetime right now, yes?"

I scoff. "It does, actually. That's what I was crying about."

When I look up, he is standing closer—there are people behind him now, pressing him toward me—and my heart skips a beat. Our eyes meet. His reflect the soft glow of the lamps outside the bar. It's getting dark, the air around us velvety. That tingle behind my knees moves to a full-on rush.

"I'm biased," he says, "but if you do it right, Madrid is an easy place to fall for. Mostly because I live here."

I smile and he smiles and the look in his eyes is so lovely it makes my stomach hurt in the best, *best* way.

"So where are you taking us tonight?" I ask. "I've heard pretty amazing things about the nightlife here. I mean, no pressure or anything."

He glances at his watch, a simple round face on a well-worn leather strap. "The bars close in a few hours. Then we will head to the discotecas—on Saturdays the best is Ático. We can start there."

"I hope Justin Timberlake will be making an appearance."

He holds up his glass, lets it tilt in his fingers. "He'd better. Otherwise I'm going to embarrass myself in front of my new friends."

I laugh. "Yeah, somehow I think you're going to put us all to shame, with or without Justin's help. I'm not proud of my white girl moves."

"But you're not afraid to show them off," he says, eyes sparking as he grins down at me.

"Hell no," I say. "Especially not after I've had a little— more than a little—sangria."

"Excellent." Rafa taps his glass to mine. "Welcome to Madrid, Vivian. I'm glad you're here."

What does that mean? It probably doesn't mean anything. We're just talking, drinking, maybe flirting too.

Even if Rafa did mean something by that, I came to Madrid to work my ass off, pull up my GPA, and enjoy some art. I didn't cross an ocean to start a relationship—a hookup, a romance, whatever—that inevitably won't last. I promised myself no more hookups, no more heartbreak.

Still.

I find myself grinning back at Rafa, wondering what his wine-stained lips would taste like.

Wondering if his kindness is a ploy to get in my pants, or if it's genuine. It makes no sense, I know—guys this good-looking, guys that smell this wonderful, don't need to be nice to awkward American girls like me to get some.

But there's something about Rafa—something about his eyes, his calm, easy demeanor, that makes me think he's different.

"Thanks," I say. "I'm glad I'm here too."

And I mean it. I do.

CHAPTER THREE

The line to get into Ático snakes down the street and around the corner. I fall back a bit, intimidated not only by the size of the line, but also by the mind-bendingly beautiful people who wait in it. The men, their hair as slick as their smiles, look like fútbol players who just stepped out of a cologne ad. The women, too, are meticulously coiffed, fashionable while revealing just the right amount of leg, of cleavage, of midriff.

I look at my rumpled skirt and tank top. I'm glad I worked all those extra hours at my nannying job this summer. I have some serious shopping to do.

The throaty *thump thump thump* of a baseline echoes through the discoteca's open doors. A ribbon of anticipation unfurls inside my chest. I wasn't lying when I told Rafa I'm not ashamed of my white girl moves. I love to dance. Like, *love* it.

I'm pumped Rafa's into dancing too. I hope I get to dance with him—even just for a little bit—so I can say I raved with a studly Spaniard. And on my first night in Madrid, no less!

Like lost little ducklings, the other Meryton kids and I follow Rafa to the front of the line. He greets the bouncer like they're BFFs, clasping his hand and pulling him into a hearty bro hug. Rafa speaks to him in low, languid Spanish, motioning to the small knot of us behind him.

The bouncer nods and unhooks the velvet rope in front of the doors. With a final wave of thanks to the bouncer, Rafa makes his way through the door.

"C'mon, guys," he says, looking over his shoulder.

He looks right at me.

My stomach does its hundredth backflip of the night. Even if I manage to become friends with Rafa over the next six months, I don't think I'll ever get used to the vibrant shock of his blue eyes.

To the way he makes me feel like I'm the only girl in the room, even though we're surrounded by crowds of fast-talking, good-looking Spaniards.

My face flushes with heat. I'm not drunk, not by a long shot—I was too busy talking to Rafa to drink much sangria—but I feel light, buoyant, the balloon inside my chest expanding with every look and every grin I share with Rafa.

I offer him one now, and he grins back.

"Are you all right?" he asks.

"Better than all right," I say. "Thanks for getting us in—that line was no joke. I was ready to cough up that twenty Euro cover charge too."

"You don't pay a cover," he says. "Not when you're with me."

"Now you're just bragging."

"I am," he says, those shapely lines around his mouth deepening along with his grin. "This is my city. I want to show it off to you."

It's dark inside Ático, the floor vibrating in time to the bass. We follow Rafa through a narrow entry passage that opens onto an enormous dance floor.

My breath leaves my lungs. I have never in all my sheltered twenty years of life seen anything like this. Mirrors line the walls and ceiling; enormous chandeliers hang above our heads, dripping with crystals that reflect the pulsing rainbow of colored lights that flash from the DJ booth. Hundreds of people fill the space, hands above their heads as they dance and laugh and sloppy make out.

The DJ bangs out some Maroon 5, and it's hard—really hard—not to start dancing myself. We follow Rafa around the edge of the dance floor, slipping into a separate room where it's much quieter. A bar is set into the far wall; everything, from the walls to the bar stools to the bar itself, is lacquered a sinister shade of black. Sultry red lights shine from ceiling. It feels like we're in a vampire bordello-slash-bar. I dig it.

Rafa and Al belly up to the bar. I stand back a few steps, digging into my crossbody bag for some cash. When I look up, I catch Rafa looking at me. This time he's really *looking*. His gaze flicks down the length of my body, lingering on my legs, and flicks back up again. It could be a trick of the red light, but I think I see his eyes darken.

Heat spikes through my center. I'd be lying if I said I didn't like his attention.

His appreciation. He's checking me out, and I kinda dig it.

"What would you like to drink?" he asks. His perfect skin glistens in the red light, emphasizing the sharp angle of his jaw.

"I was going to buy you one, actually," I reply. His blatant interest emboldens me. I take a step forward, my heart unsteady in my chest. "You got us in here for free. I owe you."

"You don't owe me anything." Rafa leans his elbow against the bar, tilting his head. "You can get the next round, maybe. I'm buying this one."

"Seriously? You guys paid for all the sangria—"

"Vivian." He levels me with a look. "Let me do more bragging, yes? I want to buy you a drink."

I roll my lips between my teeth. Truth be told, I'm taken off guard. Guys at Meryton never—*never*—offer to buy you a drink. Sure, they'll give you a plastic cup of jungle juice at a party, but beyond that, you really can't expect much.

I also have no idea what to order.

"Okay," I say. "What are you drinking?"

"Cuba libre," he replies. He takes a step to the side, making room for me beside him at the bar. "Rum and Coke. D'you want one?"

I slide up next to him. We're so close I can smell his aftershave again. "Sure. Yeah. That sounds perfect, thank you."

Rafa waves down the bartender and orders our drinks. I watch with my heart in my mouth. The way the words roll off his tongue—God, what I would give for him to whisper sweet Spanish nothings in my ear all night.

Naked.

His teeth nicking the place where my ear meets jaw.

I blink, willing my pulse to slow its rapid-fire pace. This is not my first rodeo. I should have more self-control. I should know better than to fantasize about things that will never, ever happen.

But Rafa is even more handsome up close. I'm transfixed by the way his collar slides down the sinewy slant of his throat as he leans across the bar to grab our drinks. Our fingers brush as he hands me the glass; the contact is fleeting, but my fingers feel singed, sparks of awareness emanating from this tiniest bit of contact.

Rafa grins as he touches his glass to mine. "Careful," he says. "They make them very strong here."

I take a sip. The sticky burn of rum sluices down my throat. I pull away, let out a pained breath. "Holy shit, Rafa. That's, like, nuclear."

"Here." Before I can protest he takes the drink and turns back to the bar. He asks the bartender to add more Coke (somehow I understand this). A minute later, Rafa is pressing a fresh cocktail into my hand. This time his fingers linger on mine. "I hope that's better."

Reluctantly I pull away to take a sip. "It is. Much better, thank you. You didn't have to do that."

Rafa waves me away. "Es un placer," he says. It is a pleasure.

For a minute I wish I knew how to stay "the pleasure is all mine" in Spanish, but on second thought I'm glad I don't. I haven't had nearly enough to drink to excuse cheesy lines like that.

The bar is getting crowded. Rafa puts his hand on the small of my back (!!!) and guides me to the middle of the room. I want his hand to stay there, I want his hands all over me, I want to hook my finger in the collar of his shirt and pull him against me. My body thrums with the desire to do all these things.

I drink my Cuba libre instead.

"So what do you think?" Rafa asks, motioning to the room. "Is it what you expected?"

He stands in front of me, hand in the pocket of his jeans, neck bent at a delicious angle as he waits for my reply. He is standing close, really close now, and I can't help but wonder if he wants to touch me as much as I want to touch him.

"It's pretty amazing," I say, looking around. "Thanks for being our guide. I know you probably didn't want to spend your Saturday night showing a bunch of stupid touristas around."

Someone slides behind Rafa, and he takes a step closer to me to move out of the way. He holds his drink above my head as his body presses against mine for one delicious, electrifying moment, his hips at my hips, my arms sandwiched between us. The warmth of his body seeps into my forearms, and I have to close my eyes against the deluge of need that swells inside me. I feel it everywhere: in the pit of my stomach, between my legs, in the black rioting space of my head. We fit so well together, Rafa and I.

Of course our bodies fit so damn well together.

"Sorry," he says.

"It's all right." I open my eyes and he's looking down at me, brow creased with concern.

"You sure?" he asks, stepping back.

I manage a smile. I wonder if he can feel the hammering of my heart. I hope, sincerely, that he can't. "I'm sure."

"Good." He leans down, lowers his voice. "And you are not a stupid tourista, even if you think your Spanish is yack."

His breath in my ear, the way he smells, the things he's saying—I can't take it.

I'm fighting back a grin and losing.

"What?" he asks, a smile splitting his face. "Did I get it right? *Yack*?"

I laugh. "Yes. You got it right. But your line would have made Justin cringe."

"It wasn't a line." He glances over his shoulder when a new song—Skrillex, it sounds like—comes on. "Speaking of Justin, do you want to dance? One sip of the nuclear rum and he is ready, I think. What about your white girl?"

"My white girl is always ready."

One side of his mouth curls into a half-grin. "But can she keep up with Justin?"

"Probably not."

"I will see what I can do to help." He looks over my head. "Alberto! Vamos!"

The other Meryton kids crowd around us. Al sidles up to Rafa; Rafa meets my eyes, smiles as he tilts his head toward the dance floor. Just as we begin to move in that direction, I glance to my left and Katie is there, wagging her eyebrows.

"What?" I ask.

"You know what," she says, nodding at Rafa. "*Him*. He likes you."

I follow her eyes to the outline of Rafa's broad shoulders and back. He cuts a dashing figure from every angle, apparently. My heart clenches.

"No he doesn't."

"Yes, Vivian, he does."

"He's just trying to be nice to his cousin's friends," I say. "He could probably smell my homesickness from a mile away."

"Exactly," she replies. "It's so damn cute watching him try to make you feel better. Chica, it's obvious. He's chatting you up, buying you drinks, flirting with you about yacking and JT . . ."

"Hey," I say, pinning her with a glare. "You were listening to our conversation?"

"Of course I was!" Katie draws back, offended that I would think otherwise. "I had to make sure you didn't need rescuing. Besides, we were all so curious. Especially Al. He said he's never seen his cousin look at someone the way he looks at you."

I look away, hoping Katie can't see the thrill that moves through me at this little offhand nugget of info.

"Look at him," I say. "I mean, he's ridiculous. That's why I started flirting with him in the first place—because he's so far out of my league. I don't have a chance in hell, Katie. And even if I did, you know I'm looking for something . . . more. Something that lasts. In my experience, guys like Rafa don't really like to stick around."

She shrugs. "Maybe you're right. But from what I'm seeing —and hearing—you've got this hombre wrapped around your finger. You don't need to do anything with him except have fun. I mean, a little public make-out sesh never hurt anyone."

"I'm pretty sure sloppy dance floor face sucking has hurt *everyone*."

"Doesn't mean you shouldn't do it." Katie pats me on the back. "Vaya con dios, amiga."

Go with God, my friend.

We're on the dance floor now, the music so loud it swallows me whole. Our group is inundated in a sea of writhing bodies, their push and pull making it difficult to move through the crowd. The smells of sweat and alcohol hang heavy in the air; the strobe lights flash, freezing the crowd one frame at a time; the floor and my breastbone vibrate with every drop of the bass.

I. Freaking. Love. It.

Katie starts to dance and I do too, the two of us holding our drinks above our heads as we shimmy our way across the floor. I can't really see much, and holy hell it's starting to get crowded, so I just try to keep sight of Katie's blonde knot at the crown of her head. I think I see Rafa up ahead, leading us to the middle of the club.

The music is so good it's intoxicating. You couldn't *not* dance if you tried. It's a mix of techno and pop and a little bit of rap. I have no idea who the DJ is, but he's amazing. No wonder Madrileños stay out dancing until breakfast. I'd skip sleep for this too.

There's a hand at my arm, and I turn to see a greasy-looking guy stumble toward me. He steps on my foot—*ef* that hurt—but when I try to pull away he only moves closer, cutting me off from my friends. He's huge, his biceps straining against the bejeweled sleeves of his T-shirt; he smells like gin and stale cigarettes. Lovely.

I try to pull away again, but this time he grabs my ass and tugs me against him, grinding his hips into my belly. I put my hands on his chest and push, but to no avail. He's got me trapped.

Panic flutters inside my chest.

"No gracias!" I shout, but either he doesn't hear me or he's ignoring me. His hard-on works an eager circle into my hip. I manage to pull my hips away from him, but then his hand is sliding up my leg, underneath my skirt. I tell him no, no, *hell* no.

His hand doesn't stop its progress up my leg.

My panic no longer flutters. It's a full-on adrenaline-laced surge that pushes my heart into my throat.

I hit the first thing I think of.

I thrust my knee between his legs with all the force I can muster, hoping to put his dick back where it belongs. "*No!*" I say.

He falls back with a yelp of pain, hands cupping his crotch. I take advantage of his momentary weakness and shove him away, smoothing my skirt as I catch my breath.

That's when the guy looks up at me, gaze flashing with resentment. Behind him his friends have stopped dancing; they're staring me down.

Shit.

I gotta get out of here, stat. I look around for my friends, but I don't see anyone I recognize. I've lost them. I set down my drink on a nearby table and keep looking.

One of the guys reaches for me. I dodge his grasp, whirling around on my heel.

And thump nose first into a familiar white button-down shirt.

"Oh God," I breathe into the *V* of Rafa's bare chest. Relief douses my panic. "Oh, thank God."

He looks down at me, his blue eyes dark with concern and something else. Something that burns a shade hotter than anger.

"Are you all right?" he asks, shouting above the music so I can hear him.

I nod my head. "I'm fine. I'm okay. Just a little shaken up, I guess."

He searches my face. "They did not hurt you?"

"No." I nod my head at the offending creeper, still bent over. "I hurt them."

One side of his mouth kicks up in a grin. "Tienes cojones, mujer."

"What?" I shout.

"I said you have balls, woman!"

"Oh," I say. "I guess so, yeah. But he doesn't. Not anymore."

Rafa laughs, his lips parting to show a sliver of white, even teeth. "Your aim, it is very good."

"Thanks. I try."

"Give me one moment, Vivian," he says. His touch featherlight, he tucks me behind him, stepping forward so that he forms a wall between me and the handsy jerk-offs.

It's a tight spot. People move behind me, elbowing me farther into the enticing slopes of Rafa's back. His muscles glide and bunch against my chest; I can smell him, the spice of his aftershave. I squirm, embarrassed, but Rafa doesn't seem to mind; he reaches around and holds me against him, his fingers splayed on the small of back (again!!!). The ties of his bracelet tickle the inch of bare skin between my top and skirt.

His shoulders vibrate as speaks to the guys. He's a head taller than his captive audience, and I have no doubt he could seriously hurt any of them if it came to blows. But Rafa doesn't raise his voice, he doesn't point or gesture, he doesn't lose his cool. He just talks, a steady stream of lethally beautiful Spanish. I can't hear most of it; I catch snatches, a few joders, one que te folle un pez.

I have no idea what any of it means, but even as the creepers flick their hands in front of their faces with lewd violence, they back off.

Rafa's hand moves from my back down the length of my arm, his fingers firm but gentle as they slide down my skin and grasp my hand. I see stars.

He looks at me over his shoulder. Our faces are inches apart. I notice, for the first time, how full his lips are. Inviting. Mine grow warm with curiosity.

"Ready to dance, white girl?" he asks.

I smile. "I'm following you, JT."

I try not to think about my hand in his. The pleasant scratch of his calloused palm against mine, how his hand swallows my own.

I try not to think about it, because it doesn't mean anything.

It doesn't mean what I want it to.

Rafa starts to dance as we approach the circle of my friends, moving his head in time to the beat. Al is here, dancing his adorable little Euro dance. He smiles at me; I smile back, my cheeks glowing with heat. I wonder what he knows about his cousin that I don't. *He said he's never seen his cousin look at someone the way he looks at you.*

Katie is here too, her eyes wide with relief when they land on me. "Where did you get lost? We went looking but we couldn't find you!" Her gaze moves up to Rafa. "But I'm glad *some*one did."

She sees that we're holding hands. She looks right at me, as if to say *I told you so*.

I shrug, shy, suddenly.

Our hands still clasped, Rafa brings our arms over our heads. He swivels his hips, slowly, slowly, as he spins me around to face him.

I was spot on: holy *mother* this guy can dance. He moves

fluidly, easily, as if he's been dancing to Beyoncé remixes since he was in diapers. For a hot minute I'm horribly self-conscious. I wish I had guzzled a gallon of magical sangria. I can't white girl dance, not in front of Rafa.

I am not prepared for how overwhelmingly sexy he is when he dances.

But he doesn't give me a chance to second guess myself. Singing along to the song, Rafa really starts to dance, pulling me closer, closer. *Closer.*

Oh, Lord.

Rafa senses my reluctance. He smiles down at me, curling his fingers around the back of my hand as he pulls me against him, guiding my body into motion with his.

"This okay?" he asks. "I know those putas de madre scared you."

Are you kidding? I want to say. Rafa's touch, his dancing, couldn't be more different from that puta de madre's, whatever that means. ("Bitch of the mother," I think?)

In reply I start to dance too, keeping my gaze glued to my feet. His eyes are on me, I can feel them, but it's easier if I don't look. It's less overwhelming this way.

The feeling of his body moving against mine is . . . everything. I've never felt anything like it. I've never had a guy this delicious all to myself. It's glorious.

And intimidating as hell.

A new song comes on, and Rafa shimmies back, guiding me underneath the arch of our arms. I laugh, loosening up. I can feel it, but I'm not quite there yet.

Good thing Rafa is in no rush. He's patient with me.

I wonder why.

And then I wonder why I'm wondering so much. I start to dance a little harder, biting my lip as I turn around in Rafa's arms, swirling my back against his front. I let go of his hand to hold my arms up; he holds his hand at my waist, my skirt damp from the condensation dripping down his glass.

The song fades into another, which just happens to be one of my favorite songs of all time—a Lil' Jon classic that is, in my humble opinion, the bumpin'-est jam to ever come out of America.

It's just the push my inner dancer needs.

I turn to face Rafa, hooking my finger in the *V* of his shirt. It's as satisfying as I imagined it would be. Singing Lil' Jon's incredibly explicit lyrics, I pull Rafa toward me, my hips working double time. His follow suit, and when we meet it's like a (sexy) bomb goes off.

He smiles, a devastating flash of lips and teeth and eyes. I unravel in his arms, allowing sensation to take over. He's smiling and I'm smiling, and as we move faster and harder, it feels like we're the only people in the room.

We dance like this to the next song and the next. They keep getting better. *We* keep getting better.

His hand brushes my breast as he sets his drink aside.

"Sorry!" he shouts.

I grin. "No you're not."

He gives me a wicked little smile and shrugs.

We keep dancing. This is not the semi-gross bump 'n' grind I'm used to back at college. This is something much, much better. Yes, there's a gratuitous amount of touching, of swiveling hips and shaking asses, but this feels—I don't know, more authentic, somehow. Like we're dancing because we love the music, we love to actually dance, not because we want to dry hump each other as a prelude to hooking up.

Rafa's chest and forehead are slick with sweat that glistens in the purple strobe lights. He tugs at his hair and it stands away from his head in wet spikes. We're both dancing like idiots. He gives me a lopsided grin, as if to apologize.

Puh-lease, I want to say. I start doing a pantomime of my

mom's favorite move—the sprinkler. Laughing, Rafa pulls a move I can only describe as John-Travolta-meets-shopping-cart. It's adorable.

He spins me away from him, spins me close, spins me underneath his arm. He is singing along to the song—it's in Spanish—a smile splitting his face, and I am laughing so hard I might burst. My feet hurt and I'm thirsty as hell, but I wouldn't stop dancing if you told me I could trade places with Kate Middleton. I'm having way more fun than anyone else on the planet right now.

Only when the music gets annoyingly techno does Rafa slow his dancing stride. He holds me against him, my front to his front, our bodies languid as we try to catch our breath. I linger in the circle of his arms, my palms resting on his damp shirt. His heart beats strongly, unevenly into my hands.

I look up at the same moment he looks down. For a minute neither of us does anything except look. I have no idea where I got such cojones—usually I'd need to look away, embarrassed by his attention, by my interest—but I meet his gaze head-on. His gorgeous eyes are full of laughter. Heat too —I see heat there.

Maybe I'm not the only one unsettled by all this touching and laughing and singing.

Maybe Rafa feels what I feel.

Excited. Nervous. Awake. I don't want this night to end.

Rafa takes my hand in his, holding it to his chest. His cheek grazes mine as he dips his head. "Let's maybe take a minute, yes?"

I look at him from the corner of my eye as he pulls back. I nod.

We look around, and our friends have disappeared. Rafa peers over my head, but no luck. We've lost them.

I can't say I'm upset. I'm glad to have Rafa to myself.

I follow his shoulders through the crowd, unable to

breathe around the enormity of want inside me. The back of his hair is a mess of wet points and licks. I want to run my fingers through them, to claim him, even for a second.

We fall through the front doors, gasping for air as if we've been underwater. People mill around on the sidewalk, smoking cigarettes, chatting in small circles. You can cut the air with a knife; it's as hot and humid as it is back home in Charlotte.

I dig my phone out of my purse.

"Holy shit," I say. My voice sounds fuzzy over the ringing in my ears. "It's four thirty! What time did we get here?"

Rafa scrolls through his phone. "A little before one, I think?"

I meet his eyes. "Did we really just dance for four hours?"

It felt like forty-five minutes. If that.

"I know," he says. "Doesn't feel like it, does it?"

"Not even close," I say.

I have a message from Katie; she sent it an hour ago. *Tried to get ur attention but u were too busy speaking body language with Rafael. Al assured me u were ok w/ him. Took cab home with guys. Text me when u are home safe [kissyface emoji] [tongue emoji] [sexy lips emoji] [thumbs up emoji]*

I bite back a grin.

"What?" Rafa asks, looking at my phone over my shoulder. He's standing close enough that our bodies barely touch. The collar of his shirt brushes the nape of my neck. Despite the heat, I resist the urge to shiver.

I press the button at the top of my phone, blanking the screen. "Nothing," I say. "It's Katie. She's just teasing me."

"But she is okay, yes?"

"Yes," I say. I gather my hair in my hand and hold it off my neck. "God, it's hot."

"It is Madrid in August," he says, unbuttoning the next

button of his shirt. He tugs at the fabric, fanning himself. "Are you hungry?"

I swallow, hard. His chest—tanned, taut, smattered with dark hair—peeks through his open shirt. I want to laugh it's so ridiculous.

"Maybe," I say.

"My favorite churrería is very close," he says. "Would you like to go with me?"

I lick my lips. I remember that I really do have nothing to lose. "Only if you unbutton your shirt again. Just one more button."

He looks at me, his face splitting into a slow, knowing smile. He runs his tongue along the inside of his bottom lip. His eyes never leaving mine, he unbuttons another button. He looks like one of those half-dressed dudes on the cover of a romance novel. Dangerous.

Delicious.

He pins me with an amused glare. "Are you satisfied, Vivian?"

"I am."

"Good." He tucks his hands into his pockets. "Let's get some churros. It is the best place in Madrid, I promise you."

CHAPTER FOUR

Despite the late (or early?) hour, the churrería is packed. It's a cute, high-ceilinged spot, its walls covered in gleaming white subway tile. The scent of fried dough cut with the sweeter smell of chocolate envelopes us as we walk through the door. I'm suddenly ravenous.

The line snakes around the perimeter of the room, but it moves quickly. Club-goers like ourselves lean against the counter as they wait to order. Rafa greets the guy behind the counter the same way he greeted the bouncer: handshake, bro-hug, something or another in Spanish. The guy nods at Rafa's nearly-bare chest and laughs. Rafa introduces me as his amiga, *Vee-vee-an*, and I wave hello. The guy looks back at Rafa and smiles, speaking in rapid-fire Spanish. Rafa shrugs, his cheeks flushing with color.

I really, *really* need to work on my Spanish. I want to know what they're saying. I want to know if they're talking about me. I have a funny feeling they are.

The guy hands us wax-paper cones overflowing with churros still hot from the fryer. He gives Rafa a small Styro-foam container I assume is the chocolate. When I try to pay,

Rafa grins at me over his shoulder as he digs a hand into his pocket.

"Maybe next time," he says.

"You said that about the drinks," I reply. "Really, Rafa, I wish you'd let me pay for *something*."

"Next time. C'mon, it is too crowded in here, let's eat outside."

His hands full, Rafa leans his back against the door and holds it open for me. Part of me wishes he would stop being so polite. It might keep the swell of happiness I feel at his every gesture, his every smile, in check. I'm helpless against the onslaught. It keeps coming, wave after wave after relentless wave, and I am all too content to let it pull me under.

We walk a ways off to the side and stop at the edge of the sidewalk. It's quieter here. A gas lamp flickers on our side of the street, putting off shadows edged in gold.

"Is here okay to sit?" Rafa looks down at my skirt. "I do not want people to see something they are not supposed to see."

"I think I'll be okay." I sit on the square curb, tucking my skirt between my legs, just in case.

Rafa sits beside me. Our feet almost touch on the cobblestone street, his suede lace-up shoes dwarf my sandals.

"Have you had churros before?" he asks, setting the Styrofoam container on the sidewalk between us. He coaxes off the lid with a broad thumb. I watch him bring that thumb between his lips, licking off a small smear of chocolate.

Oh dear.

I clear my throat. "Once, in high school. My Spanish teacher brought in the packaged ones—you know, the kind wrapped in plastic? They weren't very good, to be honest."

Rafa makes a face. "Why anyone would eat that stuff, I do not know. Those are not real churros. But these—these are the best."

"So I'm supposed to dip it in the chocolate?"

"Yes," Rafa says, showing me how it's done. "The chocolate—how do you say—completes the churro. Like the icing for a cake."

I smile, dunking my warm churro into the thick chocolate sauce. It takes some handiwork to keep the chocolate from getting all over the place, but somehow I manage to bite off an embarrassingly huge chunk of my churro without staining my shirt.

Rafa watches me, waiting.

"Qué piensas?" he asks. *What do you think?*

"It's delicious," I say around a mouthful of churro. "Like, *really* freaking good."

Rafa was right; the churro itself is yummy, kinda like an unglazed donut. But it's the chocolate that really makes it. This is no ordinary chocolate sauce—it's thick and gooey, just the right consistency for dipping. I'd compare it to a ganache, maybe, or especially decadent hot chocolate.

Rafa smiles, inhaling the last bit of his second churro. "See? I told you. The best churros in all of Madrid. It is our tradition here. We dance all night, and then we get churros before we go to bed."

"In the States we have street meat," I say. "Hot dogs and stuff."

He laughs. "Oh, yes, I've had your street meat. I like it."

"But you don't love it."

"Not like I love churros," he replies. "You have to agree, Vivian, these are much better than your hot dogs."

Tucking into my second—or maybe it's my third—churro, I nod. "Way better."

Rafa looks at me, his grin deepening. "You have chocolate on your face. Here." He points to his left cheek.

Ef. I bring the heel of my hand to my face, trying to wipe it off.

"Did I get it?"

"No," Rafa says. "The *other* left cheek."

I try the other left cheek. Rafa shakes his head. He points to my face. "There."

"Here?"

"No, there."

"Did I get it?"

"No, *there*."

"There where? Where the hell is it?" I'm wiping my fingers all over my face, trying to find this stray speck of chocolate. "God *damnit*, Rafa!"

Rafa is laughing now, and I am too, the kind of laughter that makes my sides ache. I probably look like a murder victim with all this chocolate smeared on my face, but whatever—I'm too busy trying to breathe to care what's going on with my face.

"Here," he says, reaching out. "Let me help you."

He swipes his thumb—that *thumb*—across the edge of my bottom lip. A charge of electricity gathers at the base of my skull and races through my body, sparks flying between my legs. My laughter dies, slowly, and I'm left looking at Rafa looking at me, his fingers hovering above my face, my lips tingling like they'd very much like to be kissed.

It's so ridiculous, I know, something straight out of a rom-com, the manly-yet-charming guy wiping a bit of ketchup, or maybe it's ice cream, off the smitten girl's face. A bit of intense, heated staring ensues, that moment of delicious hesitation before the guy leans in and plants a wet one on his lady love.

Who knew such romantic things happened in real life too? I am in this ridiculous moment *right now*. And I have no idea what to do.

My heart is pounding.

Rafa's blue eyes search mine. His teeth flash between

parted lips. I wonder what he would taste like. What it would feel like to run my tongue along the seam of his perfect lips, to take that bottom lip between my teeth.

Say yes, a voice whispers inside my head. *Let him kiss you.*

I think he's leaning closer. The heady scent of his aftershave envelopes me, and my eyes flick to his lips. Those intimidatingly perfect lips.

I don't know why I do it. I'm embarrassed, maybe; more likely it's fear that has me pulling away, abruptly, my cheeks burning as I finger one of my churros. What if I forgot how to kiss? What if my breath smells? What if my eyeliner is smudged and I look like a raccoon? I am certainly no smitten heroine. I can't afford to be.

I guess the cojones I had at the club have shriveled up and died.

Regret tightens at the back of my throat. I scramble to think of something to say to break the ice that has spontaneously formed between Rafa and me.

"Those guys who were bothering me, back at Ático," I say. "What did you say to them?"

Rafa tucks his last churro into his mouth and crumples the wax paper in his hands. "I told them to leave you alone"—he grins—"in so many words."

"What does 'que te folle un pez' mean? Am I saying it right?"

"Oh, you're saying it right," Rafa laughs, shaking his head. "If you translate it word for word, in English it means 'I hope you go fuck a fish.' Basically our version of 'go fuck yourself.'"

"Wow," I say. I love hearing him say *fuck*. It's face-meltingly sexy. "Wow, that is a lot worse than I thought it was. And way more awesome."

"It is a good thing to remember, yes? For when people bother you. What do you say to guys in English? When they bother you like that, I mean."

I make a sound of amused disbelief, something between "tssshh" and "ha!"

"What?" Rafa asks. "Is it very bad, what you say to them?"

"I don't have to say anything. Guys back at Meryton—well. They definitely don't bother me. They don't know I exist."

Rafa stares at me like I *do* have raccoon eyes. I swipe my fingers under my bottom lashes, just in case.

"I don't believe it," he says.

"Where I go to college, the girls are competitively perfect. Trust me, Rafa, I've never gotten so much as a second glance."

"But that is impossible. I gave you a second glance. And a third. And more than that." Rafa shrugs, holding his knees in the circle of his arms. "I hope you do not mind me telling you this. But I like to look at you."

"I noticed," I say, blushing. It's on the tip of my tongue: *I like to look at you too*. But I can't bring myself to admit such a thing to such a handsome Madrileño. Everyone likes to look at him. What do I matter?

"I will stop, Vivian, if you don't like it," he says. "You know how to tell me to go fuck a fish now."

There will be no fucking of fishes.

I like how he looks at me. A lot.

I really, really regret not going in for the kiss. It was the perfect, most romantic moment, and I ducked out of it like a coward.

I roll my wax paper into a ball. I am full, deliciously so. Rafa holds out his hand.

"Oh," I say, placing the ball in his open palm. "Thanks. You can call me Viv, you know."

Rafa tosses the paper in a trash can and swivels his head to look at me. "But I like Vivian. It is such a pretty name."

"It's pretty when you say it," I reply. "I feel like that *Vee-*

vee-an is my Spanish alter-ego. She chain-smokes and dresses like Coco Chanel."

He smiles. "She splits her time between her penthouse in Barcelona and a yacht off the coast of Cádiz."

"I have no clue where that is," I say, laughing. "But yes. That is *Vee-vee-an* to a T."

"But this Vivian you are now, she is such a good dancer," Rafa says. "And she defends herself very well."

"I got that guy in the balls."

"I noticed," he says. "I like her. You. Just like you are, in this moment. And in that moment too, when you got the guy in the cojones."

If this was any other dude, on any other night, I'd think the things Rafa is saying are nothing more than cheesy lines to get in my pants. I'd think he was laying it on thick, so shameless in his agenda to get laid. A 6 a.m., last-ditch effort with the last girl standing.

But coming from Rafa—how he speaks them, how he looks at me when he says them—these words are sincere. Powerful in their simplicity. Like he has no agenda, other than to compliment me, and make sure I don't have any chocolate on my face.

No agenda other than to have fun on a Saturday night in Madrid.

Herds of scantily-dressed people, heels clomping against the cobblestones, filter past us. They laugh and smoke, and a few couples even put on a show, fondling each other like they mean it. I look up; the sky has faded to grey, just light enough to make out wisps of cloud scudding overhead.

Rafa checks his watch. His skin glows in the soft light.

"It's almost six." He rises, brushing off his jeans. "We should get going if we want to catch the first Metro."

I can't remember the last time I witnessed six a.m. Back on campus, a late night usually meant two or three a.m.; we'd always try to schedule our classes so we didn't have to wake up before nine. Six was no man's land.

I feel badass, frankly, for making it out so late. Everyone else left hours ago.

And still it feels too early for the night to end.

Rafa reaches down and offers me his hand. I take it. He pulls me up beside him, my leg bumping against his. For a minute our eyes meet. I'll never get used to how beautifully blue his are. They are the K.O. punch, every time.

I want to kiss him, badly. My heartbeat thrums through my body. Do I take a chance? Or do I let the night end on this heady, anticipatory, *safe* note? I already count tonight among my most favorite nights ever. Why risk a kiss that could ruin the memory of the wonderful hours I spent in Rafa's company?

It's a classic case of damned if you do, damned if you don't. I'll regret not kissing Rafa. But there's a chance—a very good chance—that if I kiss him, I'll regret that more. Maybe he never wanted to kiss me in the first place; maybe he pulls away, tries to be nice in a horrifically awkward way.

Maybe the kiss is so wonderful I'll start falling for him on the spot. Rafa looks like he would be a lethal kisser, thorough and patient and intense, all at once.

But Lord knows I need to fall for another unattainable guy like I need a hole in my head. I've done the sorta-kinda-relationship hookup thing, and I ended up with a broken heart. I'm terrified of getting hurt like that again. If I'm going to get involved with someone, it's gotta be real, and it's gotta have forever potential.

Rafa, with his handsome smile and panty-dropper charm, doesn't seem like the forever type.

He offers me a quirk of his lips. He hasn't let go of my hand. In fact, his fingers, thick and calloused, slide between mine, locking my palm in place against his. He's still looking at me, his eyes and his face soft.

Kiss him.

"So," he says. We start to walk, hand in hand, down the street. "What did you think of your first night in Madrid? Was I a decent guide?"

I blink. I swallow. I can't concentrate on anything but our hands swinging between us. His touch is gentle and sweet. Around us the air has finally cooled; my skirt ripples in a slight breeze.

I wish I could capture this moment and squeeze it into a bottle, uncorking it whenever I want to feel the way I feel right now.

Kiss him.

"The chocolate incident notwithstanding," I reply, "I'd say it was pretty awesome. You were right about the sangria—it *is* magical. My white girl jammed out. I learned some amazing Spanish swear words—thank you for those."

"Happy to be of service."

"The churros were ridiculous. The music was sick." I look at him. "But as for you . . ."

There it is again, that smirk at the corner of his lips. "Come on, Vivian, you must give me some credit here. Look at this!" He brushes the fingers of his free hand across his bare chest. "I am practically naked, all for you. I am no Justin Timberlake, but I worked very hard on my chest hair, and I think it deserves a little bit of appreciation, yes?"

I slow my pace and he slows too. *Kiss him.*

I look down at said chest hair, peeking through his egregiously unbuttoned shirt. "It is very nice hair," I say. "It's no Austin Powers bath mat, but I like it."

"He is a tough guy to beat," Rafa says. "Maybe when I am older I will be so lucky."

I don't know how we arrived at this topic of conversation,

but I'm over it, I'm over talking, I just want to kiss him. I remember what Katie told me at the beginning of the night. *Talk to him. You have nothing to lose.*

I'm holding hands with Rafa right now because I had the *cojones* to talk to him. Who knows what will happen if I kiss him?

Sure, it could bruise my ego, and my memories of tonight.

But he's looking at me again and oh God those freckles and his shoulders and the dark messy waves of his hair and the way he smells and now he's teasing me about my sweaty palm and running his thumb across the back of my hand and I can't, I can't, I just *can't not kiss him.*

Rafa pauses at an intersection, looking both ways down a deserted lane. There's a tiny little alcove, a quirk in the building's architecture, just up ahead, obscured by a tree. The perfect place for a little late-night make-out sesh.

We cross the street—I'm on the outside—and when we step up on the curb I give Rafa's hand a tug. He turns to face me, the laughter softening in his eyes. My heart is pounding so hard inside my head I think it might explode. I take a step closer.

"Are you okay, Vivian?" he asks.

Not okay. Definitely not okay. But I'm going to do it anyway.

I've never made the first move before—at least not when I was this sober— but I know if I don't just go in for the kill, I'm going to mess it up.

I rise up, slowly, on my tiptoes. Our faces inch closer. He keeps looking at me. I feel the heat of his gaze on the rise of my cheekbones. But I can't meet his eyes, so I focus on his lips instead. The scent of his aftershave hits me and I know I've made the right decision.

Or maybe the worst decision ever.

My body slides up the tall length of his, our clasped hands

trapped between us. I love the solid warmth of his body, the delightful shock of being this close to someone.

And then I kiss him.

I close my eyes and press my lips to Rafa's mouth and I kiss him.

The second I do it, I think *oh my God, what a fucking idiot fish I am, what in the world am I doing, stop now, stop while you're ahead.*

It's excruciating, that first second.

But the second—er, second—is much better, because Rafa starts kissing me back.

His lips melt into mine, slightly parted, perfect for kissing. My heart flutters inside my chest. The kiss is slow and a little timid, like neither of us want to go too far or reveal too much. But I don't mind it. I like slow, especially with Rafa. It allows me to savor every heartbeat, every feeling, every damn delicious thing about him.

Rafa pulls back. My stomach flips. I wait for him to bumble an excuse, to tell me he can't because he has a girlfriend, he has to get home, he thinks I smell.

But when I open my eyes, he's grinning. Relief, warm, spreads through me.

"For a minute, I believed you didn't want to do that," he murmurs. "Back there, after the chocolate incident . . ."

I shrug, bashfully. "I did. I do. I do, Rafa. I just . . . gah, I was just being an idiot."

He brings our joined hands up between us, settling my hand on his chest. I can feel the *pound pound pound* of his heart. Something about it furiously working makes my own skip a beat. I'm the one who is making him feel this way. I'm the one he feels this—whatever *this* is—for.

I look up, startled, a little scared. Rafa brings his hands up to my face, his fingers gliding with erotic ease to rest just beneath my earlobes, in my hair, on my cheeks. He angles his head, his lips hovering less than an inch above mine.

A current of desire rips through me. I have never felt anything like it.

Rafa holds me there, an inch from the kiss I want more than my next breath. His nose brushes mine as he looks at me and looks at me and keeps looking, his eyes glassy with heat. He's making me wait.

"I didn't know if *you* wanted to do that," I say.

One side of his mouth curls into a grin. "Do you not remember? I kissed you first, Vivian."

My cheeks burn with the memory of the quick, sweet kisses he gave me when we first met at the bar.

"But those were polite kisses," I say. "Hello kisses."

"But still kisses. I have been waiting to do it again all night."

He bends his neck and presses his lips to mine. My eyes flutter shut, a poignant rush of sensation moving from where our mouths meet to where my legs do. His mouth moves over mine, opening me to his every stroke, every pull and nick and bite. In a handful of heartbeats Rafa makes the kiss his own, holding my head in the cradle of his hands as he moves over me. He tastes like chocolate, just a hint of sweet sangria.

Behind my closed lids, a confetti of sparks ignite and sparkle.

Whistles and catcalls erupt somewhere behind us. Rafa slows, but his lips never leave mine. He wedges my legs between his own, and in one swift, strong movement, he swivels me around, reversing our positions so that he is between me and the street. I sense him hunching his shoulders forward, blocking me from sight, pressing me into our little make-out alcove.

I don't have time to think or catch my breath. Rafa keeps kissing me, and the kiss keeps getting better. Deeper. Our first kiss was timid, but this kiss—this kiss is anything but. My head spins as I try to keep up with him. He's slow and fast and insistent and soft, all at once. I lose myself in him, my mind a blessed blank. He's just as good a kisser as I thought he'd be.

Better, even. There is something incredibly sexy about the way he moves. He's confident without being overbearing. Yes, the kiss is his, but that means I'm his focus. He lavishes me with attention and care, his tongue working to open me to him, and I open, willingly, wildly.

This is how everyone dreams of being kissed. With abandon. With feeling. I grasp his forearms, my fingers digging into his bare skin as I hold on for dear life.

There is nothing safe about Rafa. Not the way he looks at me or the way he dances or how I feel when he touches me. Definitely nothing safe about the way he kisses me.

But I feel safe with him anyway. Safe to be myself. Safe to kiss him back without worrying about what happens next.

I feel safe because we'll probably never see—much less kiss—each other again. He's way out of my league. And I don't want to fall for a guy I'll just have to leave in a few months. I don't want to get hurt again. I can't bear it.

This is just a kiss, I tell myself.

It's just one kiss he won't remember, and I will try to forget.

Still. There's this rush between my skin and bones that whispers to me, telling me this is no ordinary kiss.

That nothing will be the same after this kiss.

CHAPTER FIVE

Rafa and I sprint through the Metro station. Still delirious from that *kiss*, we giggle our way down an escalator that looks like it's about a mile along. Down here the air is muggy and a touch too warm.

Or maybe it's me that's a touch too warm. I'm a little shaky, dizzy too, like I've had too much caffeine. My heart pops around in my chest.

I follow Rafa to a bank of turnstiles. Even in the blaring fluorescent lights, he is gorgeous. His shirt is somehow still crisp, the muscular roll of his shoulders straining against the starched white fabric. My dizziness spins to new heights. I wonder if I have vertigo.

I start to turn for the ticket machine, but Rafa grabs me by the elbow. "No," he says. "You come with me."

"Seriously? You paid for everything tonight. Which very sweet of you, Rafa, but really, I can buy my own Metro ticket."

"Maybe next time."

"You keep saying that."

"It's more fun this way. Trust me."

He tucks me into the curve of his body, my back to his front, and with his hips (oh, sweet heaven) he nudges me into one of the turnstile stalls. He slips his arms underneath my own, trapping me against him. I understand, suddenly, what Rafa's about to do.

"But you can't sneak me in," I whisper, glancing around. "There's gotta be cameras everywhere—they'll see us! I don't want to go to Spanish jail before the semester even begins."

"We'll be fine. It's much quicker. Stay close."

Rafa holds his pass to the scanner until it beeps. Together we push through the turnstile, my vision going blank at the sudden, searing contact of our bodies as we stumble out on the other side.

At the same time, it feels like the most natural thing in the world—his palm moving up the length of my spine, stopping to grasp the nape of my neck between his thumb and forefinger. He touches me easily, like we've been at this for a while; like we haven't just met and made out on the street.

The ground rumbles beneath our feet.

"C'mon." Rafa starts walking, hanging a right. "I think your train is about to arrive. It's the red line, remember? It will take you right to the Retiro stop, and then all you have to do is cross the street and you will be at home."

I nod. On the way to the station, Rafa helped me figure out the closest Metro stop to my señora's apartment. Thankfully I don't have to switch trains or make any complicated maneuvers—even with a super knowledgeable and super-hot Madrileño at my side, I'm a little nervous about my first Metro ride.

We stop at the edge of the platform. A couple people mill about the quiet space, a guy in a suit, another in scrubs. Two girls, dressed for the club, doze off on a bench.

I am hyperaware of Rafa's hand on my neck. I like the way he touches me. I like being held like this.

It's six in the morning and I am stone-cold sober and I do not want this night to end.

"You will ask for help if you get lost, yes?" Rafa asks. "Not everyone speaks English, but most young people like me will understand it."

"Thanks," I say, looking up at him. "For everything. I had a really, really fun time tonight. I think you're right—I'm going to like it here."

We look up at the sound of an approaching train.

"Your phone number," Rafa says. He's blushing a little bit. "Can I get it? Maybe we can do the Sorolla Museum together. It's fun for me too, showing you around."

I look at the station's cave-like mouth. The tiled wall glistens as the train's headlight hits it.

Rafa is a really cool guy. And the fact that he's asking for my number makes him even cooler.

I shouldn't give it to him. This whole night happened because I thought—I knew—I wouldn't see Rafa again. I never expected to have so much fun together. I never expected him to like me as much as I liked him.

But here we are, his hands on my body and my heart thumping in my chest. I glance at him from the corner of my eye. He's *so* cute.

I do it, quickly. I give him my number, and he types it into his phone. "I don't know if it will even work," I say. "I'm not entirely sure how the whole country code thing changes it, so . . ."

"Then I give you my mine." Rafa grabs my phone and types his number on the keypad. He hands it back and meets my eyes. "If you do not hear from me, it is because the number you gave me is wrong. You must call me then, yes? I want to see you again."

The backs of my knees tingle. "I'd like that."

My train is here. It hisses to a stop. The doors glide open.

"Thanks again. For everything," I say. "Buenas noches, Rafa."

Good night.

Rafa offers me a lop-sided grin. He bends down and presses a kiss into my cheek. "Buenos días, Vivian."

Good morning.

I take a seat on the train facing away from the platform. I don't want Rafa to see the hugely embarrassing smile I'm sporting at the moment.

But at the last minute, after the doors shut and the train is pulling away, I sneak a glance over my shoulder. Rafa is still there, rakishly handsome in his unbuttoned shirt, watching me with his hands in his pockets. He takes one hand out and holds it up, splaying his fingers in a sort of wave.

I wave back, my face alive with the memory of those hands on my skin.

I look down at my phone.

Rafa saved his number under the name Justin Timberlake.

It's only six, and already he's made my day.

Back at Stella's apartment, I have trouble falling asleep. Even as my body is restless with excitement, my heart throbbing as I relive the kiss a hundred, a thousand times, my head knows better.

I met Keith the first week of my sophomore year back at Meryton. Like Rafa, he was cute and charming, and from the first night we played flip cup together at his frat house, I knew I wanted him.

We sexiled our roommates so much they hated us by the end of the semester. In retrospect, I see the warning signs—

he only texted me late at night on the weekends, we never went on a real date like the dinner-and-a-movie thing—but I was so obsessed with him, so eager to find the "one" and fall in love, I ignored them.

When I fall, I fall hard. And I fell *really* hard for Keith. I was naïve enough to believe people who connected like we did—people who really liked to hump each other on a weekly basis—became boyfriend and girlfriend. I wasn't hooking up with anyone else. I didn't *want* to hook up with anyone else. I wanted Keith.

But Keith didn't want me. Not like I wanted him, anyway. And that was devastating. I remember the inconsolable sobs I muffled in my pillow, the unrelenting pain, and the months of looking for him, pitifully, everywhere I went, wanting to be with him more than I wanted anything else.

I remember my lightheaded panic when I heard he hooked up with a girl in my dorm. It was horrible, trying to pretend I'd moved on too, when just *seeing* him at the dining hall sent my heart skittering.

I promised myself I wouldn't let anyone devastate me like that again. I promised myself I would protect my heart, and not fall for a guy who couldn't, or wouldn't, stick around for the long haul.

A guy like Rafa. If I fall for him, and if by some miracle he falls for me, we'll only have six months together before an ocean—an honest to goodness *ocean*— separates us permanently. I've already been through the special hell of having to let a guy go, a guy I really liked, after one semester together. I'm not gonna do it again.

I just wish I could stop thinking about that damn kiss.

———

That Afternoon

"Viv."

I stir at the poke on my forehead, my senses blinking awake. The first thing I notice is the heat; I feel the sun on my face. Drool trails down my cheek onto the pillow. I can smell the cigarette smoke in my hair. My lips are sticky with the taste of sangria.

Rafa. I wonder if he texted me.

"Viv!" Poke poke. "Hellloooo, Vivian!"

My eyes fly open. Sunlight streams through the window, blinding me. My eyes smart, neon dots and streaks blurring my vision. Something—someone—is bouncing on the trundle bed beside me, her finger poking frantic Morse code onto my forehead.

I catapult upright, my entire being lighting up with excitement.

"You're here!" I cry, tugging Maddie into a bear hug. "Oh my God, oh my God, oh my God, I can't tell you how happy I am you're here!"

"Oh my God, you are *crush*ing me!" Maddie laughs, the two of us clinging to one another like the survivors of a shipwreck. You'd think we've been apart for years, decades even, when we've only suffered a three-month separation. Summer has a way of feeling like forever when you're in college.

I inhale the familiar coconut scent of her shampoo. I remember Maddie telling me she used it as lube once, when desperate times called for desperate measures and how hard we laughed when she divulged her then-boyfriend called his junk a "piña colada COCKtail."

Already I feel twenty times less homesick.

"We're freaking *here*," she says into my hair. "How insane is that?"

"It doesn't feel real, does it? You get on a plane in Philadelphia and wake up halfway across the world. I feel like I was teleported here. I keep expecting to run into a Klingon every time I turn a corner."

"Dude, forget Klingons. Is it just me or is everyone in Madrid ridiculously hot? I was totally creeping on guys *and* girls out the window on my ride in. They dress like . . . I don't know. Like they're going to some royal nightclub or something."

My heart seizes. Ridiculously hot doesn't begin to describe Rafa. I can picture his face clearly, the shapely lines of his face deepen as the corner of his mouth quirks into a grin. I feel the starchy weave of his white shirt, the tickle of his Prince Harry bracelet on the small of my back.

I shiver.

"You okay?" Maddie asks. "It's hot as balls in here."

"Yeah," I manage. "Yeah, fine. Sorry. Madrileños are totally hot. And the way they dress . . . it's pretty insane. We have some shopping to do, that's for sure."

"I still can't believe we're here. I've been looking forward to this semester for, like ever, but it always felt so far away, you know? And now it's happening and I can't really process it yet."

"I know. Studying abroad always sounded so sexy when everyone talked about it back at Meryton. The travel, the partying. Writing a paper on a Picasso you could actually see at a museum down the street. I mean, I wanted to go abroad if I could. But now that I'm here—it's exciting. And *weird*."

"Totally weird," Maddie says. "I almost puked during the cab ride because I was so nervous. The driver kept watching me in the rearview mirror. I think he knew."

"I think he was checking you out." Guys are always checking Maddie out.

"Doubtful," she says. "So, hey, Viv, I love you like a sister and everything. But are you ever gonna let me go? I kinda can't breathe."

"But I don't want to let go. We're sharing a marital bed now, which means you're my wife and you have to hug me. Plus I haven't seen you in, like, forever. And you smell good."

"You smell like a bar."

I grin. "I do."

I let her go, propping myself up on my pillows.

Maddie pulls back, crossing her legs on the bed beside me. She tucks her curtain of shiny brown hair behind her ears, and when I look up it's all I can do not to gasp.

Her pretty dark eyes are sunken and ringed with purple; they are dull and bloodshot. Her eyelids—no, her whole face —is swollen, like she just cried for the whole eight hours of her flight.

She looks like she got punched in the face.

A knot tightens in my stomach. We chatted a lot over the summer, mostly about study abroad stuff, a little harmless boy stuff too. She never let on that there might be a problem. But it's obvious that something is seriously wrong.

This is not the Maddie I saw three months ago at the end of sophomore year. That Maddie was stretched out on a blanket in Meryton Gardens, sneaking sips from a margarita-filled thermos we passed between us while we laughed about the costumes we'd made out of trash bags and bungee cords for that night's party. Sure, she was stressed about how she'd done on her exams, but she was happy. Vibrantly so.

For a minute I don't know what to say. It's not just her appearance that makes me think something's wrong. There's a sadness about her, a heaviness I sense in the slump of her shoulders and the way she wraps her arms around her waist, that makes me think it's more than jet lag.

"Mads," I say.

Her eyes glisten. She winces against a rush of tears. "I know, Viv. I know I look like shit."

"Stop it." I reach across the bed and put my hand on her

knee. "I just want to make sure you're okay. We don't have to talk about it if you don't want to. But I'm here if you need someone to listen. Always."

And I mean it. After Keith told me about his girlfriend, I was in bad shape. Like, really bad. I couldn't eat. I couldn't sleep. I couldn't stop crying. But Maddie stuck by my side through the whole horrible thing, showing up to our dorm room with a three-pack of boxed tissues and a handle of good vodka. She stewed with me in man-hate while we passed the handle back and forth. In the weeks and months that followed, she really helped pull me back together. Of course I'm going to offer to do the same for her whenever she needs me.

"Thanks, Viv. I really appreciate that." Her voice is thin. She takes a deep breath, lets it out. She meets my eyes. "My parents are splitting up. It's nasty. And, um . . . they're gonna put our house on the market and my dad moved out last week, so it's, like, official."

Shock pulses through me as the information ricochets inside my head. *Holy shit*. Mr. and Mrs. Lucas are getting divorced. Maddie's parents—her picture perfect, generous, handsome parents—are getting a divorce.

"Oh my God," I say, grabbing her hand. "I'm so sorry. Maddie. My God! What happened?"

Maddie heads off a tear with the back of her thumb. "Stupid stuff. Horrible stuff. It was, like, totally out of the blue. Mom was so hysterical she could hardly speak."

"What the hell?"

"It's awful, Viv. Just really, really awful."

I swallow the lump in my throat. "So, like, did your dad do something, or was there a specific argument they had?"

Maddie shrugs. She plucks at the tiny wet dots her tears make on the cotton blanket. "It sucks. I can't stop crying. I try to keep it together around my brother—he's really freaked out by the whole thing—but it's hard." She scoffs. "I used to think that when parents got divorced, there was always this *Leave It to Beaver* moment. You know, when the mom and dad sit the kids down at the dinner table and give them the whole 'we still love each other, but . . .' spiel. Then the mom and dad play nice and take the kids out for ice cream and maybe buy them a pool because they feel so bad about everything. That *definitely* did not happen at my house. Everything was so perfect before. And now . . . well. My family's the opposite of perfect."

"I'm sorry," I say, giving her hand a squeeze. "I can't imagine how that feels. I mean, wow. D'you think you need to be home this semester? Maybe be with your mom? Your brother?"

"Fuck no!" She laughs. "I don't want to be home with those crazy assholes. I love them, don't get me wrong. I miss them. A lot. But honestly, Viv? I think it's good for me to be away from the whole situation. And I wasn't about to miss out on a semester in Spain with you. Aren't you glad I didn't leave you to deal with our señora's crazy fucking dog alone?"

"Ohmigod that dog *is* crazy. I locked myself in our room yesterday because I was terrified of him."

"Don't worry. We have six whole months to figure out how to kill him and make it look like an accident," Maddie says. "Anyway, I think being here will keep my mind occupied, you know? Classes and travel and all that stuff."

"I don't disagree," I say. I notice she isn't answering my questions. Not directly, anyway. Something is going on that she's not telling me. Something bad. "But I'm here for you if you change your mind or need to vent. You know I'm happy to listen. If you're okay, I'm okay."

"Oh, puh-*lease*, you're gonna make me gag with all that Dr. Phil crap," she says, and we laugh. It's a particular gift of hers:

cracking us up in the middle of our emotional and existential crises. (Back at Meryton, we had them on the regular.)

"I wonder how Dr. Phil would feel about us drowning our problems in sangria."

Maddie stretches her legs out in front of her, plucking the socks off her feet with her free hand. "I know I feel pretty damn great about it."

"I had a feeling you might." I give her hand one last squeeze. "Really, Mads. I'm sorry about your parents. As your wife, I want to be there for you."

She offers me a smile. "You've always been my better half, Viv," she says. She slides to the edge of the bed. "C'mon, let's talk about something else. Anything else. I gotta do a little unpacking, and then I say we go sample some of that sangria."

I lean back on the pillows. Wow. Just *wow*. I feel terrible for Maddie. I can't imagine what it must be like, to have your family fall apart on you. To see your mom hurt like that. I take for granted that my parents have their shit together, and that they get along. Just thinking about them splitting up makes me want to cry.

"Stop thinking about it," Maddie says, unzipping her suitcase. "If you're thinking about it, I'll think about it too. I didn't sleep at all on the flight because I was thinking about it. I'm sick of it."

"Okay," I say. "What should I think about then?"

"Taking a shower, maybe?"

I grin.

I wonder what time it is. If I got home at six thirty, that means I'd need to sleep until, oh, at least noon to not feel like a zombie all day.

I glance at my phone. A surge of nervous anticipation prickles through me. *Did* Rafa text me? I want to know, badly.

And the fact that I want to know so badly is all the

evidence I need that giving Rafa my number was a bad idea. If he texts me, then what? What in the world do I text back? "Hey, thanks for the churros, let's pretend the kiss never happened, sorry but I'm looking for true love and there's no way true love can work with you. Mostly because you live in Spain and I don't want to fall for a guy I have to leave, but also because you're ridiculously hot and probably all the girls touch your peen on the regular."

I mean, I'm done sharing penises with other girls. I want my own already. One that belongs just to me, forever and ever.

But if Rafa *doesn't* text me, then I'm going to feel like shit. The things I felt with his hands on my face were . . . potent. Extraordinary. Even now, my pulse flutters at the memory of that damn kiss. The look in his eyes just before he sealed the deal. The way he tasted as his mouth moved over mine.

I know it was just one night. One kiss. But nights like that don't happen very often for me. I don't have a ton of experience with guys, but I know that what I had with Rafa was special. We hit it off, big time; we connected in a way I haven't connected with another human since Keith.

Knowing he doesn't feel that way about me will be kinda crushing.

Still, I feel a small buzz of excitement as I reach across the bed and grab my phone from the desk, tugging it off the charger.

"So you obviously had a late one last night," Maddie says. She lifts a stack of folded shirts from her enormous suitcase and puts it in a drawer. "I want to know everything. Where did you go? What did you do? *Who* did you do?"

"We went to this cool little bar in a neighborhood called Chueca," I begin. "A couple people were there. Al, Katie . , . and there was this guy . . ."

My phone screen lights up. 1:43 p.m. I have never, ever slept this late.

There are the usual alerts—social media stuff, a missed alarm that I forgot to reset—a missed call from my mom, a reply to the text I sent Katie when I got home, and two texts from Maddie.

That's it.

No text or missed call from Justin Timberlake.

My heart plunges into an icy well of disappointment.

For a hot minute I indulge in the fantasy that the number I gave him didn't work, and that I have a romántico text waiting for me somewhere in the international cellular ether. But if Katie's texts came through, and so did Maddie's . . . I mean, wouldn't Rafa's too?

What did you expect, I scold myself. *It was one night. One kiss.*

I've been in this position often in the past few months, meeting a cute guy on a Saturday night, maybe making out with him, laughing and flirting and having a good time. Not once—literally, not one freaking time—has anything ever come of it. I don't know why I would think a cute guy would be interested in a relationship, would be interested in *me*, after the experiences I've had. I know better than to get my hopes up.

"A guy? Like, a *guy* guy, or just a guy?" Maddie's head pops up over the open flap of her suitcase. "Viv, did you make out with a random Madrileño last night? Please, please tell me you did, and that it happened in a public place."

"What?" I look up from my phone.

"The guy you said was at the bar last night. Was he cute?"

"Oh," I say, swallowing. I don't know why, but I really don't feel like talking to Maddie about Rafa. I guess I was right, what we had was a one-night (make-out) stand. Why tell her about a guy who obviously doesn't want to see me again? I gotta move on or risk getting hurt again, the way Keith hurt me.

"Oh, yeah, um. It was nothing. He was nothing, I mean. Just some random dude who was there, Al Montoya's cousin or something." I toss my phone across the bed. "So, tell me about the rest of your summer. I know your internship was kinda boring—how did the review go?"

CHAPTER SIX

Wednesday
First Day of Classes

I don't think I've been this nervous going to school since I started kindergarten. I hardly sleep, and when I wake up I can't eat the cereal Stella left for us on the kitchen counter.

I would, however, *kill* for a cup of coffee. Taking your coffee to go is considered a sacrilege in this country. Here, everyone drinks these tiny cups of weapon-grade espresso. It seems there is not a single place that sells American style brewed coffee in all the land.

Needless to say, I've had a wicked headache for days now.

While class itself terrifies me, the Meryton in Madrid program is pretty sweet. The director, Elena, is a thirty-something Madrileña who is the kind of beautiful I want to be when I grow up. We met her during orientation on Monday. She talks in lovely, lisping Spanish, and emphasized again and again the importance of *experience*. One of our required classes is actually an "experience" class, where the program takes all fifty of us around Spain—Barcelona, Seville, Toledo, and Granada are on the schedule—to show us some of the oldest and most beautiful architecture, historical sites, and *art museums* in the world.

I mean, how ridiculously cool is that?

On my way to class, I run into Al. My stomach does a backflip. I wonder if he knows about Rafa and me.

Al kisses me on both cheeks.

I shoot him a look. "Really? Not a week in Madrid and already you're using the double kiss?"

"I've been here since the beginning of August, thank you very much," he says. "And yes, I happen to think the double kiss is a much better alternative to the awkward hello hug."

"Very true." I adjust my bag on my shoulder.

"So how'd it go with Rafa? He's been working all week, so I haven't had a chance to talk to him. But you two pulled quite the Houdini on us at Ático on Saturday," Al says, wiggling his bushy eyebrows.

Heat rushes to my face.

"Rafa's a nice guy," I offer. "It was nice of him to show us around."

One of Al's bushy eyebrows pauses mid-wiggle. "Nice? That doesn't sound promising."

"No," I say, pushing through the crowd that clogs the hallway. "I mean it. After Ático, we just went to grab some churros. Then we went home. End of story."

Al holds up his hands. "I didn't mean to pry, V. I'm just having a little fun with you. My cousin *is* a nice guy." He shrugs. "It would be cool to see two of my favorite people hit it off, that's all."

It would be so, so cool. But we're both getting our hopes up for nothing. I haven't heard a word from Rafa in the four days since we kissed in the street. I'm not an idiot; I know what that means. This is not, as Maddie would say, my first rodeo.

"Come on, Al," I say. "A guy like Rafa probably has his pick of the ridiculously hot Madrileñas who inhabit this city. I bet they throw themselves at him."

"I'm not telling you that girls aren't into Rafa. But he isn't like that, V. He's not into that scene. I mean it when I say he's a nice guy."

I scoff. "Nice guys don't look like that."

"You'd be surprised." He meets my eyes. "Things are much different here than they are back at Meryton. Try to keep an open mind."

Of course my very first class on my very first day at San Pedro is in a huge lecture hall. A hundred or more students fill the auditorium-like space. I sit in a far corner with a handful of other Meryton in Madrid kids, so anxious I can practically chew on my stomach.

Then the professor comes in, a young-ish looking guy in a tweed blazer and tailored pants, and after several attempts finally quiets the class. He introduces himself, and dives right into complex economic theory—*in Spanish*.

Not just any Spanish. *Spanish* Spanish. It's completely different from the slow, measured Spanish of our classes back at Meryton. This is no-holds-barred, wow-I-am-so-lost, what-the-hell-did-he-just-say Spanish. The kind of academic Spanish used to explain Keynesian economics in the context of prewar Europe.

Oh. *God.*

I record the lecture on my phone, even though I don't think I'll ever understand it. I scribble half-baked notes in a notebook while my mounting frustration collects in a lump at the back of my throat. *This is not what I signed up for. I am never going to pass this class. I am not ready for this. Why did they let me come to Madrid if they knew I would sink like a stone?*

And what the fuck does "renacimiento" mean?

By the end of the lecture, I am exhausted and overwhelmed. A pack of TAs, arms laden with our graded take-home exams, troll the aisles as they call out names. I hear *Vee-Vee-An* Bingley from across the room. Heart thumping, I gather my things and head that way.

I see the big, fat C- scrawled in red pen across the top of my exam before the TA even hands it to me. I suddenly can't breathe around the lump in my throat. I need to find a bathroom, stat, before I embarrass myself. I've already made out in public; I'm not about to cry in public too.

I'm upset mostly because of the awful grade. This is supposed to be the semester I improved my GPA, not tank it.

But I'm also upset because I could have worked harder. Don't get me wrong, it took me days to complete the exam. Answering the questions would have been difficult enough in English, having to translate the answers into Spanish was nothing short of a Herculean task. But I didn't give it one hundred percent. I struggled to truly engage with the material. Econ can be so . . . boring, I guess. I start to glaze over halfway through my assignments, which never happened before I started studying Econ.

I have to get my shit together. My internship prospects, my future—it's all on the line.

I stuff the exam into my bag. Keeping my head down, I slip out of the hall and make for the only bathroom I know about in this freaking hamster maze of a building. I hit the stairs and head toward the cluster of classrooms and offices designated for Meryton in Madrid. My vision is blurry with tears, and my head is pounding. I wish Maddie and I had similar schedules so she could come give me a hug. (She's an architecture major, so we're rarely in the same class.)

I'm moving so fast I don't see Elena, the program director, until I almost walk right into her at the bottom of the stairs.

"Ah! *Vee-vee-an!*" She takes my hand in hers and gives it a quick shake. "It is lovely to see you again."

I blink back my tears, hoping she can't see them. Elena was beautiful from afar. Up close, she's unbelievably adorable, her fashionable lob—a long bob—tucked behind her ears, her pencil skirt and collared shirt Madrileña chic.

"Nice to see you too—"

"Elena. You all must call me Elena. Do you have a moment? I would like to speak with you about the tutor you requested."

"Sure," I say. My voice is embarrassingly thin. I clear my throat. "Sure, Elena, no problem. My next class isn't until two, so I have plenty of time."

"Vale," she says, waving me to follow her. Her heels sound an authoritative beat against the linoleum floor as we walk. "So what do you think of Madrid so far?"

"It's good. Beautiful. Though I'd be lying if I said I wasn't a bit . . . overwhelmed."

She smiles warmly. "This is very normal, Vivian. Madrid is a big city, and very different from what you are used to. It is all part of the experience. Give yourself some time, and I think you will someday love it. What about your *señora*? Is Stella treating you well?"

Wow, Elena really knows her stuff. I guess it's her job to know who and where we are as director of our program, but still, it's nice to know someone's looking out for me.

"Yes, very well so far," I say. "The apartment is beautiful, and Maddie and I love the location."

"The Salamanca neighborhood is very nice. And you are across the street from Retiro, no? It is my favorite park in all of Madrid."

I follow Elena into a little square of offices. Here the floor is carpeted, and her steps are muted. "We haven't been able to explore Retiro yet. But that's on our to-do list this weekend."

"Excellent. It is a good place to do all things. When I was

a student like you, I would find a quiet place there and study."

She leads me to an office all the way at the back of the square. Through the open door I can see a desk covered with neat stacks of paper and a laptop. Elena motions for me to sit in a chair in front of the desk as she walks briskly to her own seat opposite.

Only when I step into the office do I see there are two chairs in front of the desk. One of the chairs—the one to the right—is already occupied by a guy.

My gaze falls on that guy's broad shoulders. There's something familiar about the sloping muscles of those shoulders, the way they fill out a light pink button-down shirt.

I spot a frayed bracelet tied around the well-tanned wrist that rests on the arm of his chair.

A pulse of heat ricochets inside my ribcage, moving up my spine to settle at the base of my skull.

Oh.

My.

God.

I inhale, sharply, the woodsy scent of his aftershave filling my head. He smells delicious.

He glances over his shoulder, revealing a chiseled jaw, half a handsome face. We meet eyes. His are startlingly, terrifyingly blue.

Just as gorgeous as I remember them. More so, if that's even possible.

"Vivian," Elena says, "I'd like to introduce you to Rafael Montoya. He's a graduate student here at San Pedro, and one of the student liaisons for Meryton in Madrid. Some of these liaisons, they organize parties, they do trips, they show our students around the city. Others provide tutoring services, which is what Rafa will do for you, per your request. He will tutor you in whatever you need help with for the remainder of the semester."

CHAPTER SEVEN

This can't be happening. This is a dream.

Scratch that. This is a nightmare. Just with a really cute guy in it.

Out of the thousands of students at San Pedro available to tutor gringos like me, surely Elena didn't pick the one guy I happened to have kissed, embarrassingly, in the middle of the street at six in the morning?

The one guy who, after that kiss, said he'd call but never did?

I couldn't be more shocked if Justin Timberlake, in all his N'SYNC, curly-haired glory, was sitting in that chair instead of Rafa Montoya.

I'm hot and cold all at once. My face burns, even as my blood prickles with cold.

"Hello, Vivian," Rafa says, his words curling with the sexi-est, chocolatey-est accent. "It is nice to see you again."

I forgot how sexy his accent his.

I can't breathe.

I am going to faint.

I wave instead. (God, why do I always have to wave?)

"Hey, Rafa," I say, managing a smile. "Great to see you too."

Elena's face lights up. "You know each other, then? That is lovely! See, Vivian, you have friends in Madrid already. This makes my job much easier—no awkward introductions."

If sweet, chic Elena only knew.

"Yes," Rafa says. "My cousin, Alberto, introduced us this weekend."

"How wonderful. Please," she says, looking at me and motioning to the chair, "sit."

I sit on the edge of the chair, gathering my bag in my lap. I wrap my arms around it, the way the stewardesses tell you to wrap your arms around your bottom seat cushion—a cushion that conveniently doubles as a flotation device—if you happen to survive a violent plane crash in the middle of the ocean. It's pointless, I know, but I cling to it for dear life anyway.

I am acutely aware of Rafa's presence beside me. Which makes me acutely aware of my every movement, every breath, every trickle of perspiration. Have I always breathed so loudly? And am I ever *not* going to be a hot sweaty mess? I swear, I haven't stopped sweating since I arrived in Madrid.

"I have spoken with Dr. Rubio, your Economics professor," Elena says, shuffling papers around in an open manila folder on her desk. "He told me you had some difficulty on the take-home exam. Was there any portion, in particular, you had trouble with? The Spanish, maybe, or the material itself?"

My mouth opens, but no words come out. If my face was burning before, it's positively en fuego now. I'm probably three shades redder than a tomato. It's embarrassing enough to have to face Rafa, but to have my shitty grades and academic ineptitude paraded in front of him is so mortifying I feel sick.

"Um." I roll my lips between my teeth. My mouth smarts with the salty tang of sweat. "Judging by the awful grade, I'd say I had trouble with a little bit of everything."

"And that's okay!" Elena says brightly. "Taking university-level classes in a different language is very challenging. It is the beginning of the semester, so you have plenty of time to learn and improve your language skills. We like to have our students start tutoring early, so they get as much out of the experience as possible. Rafa is the best of the best; he's been tutoring our students for years now, with great results. I have no doubt he will help you ace all your classes this semester."

I nod my head. "Okay. Okay, yeah, that sounds great. Thank you."

That lump in my throat has swelled to moon-size proportions. My underarms are sticky with sweat. I just want to get the hell out of here so I can lick my wounds in private. Holding it in is making my whole body ring with misery.

Elena curls her hair behind her ear. "I think it is best to start with several tutoring sessions a week, depending on the schedule. I looked at yours, Vivian, and I noticed you are perhaps taking a fifth class?"

"Yes," I say. "Art history. I was thinking of dropping it anyway, and with this awful start in my econ class, I think it's probably best just to stick to four—"

"No."

Elena and I both look up at Rafa's single-word sentence, delivered with such firmness and finality I forget, for a second, the embarrassment raging through me.

"You said you were interested in art," he says, meeting my eyes over the slope of his shoulder. I can't decide if I like him in the pink or the white shirt better. He looks devastatingly handsome in the pink. "If you are interested in it, you should study it while you are here. I know the professora who teaches that class, and she is very good. You will regret it if you only take economics in Madrid, yes? That, you can study anywhere. But Goya—Sorolla—those guys you can only study here."

Sorolla. Rafa said he'd take me to the Sorolla Museum. Is that why he's bringing him up again? Or does he not remember?

"That is true," Elena says. "It is an amazing class, and Rafa is right, the woman who teaches it is very well known. If you have the time in your schedule, I recommend you take it, especially if your passion is art. But if your passion is economics, then perhaps not?"

Despite what my major says, economics is definitely not my passion. Far from it. I want to take the art class, I do, but I'm worried I'll fall behind all the other econ majors vying for those I-banking spots if I drop an econ class to do it. I can always just visit the big art museums on my own, read some books on Picasso in my spare time . . .

Ugh. I'm so confused. Which only upsets me more.

"Let me think about it," I manage.

Rafa's looking at me again. The heat of his gaze seems to peel back layers of clothes and skin, exposing all the things I'm feeling. His eyes are soft—with sympathy, or maybe with understanding. The kindness I see there makes me want to burst into tears.

I slide farther onto the edge of the chair.

"Very good," Elena replies. "The drop period doesn't end until the middle of September, so you have plenty of time. In the meantime, I want you and Rafa to meet at least twice a week. After mid-term examinations, we will reevaluate your needs, Vivian, and go from there. Is that good?"

I nod. I need to head this off, I know I need a different tutor, someone less . . . ridiculously hot. I should ask for these things. But I worry if I try to talk I'll only end up crying.

"Okay for me," Rafa says. "Thank you, Elena."

Elena offers us a smile, the skin around her eyes crinkling with pleasure. "Buena suerte, chicos." *Good luck, guys.* "Let me know how it goes."

Swallowing, I croak my goodbyes and leap out of my chair like it's on fire. I make a beeline for the exit: out of the office, down the hall, down two flights of stairs. If there's one thing I've noticed, it's that Spaniards take their time; they don't rush around like idiots the way we do in America. San Pedro students are no exception. I get a few bald stares as I dart in and out of the crowd that clogs the stairwell.

I push through the front doors and stumble out onto the wide concrete courtyard. It's crowded with knots of kids chatting, smoking, leaning over open textbooks for some last-minute cramming. I'm jealous of these people going about their normal mornings in their normal country of residence. I don't know if I've ever felt more lost, or alone.

With shaking hands, I dig my sunglasses out of my bag and shove them onto my face.

And then I finally let myself cry. I can't stop sweating, and now I wonder if I'm ever going to stop crying, or if this semester is just going to be one huge sobfest.

My throat swells and my eyes burn and there's no doubt in my mind I'm making an ugly cry face. What. A. *Day*. And it's not even eleven o'clock yet.

I move across the courtyard, desperate to get out, to be anywhere *but* here. I don't pay attention to where I'm walking, and my flats catch on a step. I fly forward, righting myself at the last minute.

Fuck this day for life.

"*Vivian!*"

I blink. Was someone just calling my name?

"*Vivian! Wait!*"

Glancing over my shoulder, I see a guy in a pink shirt dart down the steps two at a time. He's flying in my direction.

People look up as he passes. A couple people call after him, but he ignores them. He's looking right at me.

I turn back to the sidewalk. *Rafa*. What in the world does he want?

I start to walk faster, wiping the tears from my face. I don't want him to see me like this. Besides, I have nothing to say to him. Not yet, anyway. I need to regroup first, need to clear my head.

I hear his footsteps behind me.

"Vivian!" he pants. "Please, I just ate lunch, I am going to yack if you don't slow down!"

Even as a grin tugs at the corners of my mouth, I don't slow down. In fact, I speed up. But whatever Rafa wants from me, he must really want it, because he catches up to me in one, two strides. He grabs my elbow, stopping me in my tracks.

"Hey," he says. He's breathing hard. "Did I use it right again? Yack?"

I look down at his hand on my arm. Sparks of electricity move through me at this smallest of touches. I don't want to feel this. I don't want to talk to him. "Yes. You used it right, again. You're a fast learner. Unlike me, apparently."

He squints his eyes against the dappled sunlight that streams through the leaves of the tree above us. He's a little sweaty, his hair sticking to his forehead. This somehow makes him slightly less intimidating.

Slightly.

He doesn't let go of my arm, and I'm not brave enough to wiggle free.

"Vivian," he says. "Are you all right?"

I try to nod, but my eyes smart with a fresh wave of tears, and my lips duck out as I begin to cry all over again.

His fingers slide up my arm, the quiet noise of skin

scraping against skin filling the space between us. "Hey." He steps closer. "Vivian. Look at me. What's going on?"

I look at him, but only after I turn my head to the side. I can't meet his gaze head on. "Just having a bad day. I'll be okay."

"Here." Rafa digs in the pocket of his jeans and offers me a rumpled tissue. "It's clean, I swear it. I just took it from Elena's office."

"Thanks," I say, holding up my glasses as I swipe underneath my eyes. "I mean it. That was sweet of you to think of me. How did you know I was crying?"

"I had a—how do you call it—a sensation?"

This time I can't help it—I have to grin. "You had a feeling."

He nods at a bench underneath the tree. "Is it okay if we talk? For a moment only."

We sit. I fill my cheeks with air, let it out. It's much cooler in the shade, thank God. I look down to see the tissue is streaked with mascara. Awesome.

"Do you remember what I told you the night we met? That you would dream in Spanish by the time you leave Madrid?"

I blink. "I do. I have a *feeling* you're wrong, though."

"No. I would not have said that if I didn't mean it. You *have* to have more confidence in yourself."

"Easy for you to say. I bet you speak what, five languages?"

"Six." He grins. "I like to brag, remember? So let me brag. It is only the first day of all the semester. You have much to learn, yes, but there is also much time. No student of mine has ever gotten less than an A in any class I tutored them in."

"Really?" I ask, picking at the tissue in my lap.

"Yes. Very really," he says. "So I am bragging more, but I took the economics class you are now, only three years ago. On the first test, I got a C too."

"No you didn't," I say. "You're just saying that to make me feel better."

Rafa meets my eyes. "No. It was terrible. I was very embarrassed, because I knew I could do better."

"Yes," I say, swallowing. "Exactly."

"And I did. I got an A in the class, but only after I received help from a tutor," Rafa says. "It is not a good thing, to go through the semester with so much stress. Let me help you."

"I was just taken a little off guard, you know?" I bite the inside of my cheek. "It's embarrassing. Like you said. The grade itself, and then having to talk about it with Elena and, um, you . . ."

He runs his hands up the length of his jeans, toward his knees. His fingers are broad, tan too, capable looking. "I understand. If you want a different tutor, that is okay."

"I haven't even thought about that," I lie.

"It was the first thing you thought about," Rafa says. "Vivian, you wear your emotions on your sleeve. When you first saw me, I thought you were going to run out of the room."

"*I* thought I was going to run out of the room," I say, and we both laugh. In an instant, I feel a hundred times better. I feel like I can breathe.

"I'm glad you didn't," he says. "I think you should give me a chance. I can help you. And we do get along okay, I think."

I look away. Above us, the tree sighs in a small, hot breeze. Why is he so intent on being my tutor, when he clearly wanted nothing to do with me after our Saturday night rendezvous? It makes no sense. Shouldn't he be running for the proverbial hills? Shouldn't he jump at the chance to get out of tutoring the girl he didn't mean to kiss?

Bottom line: why does he care about me or my Spanish or

my grades in the first place? So much so that he chased me across this little city block of a campus?

"You have a lot of opinions," I say. "You think I should take the art class. You think you can get me an A in econ. You think you are the best tutor to ever live."

He shrugs, a rakish grin tugging at the edges of his mouth. "I am. It is plain and simple. You are upset. It is clear you care very much about your grades. I am the best one to help you. So let me help you, Vivian."

It's the stuff dreams are made of: a super-hot foreign dude begging me to give him a chance. I don't know what angle he's playing, but he plays it well. He doesn't try to hide his concern. His eyes glisten with it, and it's really, really hard not to fall into him, not to fall under his spell the way I did Saturday night.

Maybe he's right. If what Rafa says about his killer tutoring skills is true, maybe he *is* the best person to help me get my GPA back on track.

Maybe I need to put my wounded ego aside and get real. I'd be an idiot to pass up the opportunity to ace this semester. I *need* to ace this semester, or my dreams of beating out other Meryton students for a prestigious post-grad gig are toast.

Whether or not Rafa cares about me like *that*, I know what my answer needs to be. I also need to get out of here, because I'm sweating through my dress and I'm starving. There's also that whole recovering-from-epic-embarrassment thing to consider, although I do feel a lot better about everything after talking with Rafa.

I loop the straps of my bag over my shoulder and stand. "Okay," I say. "Let's do it. My GPA needs all the help it can get."

"Vale. You will not be disappointed."

But you've already disappointed me, I want to say.

"I gotta run," I say instead. "Um, I assume Elena gave you my email and everything so we can get in touch?"

Rafa stands and slides his hands around his belt to the small of his back, tucking his shirttail into his jeans. I can't help it, I check him out as the muscles in his back and arms strain against the fabric of his shirt. There's just something so . . . right about it. Already my pulse is accelerating toward a sprint.

"Yes," he says, straightening. "Of course."

"Great. I'll see you around."

I start walking, stiff with the awareness that he's watching me. I'm being rude again, I know I am, but I feel like I got massacred this morning. I need a little breathing space.

Space Rafa refuses to give me.

He jogs to my side. I wait a beat for him to say something. I wait another. He waves to a passing girl. *Qué tal, Marta*, he says. She's very pretty.

"You never called," Rafa says, softly.

My heart skips a beat. "Neither did you."

"I did. I called *and* I texted." He sticks his hands in his pockets. "You think I would not call you after all the fun I had with your white girl?"

I want to smile at that. I want to believe him. So do the butterflies that have suddenly taken flight inside my belly.

Stop it, I tell myself. Even if Rafa is telling the truth—even if he's different from every other guy I've been with—falling for him can only end in heartache. I don't want to go through all the pain and loneliness of leaving behind the guy I thought was the one. Keith fucked with my head and my heart, and I can't go through that again. Now, more than ever, I have to keep things professional.

Platonic.

"Here, I will figure it out for us—we will need to text for the tutoring." He pulls his phone out of his pocket, slowing our stride as he types furiously on the keypad. "Is this your number?"

He holds the phone out to me.

My heart skips a beat as my eyes move over the last four numbers. They're scrambled, a 4 where a 6 should be, the last two numbers reversed.

Rafa was right. We were in a rush at the Metro station, and either I gave him the wrong number, or he typed it into his phone incorrectly.

Which means it's entirely possible he *did* call, or text, or both on Sunday. I just didn't get them.

"Shit," I say. "It's not the right number."

"Vale, you type it this time."

I take the phone, reentering the correct number with fingers that tremble ever so slightly, and hand it back to him.

"*Vale,*" he says. "I'll send you a text—see if it works now."

On cue, I feel a vibration in my bag. I open it, digging around a bit until I find my phone. My pulse hiccups when I see "Justin Timberlake—Text" pop up on the screen.

I slide my thumb across the screen to read the text.

Estás guapa con este vestido.

I look up. I know guapa means cute. Pretty.

"You look pretty in that dress," Rafa translates.

"Oh." I look down, stupidly, at said dress. It's a black midi-dress, falling just below my knees. I belted it to make it look more stylish—more Madrileño. "Thanks."

My gaze slides up the length of his body. The words are out of my mouth before I can stop them. "And you look guapo in pink."

"Gracias." Rafa flashes that lady-killer grin of his, the lines around his mouth deepening in handsome pleasure. "Already you give adjectives the correct gender. See? Your Spanish is not so bad."

"I've got my adjectives down," I reply. "It's just everything else I need help with."

He holds out his phone. "I can resend the text I sent you last weekend if you like it?"

I meet his eyes. Oh, how I want to know. I really, really want to know what he said in the text he sent me after we spent a magical Madrid night together. My heart throbs with the desire to know if he felt the way I did.

"Here," he's saying. "Give me a minute only."

A smudge of movement catches my eye. I glance over Rafa's shoulder to see a couple of Meryton students I recognize from my econ class. They're chatting, smiling, probably flush with the satisfaction of having aced their take-home exams. Everyone at Meryton seems to get economics but me.

My heart ceases its throbbing and sinks.

I not only have to get economics, I need to ace it. In Spanish. And to do that, it's probably best if I keep my raging Rafa boner in my pants so I can focus on the actual work during our tutoring sessions, instead of focusing on Rafa's ridiculously wonderful—well, his wonderful everything. If I focus on that stuff, chances are I'll fall for him, and I definitely can't afford to do that.

Besides. I freak out when I just *see* the guys I've hooked up with on campus. I can't imagine having to sit down and talk post-war economics *in Spanish* with the guy who fingered me the night before. That's, like, gotta be one of my worst nightmares. I seriously won't learn a thing.

"Really," I say, sweat trailing down my temples, "that's okay. Look, Rafa, I appreciate it, I do, but . . . um. I can't—I'm not looking for something short-term—I, like, don't want to start something we can't finish, you know? Don't get me wrong, I had a great time. Like, a *really* great time, but . . ."

"Something we can't finish?" he asks at last. "But we have

many months, no? And is not some of the fun to live in the moment? See where it goes?"

"I've done that." I bite my lip. "And it didn't work out. I'm sorry, it's just . . . it's a long story. But it hurt, and now I know what I want, and it isn't . . . um, that."

He looks at me with questioning eyes. "You are very sure."

"I'm sure."

"But we had so much fun, Vivian," Rafa says. "I want to have fun again."

"We can have fun," I say. "Just as friends, though."

He looks at me for a long, excruciating moment. I hate seeing the hurt in his eyes. I hate saying that word—*but*—it doesn't feel right, *but* I know I'm making the right decision.

"Vale," he says at last. "We will be just the friends."

I look away. "Cool. If you wouldn't mind texting me some times you're free to meet for tutoring, that'd be great. I'd like to start as soon as possible."

He draws back a little. I wonder if I've really hurt his feelings.

"Okay," he says. "If that is what you want."

"It is," I say.

"Okay. I will see you soon, then."

"Great."

"Great."

He keeps walking with me. Again I get the sense he wants to say something, but he's struggling with how to say it. Whether it's a good idea to say it at all.

Part of me is curious, ravenously so, for him to say it, whatever it is. *Tell me what you said in your text. Tell me you like me and want to see me again. Tell me you haven't felt the way you felt with me Saturday night in a long, long time.*

Another part of me—the rational part—doesn't want Rafa to say anything. Because it doesn't matter. Even if Rafa is different from every other guy I've been with—even if I'd be the star, and not the one-night stand—he lives in Spain. We'd be together for, what, five, six months? And then it would have to end. There's no way we could be together, really together, without it ending in heartache.

"Great," he says at last. "Hasta luego, Vivian."

I'll see you later.

"See ya." My throat swells inexplicably as I say it.

Rafa veers to the right, back toward campus. I keep walking, even though I have no idea where I'm going.

CHAPTER EIGHT

That Night

Maddie and I stare at our plates. Stella is not in the kitchen—she left a note, saying she was heading out for dinner—so neither of us bother to hide our disgust.

"What. The hell. Is that?" Maddie asks. She pokes at the blob with her fork. It looks like a scoop of mayonnaise, dotted with a confetti of frozen peas and sliced carrots. There is no meat, no salad, no wholesome, homemade meal.

There is just mayonnaise.

"I have no idea," I reply, curling my lip. "But I'm pretty sure it is not delicious."

Maddie gives the blob a whiff before shoving her plate away. "I'm sorry, but I just can't eat this shit. I mean. I know they warned us the food might be weird. But this is, like, beyond."

We look up at the sound of the closed door rocking in its frame. Chiquitin is on the other side, scratching to be let in so he can bite us and probably steal our dinner. I'm tempted to shove the mayonnaise in his face and run.

"Wanna try to grab food somewhere?" I turn back to

Maddie. "Katie sent me a text a little while ago, saying she was going to meet up with some girls for a glass of wine. I think they want to go to a place in our neighborhood."

"Hell yes. I think we could both use a glass or four of some vino."

Maddie stands. She steps on the trash can's pedal, the lid flying back to hit the wall with sold *thwunk*, and tilts her plate over the can, watching as the blob slides slowly, *slowly*, off the plate. "Ugh," she says. "It's like a science experiment gone wrong."

My stomach grumbles. I sigh. We are a long way from the dining hall at Meryton, with its salad and sushi and soup stations. God how I miss that soup.

This is going to be a hungry semester.

The restaurant is a cute little place on a street not far from our apartment. It's past nine o'clock, but the place is bustling, the smells of sautéed garlic and olive oil wafting through the open windows.

Katie managed to nab a table toward the back, and Maddie and I wedge our way across the restaurant to get there. I glance at the food people eat as I pass. It looks delicious, if unfamiliar, much better than Stella's mayonnaise blob. Everyone—and I mean everyone, even the obviously underage kids who I guess don't have bedtimes—is drinking red wine.

"Hey, chicas!" Katie says, rising to give us hugs. She introduces us to the two girls sitting with her, Rachel and Laura.

I don't know Rachel, although I recognize her from campus. But Laura I do know. Well, kind of. We've rubbed elbows at a couple Panhellenic meetings—she's in one of the "core four" sororities at Meryton, which supposedly count the hottest, richest girls as members.

Laura appears to be both hot and rich. Maddie and I try not to stare as we take our seats on the bench across from her. To say she's gorgeous is an understatement. She catches everyone's eye, from the waiters who pass by to the well-dressed women at the table next to ours. She's rocking a stripped-down California hipster vibe, with long dark waves that perfectly complement her flawless perma-tan. A stack of gemstone-studded David Yurman bangles wink in the low light as she picks at the straps of her teeny-weeny tank top.

I know assuming makes an ass out of you and me, but I can't help but *ass*ume she's one of *those* girls. You know, the girls like Kelly from 90210, girls who drive brand new BMWs, who only party with the right guys in the right frats, the girls who are shallow and super aware of their social superiority. *Those* girls form a small but influential clique at Meryton.

I'm a little intimidated by her, to be honest.

The girls look as exhausted and overwhelmed as I feel. When the waiter comes, the five of us stare at our menus, waiting for someone else to speak up first. I'm pretty decent at reading Spanish, and I know the words for basic foods— apple, chicken, beer, olives. But the menu might as well be written in Elvish for all I understand. Gambas al ajillo? Albóndigas? Morcilla?

What. The. Fuck?

At last Katie looks up at the waiter. "Vino," she says. "Por favor, mucho, mucho vino." *Wine. Please, a lot, a lot of wine.*

"Vino tinto de la casa?" he asks. He points to a line item on my menu.

The girls and I look at each other. Some kind of wine of the house? Whatever it is, it's two euros (what?!) a glass. It's cheaper than ordering a soda or a bottle of water.

Wine is literally cheaper than water in Spain.

This may be a hungry semester, but it will not be a sober one. A fair trade-off, I think.

"Vale," Rachel says. "Right now I would slap around a bag of Franzia, so whatever that tinto stuff is, I'm sure it will be fine."

I like Rachel already.

The waiter returns with several glasses of red wine in his hands, the long, lithe stems tucked between his fingers. I lick my lips. My eyes are sore and tired from crying during my multiple crises today. A glass of anything alcoholic sounds heavenly.

"I don't think I've ever had red wine," I say, sticking my nose into the glass because I guess that's what you're supposed to do. "It smells good."

Maddie makes a face. "I've had it before. It's all right. Kind of an acquired taste, I think. Considering I usually drink really bad whiskey sours out of plastic cups when I go out, red wine feels fancy."

"Oh, whiskey sours," Katie says. "Worst hangovers *ever*."

Laura shakes her head. "Not as bad as cheap champagne. I was bedridden for two freaking days once. I'd say never again, but that would be a lie." She holds up her glass, almost blinding me with those bracelets. "A toast, to making it through the first day of classes without dying."

The waiter, passing by our table for the fiftieth time to check Laura out, stops and shakes his head. "No no no. Así es como lo hacemos en España."

This is how we do it in Spain. I think.

He swipes an empty glass from a nearby table and holds it up. "Arriba."

We hold up our glasses. "Arriba," we repeat.

"Abajo," he says, sweeping the wine down to his chest.

We do the same. "Abajo."

He moves his glass to the center of the table. "Al centro."

"Al centro," we say, clinking glasses.

"Al dentrooooo!" The waiter brings the glass to his lips.

"Al dentrooooo!" we say, smiling as we gulp at our wine like the underage American chicks we are.

The wine is . . . not bad, I guess. I sputter a little bit. You definitely can't drink this stuff the way you drink a crappy whiskey sour. It's meant to be sipped, which will take a little getting used to.

Maddie smacks her lips. "That's . . . interesting."

"I mean, everyone seems to be drinking it," Katie says, glancing around the restaurant. "There must be a reason."

"I say we just keep drinking until we like it," Laura says. "Or we fall over."

We laugh at that, and I feel the tangled knot of worry at the back of my head begin to unravel. So maybe Laura is a *little* less Kelly, a little more cool.

A little.

"So." Rachel lets out a sigh as she places her hands on either side of her wine glass, sliding it onto the table. "Can I just say that ever since I got to Madrid, I'm having trouble shaking this giant sense of WTF? Like, what did I do to myself?"

I am so relieved to know I am not alone in my foreign-land struggles I almost reach across the table and pull Rachel into a bear hug.

"Yes," I say. "Yes. Totally. Everyone back at Meryton raved about their experience abroad. They made it sound like the best thing ever. Maybe it will be, I don't know. But right now it's all I can do not to cry every ten minutes. I'm, like, completely overwhelmed."

Maddie wraps an arm around my waist. "Aw, Vivitar, I'm sorry. No more crying. Only more drinking."

"I get it," Katie says. Her lips and teeth are already stained purple from the wine; she makes it look adorable. "It's horrible to say, but after I got out of my first class today, I wished this semester would go by quickly and just be over. Keeping up with the professor was exhausting."

Laura nods, the wine slipping forward in her glass as she sips it, thoughtfully. "I'm with you girls. I, like, didn't sleep at all last night because I was so anxious about everything. What if I'm the dumbest kid in class? Or what if the Spanish deodorant I got at the farmacia doesn't work and I pit out my shirt and everyone knows it was me who stunk up the classroom?"

OMG yes, I think to myself. *I worried about the exact same thing.*

"But don't you remember, that first month or so of freshman year at Meryton, feeling so out of place? Wanting the four years to be over so you could go back home?"

"I do," I say. "But now it's the opposite. Not that I hate to go home to my parents. But Meryton is home now."

"Exactly," Laura says. "I feel like that's how it's going to be here. I don't think Madrid will ever really feel like home, per se, but I do think we'll fall in love with it. We didn't come here just to pass the time and get the hell out. We came here to experience life in a different country."

Maddie swirls the wine in her glass. "You're right. And the more we make the effort to experience things, the more we'll fall in love with Spain. I hear you, *Laurencita.* But these first few weeks are going to be hard. Sometimes it just flat out *sucks.*"

The waiter with the wandering eye returns, sliding a couple bowls of green olives onto the table, along with a small platter of white cheese.

"And sometimes," Rachel says, spearing an olive with a toothpick and popping it into her mouth, "it's magical. Alcohol plus cheese plus olives, and on a Wednesday night? Hell yes."

Rachel is right. If we were back at Meryton, we'd probably be holed up in the library, trying to ignore the internet while highlighting the hell out of our textbooks.

This—the five of us getting buzzed on a school night in a local tapas bar— is something that would've never happened in North Carolina. This is new, an experience. One I'm really enjoying.

"So, Katie," Rachel says around a mouthful of cheese, "tell me about this guy Rafael. You know, Alberto's cousin or whatever. I heard you went out with that whole group on Saturday night. People keep talking about how insanely hot he is."

Heat rushes to my face. *Oh no.* Not this guy again. I can't get away from him. I bring my glass to my lips, trying to hide behind it. *People are talking about how hot Rafa is?* When did this happen?

And why do I feel an unworthy—and unwanted—prickle of jealousy at the mention of his name? Didn't I just tell him I wasn't interested in anything more than his tutoring services this morning?

Katie meets my gaze across the table and grins. "You should ask our friend Vivian here. She hung out with him for a while that night."

"You did?" Maddie turns to me, eyes dancing with curiosity. "Oh my God, you *did* make out with a stranger in a public place, didn't you?"

I'm glad it's dark in the bar, so the girls (hopefully) can't pick up on my burning discomfort. I chug my red wine. I feel the start of a happy buzz in my legs.

"Um," I say. "I mean, yeah, we talked for a little while. But that was it."

"Was it?" Katie's grin broadens. "He was *into* you, chica. You guys should've seen the way he was looking at Viv."

I can't help but ask. "How was he looking at me?"

"Like he wanted to eat you."

93

"No he wasn't," I say, averting my eyes. I try to blur the image that pops up in my head, the one of Rafa looking down at me just before he swallowed my soul in the kiss to end all kisses. But I see it clear as day. Even now, it makes my stomach flip—that gleam of interest in his eyes, the dark hint of sex.

I need another glass of wine.

"Rafa is cute, sure . . ." I begin.

Katie arches a brow. "Rafa? Y'all are already on a nickname basis?"

"Everyone calls him Rafa," I reply. The girls are watching me now, intently, waiting for me to reveal a delicious, or maybe embarrassing, tidbit. They'd flip out, in a good way, if I told them about the kiss. About the things Rafa did and said. The chocolate incident would slay them, I know it would, the way it totally slayed me.

But then they'd know my feelings for him are more than friendly. I can't admit to those feelings. I can't admit them to myself, and I certainly can't admit them to other people. Admitting them would make them real. And having real feelings for Rafa is out of the question. My heart can't take it, not again—falling for a guy I ultimately can't have.

"Sorry, ladies, nothing exciting to report. We talked, danced a little. Then we went home." I swallow. "He's actually going to tutor me this semester in Spanish and econ."

The girls jump in disbelieving unison.

"Hot for teacher?"

"Yes, please!"

"God, I've always fantasized about hooking up with one of my professors. The older man thing . . . I can't even."

"I'm so jealous."

"Please, *Rafa*, teach me *everything* you know. And I mean *everything*."

"Tell me, Rafa, how do you say 'I want to fuck your brains out' en Español?"

"So, you sex goddess, how did you finagle this little student/teacher situation?" Katie asks, when the five of us finally stop laughing. "Did you give him the best head of his life?"

"I didn't," I say. "Really, nothing happened on Saturday. Elena assigned him to me this morning. I'm already on the verge of flunking econ, and my Spanish is pretty awful, so . . . yeah. They want me to start getting tutored ASAP." I roll the stem of my empty glass between my thumb and forefinger. "There will be no hot for teacher, and definitely no head. I'm gonna be honest—I'm a little tired of the hookup thing. After all the shit I've been through with guys, I kinda want something a little more serious. And even if Rafa *was* serious, we'd have to break up at the end of the semester, which would totally suck. Hooking up with him would be a dumb move."

"Or maybe the best move ever," Rachel says.

"Not for me," I say.

Laura flags down the waiter—it isn't hard—and orders us another round of vino tinto de la casa. "But what if he really digs your vagina?"

"Yeah," Maddie says. "What if he makes you come ten times a day?"

I laugh. *If only*. "Not gonna happen. I'd rather make myself come ten times a day and still keep my heart and my GPA intact, thank you very much."

"Have it your way." Maddie sips at her wine. "But if Rafa is as hot as people say he is, then someone has to take one for the team. Maybe I'll say hello the next time he's around."

There it is again, that stab of jealousy. The idea of Maddie —cute, effortlessly smart, brilliantly flirtatious Maddie— hooking up with Rafa makes my stomach clench. I hate it. I don't know where this sudden flush of hate comes from, but it's there. I sip my wine but it does not dissipate. Maddie usually gets what she wants when it comes to guys. I have no doubt Rafa will fall under her spell in five minutes flat.

I just told the girls I wasn't interested in Rafa. Maddie has every right to go after him. As do the other girls. I'm the one who has no right to feel jealous if they actually do say hello to Rafa, or if something does actually happen between them.

I thought I was making the right decision by keeping things platonic with Rafa—by telling the girls that nothing happened. It has to be the right decision.

Why, then, won't this terrible feeling in the pit of my stomach go away? Rafa doesn't belong to me. He never did, and never will.

I drink more wine and change the subject. I've always loved my girlfriends; the relationships with my girls have always been very important to me, and I'm proud of the tight-knit circle of friends I've accumulated over the years. Considering how guys have treated me, I'm one hundred percent chicks before dicks. Feeling these ugly things about one of my besties is unsettling. She deserves better.

We drink, we laugh, we get our red wine buzz on. Eventually our conversation about Rafa feels distant enough that I can start to enjoy myself again. We have a wonderful time, and vow to do it again next week—same place, same time.

I have a sensation, as Rafa would say, that I'm going to like this little Wednesday night tradition.

CHAPTER NINE

Friday Afternoon

I march through the sketchy tunnel that links my neighborhood to Retiro Park, my bag tucked firmly against my ribcage. It smells like pee; a couple dudes loiter toward the exit, offering me hashish as I pass. No gracias, I murmur. I make a mental note to never take the tunnel again.

When I emerge into the late afternoon sunshine, my pulse is skittering. A little bit because of those subterranean drug dealers.

But mostly because my first tutoring session with Rafa is about to begin.

I tuck my hair behind my ear, beseeching the humidity to be kind for once. I tug at my dress—this one is shorter, a little flowy. I should've worn jeans. I should've told Rafa I'd preferred to meet in the library for our first tutoring session. The park is busy and loud. A *lot* of people mill about the gorgeous grounds. I wonder how much we're actually going to get done here.

I take a breath through my nose, let it out through my mouth. The clean scent of cut grass fills my head as I adjust my sunglasses. I am so, so nervous. I haven't seen Rafa since we had that horrendously awkward conversation in the court-yard outside San Pedro on Wednesday.

Calm down, I tell myself. Rafa is just a tutor, nothing more. I should view him no differently than I view my professors, or the TAs in my classes.

But my heart knows better. It flaps around inside my chest, a caged bird attempting escape. For a minute, I contemplate tucking tail and running. I can tell Rafa I'm not feeling well. We can reschedule for sometime early next week, when I'm more prepared for the onslaught.

Then I see him.

And all my plans go up in smoke.

He's not far, just far enough that I can appreciate, quite thoroughly, his overwhelming handsomeness. The air goes still as I drink him in.

Forget tall glass of water. He's a jug of the juiciest, most potent sangria ever. I'm catching a buzz just looking at him.

Rafa leans against a concrete newel, his ankles crossed carelessly, the licks of his brown hair gilded by the sun. He's wearing a pair of Wayfarer Ray Bans, which somehow make the angles of his jaw appear sharper, more chiseled; his smooth skin catches the light, gleaming invitingly.

The thought is there before I can catch it, smother it.

I want. Badly, I want.

There's a blanket rolled underneath his arm. He's got both hands tucked into the pockets of his jeans. He's wearing—oh God, oh *God*—a heather gray T-shirt that looks broken in and soft to the touch. He fills it out nicely, the fabric stretched over broad shoulders and shapely arms.

My breath leaves my lungs as my gaze travels up and down the long, lean lines of his tall frame. Up and down. Up and down. I never, ever want to forget the way he looks right now. This is it, the moment when Edward drapes his arm across

Bella's shoulders and walks her into school, when Darcy meets Lizzie's gaze across the ballroom, that breathless, sigh-inducing moment when anything is possible.

When anticipation is at its thickest.

I've never been inside a moment like this before. I don't know what makes this one different from all the moments I've shared with other guys. But it's literally and figuratively a world away.

Rafa looks in the opposite direction, toward the crosswalk I should have taken instead of the tunnel. He's waiting for me. Catching him unaware like this, seeing him before he sees me—it's nice to have this moment to myself. A moment of appreciation, and of longing.

Longing that I have to bury the second he looks my way.

This isn't a love story.

This is a tutoring session.

But he is so handsome it hurts. How in the world am I supposed to *not* want that?

Rafa turns his head and looks right at me. His face splits in a smile, the lines around his mouth deepening in the most egregiously cute way imaginable.

In true gringo-Vivian style, I wave. The waving has to stop, I know. Eventually I'll think of some other, cooler way of greeting hot Spaniards, but for now the wave will have to do.

Rafa rocks against the newel, standing, and makes his way toward me.

"Qué tal, Vivian?"

What's up?

"Not much," I say. I wonder if the smell of his aftershave will ever stop turning me on. It's delicious, making me want to press my body against his body and bury my face in his neck. "Thanks again for meeting me on a Friday afternoon. Probably not how you wanted to start your weekend."

"No pasa nada. No worries. It is a beautiful afternoon, vale, and we have all of Saturday and Sunday to do the other things." He glances over my head, toward the direction I just came from, and his smile dims. "You took the tunnel?"

"I did. Why?"

He looks down at me. I can see the outline of his eyes through his sunglasses. His eyelashes cast long, boyish shadows across the skin beneath his eyes. The sun has darkened his freckles. "It is not safe. You should have told me to meet you on the other side. I would have walked with you if I knew. Always use the crosswalk, vale? Unless you are with me."

"Vale," I say. I'm taken a little off guard by his concern—it's nice, to have someone care like that. Too nice. "Should we get started?"

"Yes. I thought we could go over there, on the grass. There's some shade, where it's not so hot, yes?"

I walk beside him, our elbows brushing once, twice. We both move to apologize at the same time. His laugh sounds as nervous as mine. There's no way he's nervous too.

Rafa veers off the gravel path onto the grass, steering me with him. The grass sighs beneath our feet as we make our way across a wide, shady green. Couples stretch out on blankets for as far as the eye can see.

At first I think they're all having very intimate conversations. But then I realize they're actually—wow—making out. I'm talking full-on public displays of ardent affection, no one bothering to hide gropes, tongues, wandering fingers. Some couples are so close to each other, someone could just throw out an arm and start an orgy, but no one seems to really care. It's like a slow-rolling ocean of long, languid French kisses.

My heart squirms inside my chest.

Rafa and I pass a couple making these little newborn-kitten noises as they try to swallow each other's heads. It is so, *so* awkward.

"Sorry," Rafa says, gruffly. "For young people in Spain, it is very normal for us to live with our parents until we get older. Much older. Like thirty years old. Apartments are just too expensive for us to afford on our own, pues . . . we do not have privacy, and there is nowhere to go to be with your girlfriend except the park. It is a nice afternoon too, so I forgot how crowded it is."

"Very crowded," I say, picking my way around a girl straddling her guy. Part of me is grossed out, the other part is jealous. This reminder of the things I did with Rafa—of the things I want to do—is making me dizzy.

We spot a couple who've finished swapping spit for the day. The moment their blanket leaves the ground, Rafa settles ours in its place. I bend down to grab a corner, smoothing the blanket over the grass's prickly surface. It's a shady spot, thank God. The sounds of the park surround us: rustling trees, laughing couples. Gravel crunches as people pass by on the path. On some distant playground, children scream with pleasure.

Retiro is a beautiful place. Although it's TBD if I'll learn anything here—although it's apparently where people come to hump each other—it sure as hell beats the library.

Rafa toes out of his Eurotastic sneakers, digging a hand through his hair as he moves. I try not to stare. Instead, I turn and sit on the edge of the blanket, unbuckling my gladiator sandals carefully, lest I disturb the passionate couple next to us.

"So, um." I dig my giant economics textbook out of my bag. "D'you mind if we start with econ? I think that's the most pressing thing I need to work on."

"Por supuesto," he says.

I look up. The sun is blinding and so is Rafa's gorgeousness. I blink back the neon spots and streaks that dot my vision. "What does that mean?"

"Of course," he replies, sitting beside me. He crosses his legs. "Another good expression to know. Although not as good que te folle un pez."

"That one might be my favorite."

Rafa smiles. "No favorites yet, Vivian. I still have a lot to teach you."

"And I have a lot to learn. Like, a lot. I'm not even joking."

"Not so much to learn as you believe." He looks down and clears his throat, sliding his sunglasses into his hair. "Things are better, I hope? School is going well, and your señora too?"

"You mean have I stopped wandering around San Pedro, looking like a hot mess while crying my eyeballs out?" I scoff. "Yeah, I'd like to think things are better."

"You weren't a hot mess."

"Oh, yes, I was."

He's grinning at me again, only this time I can see his eyes. Oh, those eyes in this light are more green than blue. "Okay. Maybe a very little bit of hot mess."

"I'm proud to say I've only cried three times since then."

"Three times! I should have brought some cava for a celebration. Next time maybe. What did you cry about?"

"Stupid things. Once, because I got off at the wrong stop on the Metro and was late to class. Another time because my señora's dog ate not one, but *two* pairs of my favorite underwear."

"Lucky dog."

Wait, wait. Is it just me, or did that sound flirty?

I swallow. "He is the worst dog ever. And the last time was at lunch today, when I accidentally dipped my scarf in gazpacho and got it all over myself."

"You cried about gazpacho?"

"If you haven't noticed, I cry about a lot of stupid shit."

"It is not stupid. Gazpacho stains!"

"So I've learned."

"Well, I am very glad you are feeling better." He takes the book from my hands, opening it in his lap, scoots a little closer. "Vale. I am going to speak in Spanish from now on and so are you, okay? Stop me if you have questions. Me entiendes?"

"Yes, I—"

"En Español, Vivian." There's an authoritative edge to his words. I kinda dig it in a way I shouldn't.

"Por supuesto, Rafa," I tease.

It takes me a minute to get over how sexy he sounds as he speaks delicious Spanish. I just look at him from behind the safety of my sunglasses, marveling at the sound of his voice, the way it makes each word feel like a caress.

There is a very distinct tightening between my legs. He is so close that our bent knees almost touch. I blink, willing myself to focus on the words themselves, willing myself to separate the things I'm feeling from the things he's saying.

I get there. Eventually. Only when I start to focus on economic theorems instead of Rafa, I lose interest. Then I get frustrated with myself for losing interest. I get even more frustrated when I can only muster the most halting, elementary Spanish in reply to Rafa's questions.

I take notes. I have him repeat things. We discuss important points over and over again. *Focus, Vivian.* I need to focus. This is important. I need to get this, or my GPA is going downtown Charlie Brown.

Rafa is more patient with me than I am with the material. He must sense my rising frustration, because he puts the book back in my lap and leans in close. He trails a finger beneath the words on the page, speaking slowly. The woodsy scent of his aftershave surrounds me.

Focus.

His finger stops at that word—renacimiento.

What does that word mean? I ask in boxy, uncertain Spanish.

"Pues." Rafa narrows his eyes in concentration, rolling his hand as he tries to think of the word. "Ehm. Renaissance. Yes, like a new birth. A rebirth."

I sigh. What I would give to be studying the Renaissance masters we covered in Art History this morning instead of this stuff.

What I would give to be reborn as someone who was actually interested in econ.

Five more minutes, Rafa says in Spanish, reading my thoughts. *Give me five more minutes and then we'll move on to something else.*

Those five minutes feel like an eternity. When at last we reach the end of the chapter, I slam the book shut with a *thwack* that sends the birds in the tree above us flying from their branches.

"No offense," I say. "But that had to be one of the longest hours of my life."

Rafa plants his hands on the blanket behind him and leans back. His shirt pulls against the muscles in his shoulders and chest. "This is your major, yes? Economics?"

"Believe it or not, it is." I sigh again. "I just really hate studying it lately. I, like, dread it the way I dread going to the gym. I'm so relieved when it's over. It's frustrating, because I've always been a good student. I like to study. Like, I love to study art history, I just wish I was interested in something more specific than that. Something I could actually make a career out of."

"But you don't like to study your major." He looks at me. Really looks. The kind of look that turns my stomach inside out.

I hunch over, settling my forearms on my crossed legs. I

pick at the grass. "Not a good sign—I know. I get scared, sometimes, that I'm doing it all wrong. My major especially. Life. Jobs. That the decisions I'm making aren't the right ones. Round peg, square hole kind of thing."

"Round peg, square hole," he repeats, a small smile tugging at the edges of his mouth. "I like that saying. It is good for people our age. Lots of big decisions we make in these years. But perhaps if you hate economics, you should think again about making it your life?"

When he says it like that, I wonder why I *haven't* thought more about making econ the center of my universe.

I shrug. "It's the most popular major at Meryton. It will help me get a good job when I graduate. It's safe." I swivel my head and see he's still looking at me. "It's what everyone else is doing. It's what I *should* do."

"But is it what you want to do?" His eyes search mine. "That is an important thing to think about too."

Oh dear Lord. Not only is Rafa ridiculously good looking, charming, and foreign. He also *gets it*. He understands.

I swallow for what feels like the hundredth time. "What are you studying, if you don't mind me asking?"

He shoots me a look. "You're changing the subject. Why?"

"You're asking the right questions," I say. "Which means they're questions I don't want to answer. So we have to talk about something else."

"Vale. But one day, I would like to hear your answers." He stretches out his legs. "I majored in journalism and Spanish literature. Not safe things. But now in my graduate studies I am working with a newspaper here in Madrid. I have always loved the sports, and so I write articles about fútbol—in America you call it soccer, yes—pieces on the matches, the players, news out of the leagues. In Europe, fútbol is like a religion, so there is much to say. The articles are part of my thesis. One day I would like to be a sports writer and a professor."

I blink. "Wait. You're a sports reporter for a newspaper?"

"Yes." He squints an eye against the fading afternoon light that streams through the trees. "Do you think it is stupid, what I do?"

"No," I say. "I think it's awesome. It's very Clark Kent of you."

He grins. "I am missing the glasses though."

"You would look good in the glasses." I sit up. "But the cape? Not so much. That's cool, though, that you're doing something you love. Something a little off the beaten path. It seems like everyone at Meryton wants to be a lawyer or a doctor or a banker, and that's it."

"Writing is my passion. So I chase after it. The way I chased after you on Wednesday."

I roll my eyes. "*So* dramatic. Now I know where you get it from—all those fútbol players rolling around the field in agony after someone taps their shin."

Rafa shrugs, his eyes dancing with mischief. "I like to chase you."

Maybe it's something in the air, the pheromones put off by the couples making out around us. But Rafa is flirting with me. And I can't help but flirt back.

"I'm very hard to catch," I say.

"I've noticed. Good thing I'm fast."

"You really do like to brag, don't you?"

"I do."

"Is that a Spanish thing?"

"It's a me thing. Just like you talking with your hands is a you thing," he says, nodding at the offending appendages.

I glance down at my hands. They're poised midair, fingers crooked for emphasis. "Yeah," I laugh, dropping my hands into my lap. "I guess so."

It could be my imagination, but I think Rafa's leaning close. The way he leaned when we were sitting on the curb, eating churros. Maybe I'm leaning a little bit too. The air between us twists, tightens, thrums with anticipation. The bird inside my chest is going nuts.

I want. Oh, how I want.

I jump when the textbook slides off my lap.

"Glad we're done with this," I say, tossing it across the blanket.

As I move I pull my dress up my legs, revealing more than a little thigh. I worry I've flashed Rafa, but just as I think to tug it back into place, I catch Rafa looking at me—his eyes sliding up my legs, his lips parting. His gaze darkens.

Flashes with something sharp.

I freeze. I'd be lying if I said I didn't like looking at him looking at me. It might as well be his hands moving over my body, the sensation is just as poignant, just as immediate. My skin breaks out in goose bumps.

I watch his Adam's apple bob as he swallows, hard. "Dios mio, tía," he scoffs, his eyes raking up the length of my legs—ankles to hips and back again. "You are killing me."

He reaches across the blanket and grasps the hem of my dress between his thumb and forefinger. He whips it back over my legs. "I don't want you to kill anyone else, vale?"

As he covers me up, his thumb knuckle glides across my thigh. I bite my lip against the pulse of desire between my legs.

He lets go of my dress, but his hand stops on my bare leg, just above my knee. He pauses.

Lingers.

Waits.

Suddenly, I'm too curious, too turned on, to stop him. I know I should to tell him to stop, stop, please, before we do something we shouldn't, but I can't. The feel of his hand on me—it's like heaven on earth. It's too much. It's not enough.

In the space of a single heartbeat, I know it will never be enough.

I don't say anything. I meet his eyes, and that is all the permission he needs. His gaze never leaving mine, his fingers start moving again, finding purchase in my skin; curling slowly, slowly, around my thigh, sliding up to the place where my legs meet. His touch is gentle but sure. Not a boy's touch, but a man's. Possessive. Naughty. No one has ever touched me like this. It's intoxicating.

He's definitely leaning in now, eyes flicking to my lips. His hair flutters away from his face in a breeze. My breath leaves my lungs and the world blurs around us and the rush of my pulse in my ears is deafening. I'm terrified.

I am overwhelmingly, acutely alive.

From the look in Rafa's eyes, so is he.

Just when our mouths are about to meet—just when I think I'm about to burst—he sucks a breath through his teeth, like he's in pain, and pulls back.

"Vivian," he says, breathing hard. He rests his forehead against mine. The gesture is so sweet, so pained, it makes my heart clench. "You said no."

For a second I'm too stunned to think of anything to say. My mind is mush.

"Yes," I blurt. "I mean I know I said no before, but—"

"I am not going to do anything you don't want to do," he says. "You said no before. But now . . . God, Vivian, you're confusing me."

I swallow, the sound embarrassingly audible. "*I'm* confusing me."

His eyes fly open to meet mine. "You said you didn't want to start something. That you got hurt before and you didn't want to get hurt again. I don't want to do something that's going to hurt you, Vivian."

He's right. This is a bad idea. No matter how badly I want Rafa to kiss me the way we kissed Saturday night on the sidewalk, I need to protect my heart, as cheesy as that sounds. It's been through enough this past year. The last thing it needs is to suffer through another disappointment, another relationship that won't last.

Rafa can't give me the *enduring* romance I'm looking for. The kind that lasts, that really means something. Even if he is being incredibly, frustratingly sweet right now.

"Right," I say. Falling back is an agony. I look away, embarrassed. "You're right. I'm sorry . . . I, um . . . I think I got carried away."

Rafa spears the same hand that was on my thigh through his hair, mussing the waves. The apples of his cheeks are bright pink. "Please, no apologizing," he says. "I shouldn't have let it go so far."

"It's not your fault," I say.

"It is good we stop," Rafa says. "If we kiss, we cannot judge all these kissing people around us."

I grin. "It *is* fun to judge."

"Almost as fun as capes and crying footballers," he says, grinning back. The friendly lines of his face take the edge off my embarrassment. God he's cute. "Want to take a look at art history? I hope you are liking it. I spoke with the profesora about you—she is excited to have you in her class."

"She is?" I ask.

"She is."

I tuck my hair behind my ear. "Thanks for doing that. I appreciate you looking out for me."

"It is no problem." Rafa shrugs. "I am your tutor. I want you to do well, Vivian. And I think you will."

We're finishing up art history, the light fading around us, when I turn to see Maddie making her way down a nearby path.

My prickle of annoyance takes me totally off guard. Not five days ago, I was so happy to see Mads I almost cried. Now I'm annoyed?

What the hell is going on with me?

"Hey," I say when she arrives at our blanket.

"Hey! Sorry to interrupt, but there's no food in the house, and Stella is MIA. Thought I'd come find you so we could grab a bite to eat."

"Oh," I say. "Oh, yeah, sure."

Maddie turns to Rafa. It's barely noticeable, the glimmer of interest in her dark eyes, but I know her too well to miss it. You'd have to be blind to not be interested in Rafa Montoya.

"I'm Maddie." She holds out her hand. "You must be Viv's tutor, Rafael."

Rafa offers her one of his heady smiles. "Nice to meet you, Maddie. Please, call me Rafa."

"It's very nice to meet you, Rafa," she says. "How goes the tutoring?"

"We're almost done. I can give you some ideas for restaurants, if you do not have one in mind already?"

"Actually." Maddie sits on the blanket beside him. "Why don't you join us? I'd love the lesson in tapas."

Rafa glances at me. Going to dinner with the two of them —watching Maddie parade her Spanish and her C-cups in front of Rafa—is the last thing I want to do. But I can't say no without looking like an asshole. Besides, this is the first time I've seen Maddie smile since our dinner with the girls on Wednesday, and I'm not about to ruin that.

"Sure," I say, my voice high with forced cheerfulness. "That would be great. Maybe we can finally discover what this mysterious albóndigas is about."

"Balls," Rafa says.

Maddie scrunches her nose. "Balls?"

"Yes. How do you say—balls of meat?"

"Meatballs!" She laughs, tossing her long hair over her shoulder. "Well. This is going to be a fun night."

"So fun," I say.

CHAPTER TEN

But it is fun, despite the knot in my stomach that tightens every time Rafa smiles at Maddie, every time she smiles back and speaks Spanish in her cutesy Colombian accent.

Rafa takes us to a crowded restaurant in the basement of a nondescript building. Inside it looks like a cave with arched stone ceilings and lamps fitted with trendy Edison bulbs. It's early by Madrid standards—a little past nine o'clock—but the place is packed with well-dressed Spaniards, laughter and conversation echoing across the cramped space.

Of course Rafa knows the waiter, who assures us we have come to the right place for the best tapas in Madrid.

So, I've never really had tapas. There are a couple places in Charlotte that serve them, but I have a feeling it's not the real deal. From what I understand, tapas are basically just appetizer-sized portions you share with everyone at the table. It's definitely a departure from how we eat in America. Here, there's no such thing as a big, satisfying main course. But I'm willing to keep an open mind.

"It's all about the picar," Rafa explains. "How would you say it in English? Ehm . . . like, picking. Picking at the food, a little bit of everything. Nibble, maybe, is the better word? Snack? You will see when the food comes."

Dishes come in waves whenever, it seems, they are ready. First we get bowls of olives and potato chips with our glasses of vino tinto de la casa. Then a platter of manchego cheese—it's good, like white Cheddar, but better—and jamón íberico.

"You guys seem to really like your ham," I say, spearing a paper-thin slice of cured meat with my fork. "What's that about?"

Rafa chews, swallows. "We are very much lovers of pork in Spain. I don't know why, really. Except that it's delicious."

"It melts in your mouth," Maddie says.

"What do you think, Vivian?" Rafa asks, meeting my eyes across the table. In the semi-darkness his seem to glow, pools of fluorescent blue-green.

"It's incredible. I love salty things, so jamón is right up my alley."

"Wait 'til you try the albóndigas," he says.

"The balls," Maddie giggles. "Who doesn't love those?"

It's all I can do not to roll my eyes.

The albóndigas are next, along with gambas—shrimp sautéed in olive oil and garlic—and pan con tomate, crusty pieces of bread spread with a tomato-ish tapenade.

Rafa explains each dish to us, pointing as he goes. He says gambas are his favorite, but nothing beats his mom's albóndigas, pan con tomate can be hit or miss, but here it's awesome because they get their bread from a bakery down the street, and he cracks a perfectly off-color joke about meatballs.

He lights up as he speaks. Maybe it's my second glass of red wine, but I'm entranced. It's obvious he loves his food, almost as much as he loves bragging and that little frayed bracelet. Ever the flirty gentleman, Rafa is a total charmer, flashing his smile to great effect. I've never seen anything quite like it. He makes us laugh, he tells us stories, and the three of us talk about our families (he's an only child, his parents are lawyers) and our favorite food. There are no awkward pauses, even though we're all stuffing our faces.

He's the kind of guy I've always wanted for a boyfriend. Handsome. Charming. Funny. Too bad he lives an ocean away from my life back in North Carolina.

I notice the beautiful people at the tables around us are chatting away too, gesturing with their hands as they burst into laughter. I'm starting to think conversation is an art, one that Americans aren't very good at and one that Spaniards have down pat, Rafa included.

He was right. I love the balls of meat so much I order another porción of them.

I'm full by the time the waiter sets tortilla on the table. But I eat the potato-omelet-deliciousness anyway, along with patatas bravas, which I'd describe as breakfast potatoes drizzled with spicy mayo. Like everything else, both dishes are a little different, but oh so good. The three of us practically lick the plates clean. My stomach hurts from so much food and so much laughter. It feels good to be this full; I haven't realized how hungry I've been since I got here.

Maybe this won't be a hungry semester, after all.

We finish the meal with these little shots of apricot-flavored liqueur. Rafa calls it a digestif, because it's supposed to help us digest the meal. They're a nice way to end the night, since the liqueur gives me a nice, sleepy buzz.

"That was really great," Maddie says as we climb the stairs and make our way through the door. It's still hot out, a little humid, even though it's after midnight.

"Really great," I add. "I was worried there for a minute I wouldn't like Spanish food. Thanks for proving me wrong."

Rafa puts his hands in his pockets and grins at me. "You are very welcome, Vivian. I told you before, es un placer."

It is a pleasure.

Our gazes meet in the darkness, lingering one wine-lazy heartbeat, then another. I've seen the way men look at the women they like—the women they want. No one's ever really looked at me that way.

Not until now.

There's a flutter in my belly, a sensation of falling, of surrendering to gravity. What I would give for the courage I had that first night, when I had nothing to lose and I stood on my toes and I kissed hi—

"So, like, you're a student liaison for Meryton in Madrid." Maddie turns to Rafa as he turns to Maddie. "Does that mean you'll be traveling with the program?"

"Yes," he says, a bit gruffly. "I'll be on the autobus with all of you to Toledo next week."

"Vale," she replies. "I'm glad we get to see you again."

"I'll be around all semester."

I look away, my sleepy buzz devolving into irritation.

"You two should head home. I know it's been a very long first week, and you are probably tired," Rafa says. He glances down the street, looking for a cab.

How does he do it? I wonder. How is he always so in tune with what I'm thinking or feeling?

"Yeah, we should get going," I say. "Our apartment's not far from here, so we'll walk."

"Really?" Maddie pouts. "I was hoping to share a cab—"

"We're walking," I say. I guess it's my turn to be gruff. "Thanks again for everything, Rafa. I'll be in touch about our next tutoring session, okay? Maybe on Monday?"

He turns back to me. "Okay. I can do any day, really. I will make the time."

"Monday is good."

"Vale."

And then he's leaning down, pecking each of my cheeks. The scent of his aftershave hits me, hard, and my heart clenches. *I want.* Even though I can't have, I want.

It could be my imagination, but I think he pauses for the tiniest half-second, his cheek brushing mine. A bolt of desire moves through my body. I don't want to feel this way about Rafa. I *can't* feel this way about him.

"Buenas noches," he says, and then he kisses Maddie too.

I don't know where it comes from—if I'm trying to make Maddie jealous by flaunting this inside joke I have with Rafa, or if I just want to flirt with him because it's fun—but the words are out of my mouth before I can stop them.

"Buenos días," I say.

He grins. "You're right. It is after medianoche, isn't it? Buenos días, Vivian."

He hails a cab, and Maddie and I begin our short walk home. For the first few minutes, neither of us says anything. I'm too dumbstruck, too confused, to attempt conversation.

I have a feeling I'm not the only girl Rafa laid out tonight with his smile and his wit and that handsome face.

"What's up with you guys?" Maddie asks at last. "You and Rafa."

"What do you mean, what's up with us? He's my tutor."

"That whole good morning, good night thing. It sounded kinda flirty. What was that about?"

"Oh." My stomach feels queasy. Maybe that digestif had the opposite of its intended effect? "It's just a little thing from the other day. Rafa can be a flirty guy I guess. That place though—the food was great, right?"

"It was fucking amazing," Maddie says. "And so is Rafa. I mean. Not only is he gorgeous, he's excellent too."

Maddie and I reserve that word—excellent—for only our most favorite people. It's basically code for "bow down before them and beg for their sexual blessing because they are creatures from a more perfect realm." Between the two of us, we've identified four, maybe five excellent people in the three years we've known each other—one of them being Mindy Kaling, because she's just the best.

So, yeah, when Maddie says Rafa is excellent, I know the well-oiled wheels in her head are turning.

"Yes," I say. "He is excellent. Totally."

Even though I'm not looking at her, I can sense Maddie narrowing her eyes at me. "You sure there's nothing between you two? You don't like him, he doesn't like you?"

"I'm sure." I don't know why I'm saying it, but I do. "I mean. He's cute, and maybe I had a little crush on him when we first met Saturday night. But like I told the girls on Wednesday, I couldn't hook up with him even if he was into it. Which he's not."

I'm pulling a Lizzie Bennett, I know, probably complicating things by not being honest with my *best friend* about how I'm feeling. I should tell her the truth. I should tell her how I feel about Rafa, about my fears that he'll just break my heart.

That he'll make a fool out of me the way Keith did.

But maybe if I keep denying the things I feel for Rafa, those inconvenient feelings will eventually go away altogether. Maybe if I keep telling my friends that there's nothing going on between the two of us, I'll start believing it myself.

I don't think I can bear the pain of another heartbreak at the end of this semester. So instead I'm choosing my heart to break now. It will hurt less.

"Why do you assume it would be just a hook up?" she asks

"Because, Maddie, it's always just a hook up for me."

She loops her arm through mine and pulls me close. "Your time is coming, Viv. You've built up the best damn boyfriend karma out of anyone ever. Don't let that dickweed Keith make you lose the faith. It's gonna happen—I have a feeling it will be soon."

"Let's hope not," I scoff. "I don't have time for that ish this semester. C- in econ, remember?"

"You and I both know you're gonna be fine," she replies. "So, hey. If you're not interested in Rafa, do you mind if, um, I have a little fun with him?"

I close my eyes, take a deep breath. This is silly. I'm being silly. I told Rafa no. I have no claim on him. I have no right to keep him to myself. With all the stuff going on with her parents, Maddie deserves a little fun. She deserves the distraction.

There is no right choice here. Either way I lose. But there is a way that Maddie can win.

"Of course not," I say.

"Awesome," she says. "I think he's going to be a good time."

I was prepared to give Rafa up because we could not be together. Because it wouldn't have worked, not the way I wanted it to.

But if I'm being honest, I was not prepared for the possibility of Rafa being with someone else.

Especially my best friend.

I'm just about to turn off the tiny bedside lamp when my phone lights up. My heart skips a beat when I see it's a text from Justin Timberlake.

Everything ok?

I furrow my brow. *Yup. Just about to go 2 bed. Why do u ask? U ok?*

That little blinking ellipsis appears at the bottom of our conversation, letting me know he's typing something. Then it disappears. A few seconds later, it appears again, like he can't decide what to say.

It's kinda cute.

U were a little bit quiet at dinero. Now I am awake wondering if u are upset about what happéned at Retiro.

A pause. Then he sends another text: *Sorry, I meant to type dinner. My phone is set in Spanish so getting the English right is tricky.*

I really, really wish Rafa would stop being so damn excellent. Then I wouldn't have to fight the squidgy rise in my chest as I read his text once, twice, five times.

I have to be real with *someone* tonight. I feel it's my duty to the universe.

Thx for checking in. I am ok. Feel confused about what happened, 2 b honest.

The wait for Rafa's ellipsis to turn into words is excruciating.

I understand u are scared. I will respect that. But I am having really great times with u. It is difficult for me not to like u more than just mi student. Also u have very nice legs.

That makes me smile, hard.

I type the words, erase them. I type them again. And then before I can second (third?) guess myself, I hit send.

Thx. U have nice everything.

But?

How do u always know what I'm thinking?

I'm learning yoú, Vivian.

Maddie turns over in the bed beside me, away from the light.

Maddie, who wants to have a little fun this semester with a hot Madrileño so she can forget about her parents' nasty divorce.

"Sorry," I whisper, and click off the lamp.

She sniffles. She's crying, I know she is; she's cried every night about her parents since she got here. But when I ask if everything is okay, she pretends to be asleep.

I need to learn econ, I type. *In Spanish.*

Ok. I told u I will help u get all A grades.

My heart sinks. *Thx again 4 fun time tonite. Balls were GREAT.*

Balls r always great. Glad u enjoyed.

I'm tempted to reply, but I don't.

I recognize these things I'm feeling for Rafa—whatever they are—they're not going away. But I can't give into them. I can't afford to give into them.

CHAPTER ELEVEN

Monday Afternoon

I step into the café, the bell above the door jangling merrily. I glance around, the strong, stringent smells of coffee and steamed milk giving me an instant jolt. The low hum of conversation hangs in the air. I feel a twinge of disappointment when I don't see Rafa amongst the crowd of young-ish Madrileños. It's been a struggle, trying not to think about him, trying not to think about what he was doing over the weekend, who he was with.

I make my way to the counter. There's a tasty looking array of pastries in a glass case, along with an even tastier collection of bottled beer. I wonder if all cafés in Spain serve a side of beer with their cappuccinos. I could definitely get on board with this cultural tradition.

The barista guy behind the counter looks at me expectantly, and my chest constricts with an anxiety I've become quite familiar with this past week. I still haven't figured out, exactly, how to order things in Spanish, never mind the fact that my accent is cringe-worthy in the extreme. Whenever I open my mouth, I just seem to embarrass myself and everyone around me.

"Um," I say. It's been a long day—three classes, plus a meeting and some grocery shopping—so I really, really want a beer. But it's only four o'clock, and Rafa and I have a lot of boring econ to get through this afternoon. If anything, I should get a coffee the size of my head so I can study without falling asleep.

"Sí?" the guy asks, brusquely.

I take a deep breath through my nose. *You can do this.* It's only coffee.

"Un . . . uh, café, por favor?"

The barista replies with a string of incoherent Spanish, something about espresso, a double, maybe, the world leche —milk—is thrown in there.

My shoulders tense. All I want is a coffee. At this point, I don't care if it's one of those tiny cups of espresso or a ginor-mous latte that could fuel an eighteen-wheeler. I just want to be caffeinated.

"Vale," I try.

"No," the guy says with an exasperated sigh. He tries to speak to me again, this time more slowly.

The creep of tears tightens in my throat. I know if I try to talk again I'm going to cry for the nine hundredth time since I started my study abroad adventure.

I open my mouth, determined to plow ahead anyway, when I hear the jangle of the bell above the door. I look over my shoulder and there he is—Rafa, his broad shoulders limned in a fuzzy line of late afternoon sun.

My limbs flood with relief, as potent and immediate as the rush that follows knocking back a shot of vodka. He smiles and I smile, his blue eyes soft as he comes to stand beside me at the counter. Now that Rafa's here, I feel safe, confident.

I feel better.

Oh, Lord.

"Hola," he says, bending down to kiss my cheeks. "Como estás?"

How are you?

I glance at the guy behind the counter. "I'd be better if I could figure out how to order a coffee. How are you?"

"Coffee? Bah, you want a cerveza, don't you?"

"No-o?" I say.

Rafa holds up two fingers. "Dos cervezas, por favor." He turns to me. "It will help the economics go by faster, yes? Easy to order too. But next time if you want coffee, I will teach you how to order it. It's very easy also, and with all the studying you want to do, I think you will need it."

I scoff, my eyes glued to my feet. "Do you always play the white knight for all your idiot American students? Coming to their rescue in cafes across Madrid?"

"No." The heat of his gaze breaks over the crown of my head, dripping slowly, like honey, down the rest of my body. "Just for you, white girl. And stop saying you are an idiot."

"Are you going to at least let me pay?"

Rafa grabs our bottles of beer off the counter, the necks tucked between the fingers of his right hand. "Next time."

Even the way he moves—the way he does things—is sexy. It's impossible not to stare.

We settle at a tiny little table in the back of the café. Rafa takes the chair, I take the booth. I crack open my econ textbook with a groan. Each minute is an eternity, but I have a better grasp of the material than I did during our first tutoring session. It doesn't hurt to have a super-hot Spanish guy murmuring nothings in your ear, even if those nothings have to do with Keynsian economics and the class divide in Franco-era Spain.

We finish our beers. Rafa stands, says he'll buy us another round.

I grab my wallet. "Absolutely not. If you don't let me pay this time, I am not going to drink it."

Rafa cocks a brow. "I don't believe you."

"Is that a challenge?"

"Do you want it to be?"

I narrow my eyes. "Don't tempt me, Rafa."

He holds up his hands. "I wouldn't dare, *Vivian*."

For a minute we stare each other down. A smile spreads slowly across his face. I bite the inside of my lip to keep from bursting with laughter.

I bolt from my seat, the table wobbling in my wake. Rafa is half a second behind me, his footfalls light for someone so tall. I glance over my shoulder, the laughter coming now, and he reaches for me, curling an arm around my waist. He tugs me against him, his deep, masculine laughter filling my ears.

"Te," he breathes, "atrape!" *Caught you!*

"Oh no you don't," I manage, twisting out of his grasp. People stare as we dart past, but I don't care. Something about being chased makes me giddy, gleeful even. It's like I'm six again, being chased around our backyard by my younger brother. I don't know why we laughed so hard then. But we did.

I'm laughing harder now. Maybe because I'm a little buzzed from the beer. Maybe because being chased by Rafa is so, *so* much more fun than being chased by my four-year-old brother.

Breathless, I reach the counter. Rafa slides into place next to me, hip-checking me away from the register. I hip-check him back, but he ignores me, digging a couple Euro bills out of his wallet. I lean against him and keep pushing. He trips on his feet, laughing, and pushes back.

The barista dude shoots us a look that could kill.

"No!" I say, slamming my money on the counter before

Rafa can pay. I glance at the barista. "Por favor, voy a pagar por dos cervezas." *Please, I would like to pay for two beers*.

Rolling his eyes, the barista takes my money and slides two green bottles across the counter.

Rafa turns to me, his face flush with laughter, eyes dancing. "Muy bien, Vivian! Even if you are using your Spanish to buy the beers I want to pay for."

I look up at him, grinning. "You gotta let me pay for something, Rafa. You're only saving me from flunking this semester. I mean, no big deal or anything." I hand him his beer. "It's the least I can do."

"Just this once, then," he says, clinking the heel of his beer against mine. "Salud."

"Salud." I take a sip. It's cold, so refreshing that for a minute I close my eyes to savor it—savor this moment, Rafa and me drinking beer at five o'clock on a Monday night in Madrid, my ribs sore from laughing so hard. This is one of those magical moments Rachel was talking about. I don't want to be anywhere else—*be* anyone else—on earth right now.

I open my eyes and see Rafa gazing down at me, a funny look on his face.

"What?" I ask.

"Nothing." He looks away, a small, almost pained grin tugging at his lips. "It is nothing. What else do you like to work on today?"

"I have an essay to write for Spanish Lit—we're supposed to choose a Neruda poem and analyze it."

"Neruda! Yes. I love him."

I slide back into my perch on the booth while Rafa takes his seat across from me.

"You love Spanish love poetry?" I ask, digging my notebook out of my bag. "I thought you liked writing about soccer."

"Fútbol."

"Right. Sorry. Fútbol."

Rafa shrugs. "I like sports, and I like art too. All kinds of writing and reading I like."

I place a packet of photocopied poems on the table between us. Rafa slides it toward him, rotating it so he is able to read the poems.

"Do you have a favorite Neruda poem? They gave us so many—half the battle is just translating them and choosing one to write about. I've studied Neruda before, but never any of the poems in this packet."

"I do. I hope it is in here. It is one of the twenty love poems—número catorce . . ." Rafa folds the pages over the staple in the top left-hand corner of the packet, searching for the poem.

"Number fourteen?" I translate. "That doesn't sound very romantic."

"Trust me, you will like it. Neruda, his poems are . . . what is the word? Fuerte. Explícito. How do you say it in English?"

I blink. "Strong. Explicit."

"Yes. Ah, here it is." He tilts the page on the table so we can both read it.

"Yikes," I say. "It's a long one."

"It is worth the effort. Vale." Rafa begins to read the poem aloud, his voice low, his tongue languid as it moves easily over each ridge and mountain and valley of the words on the page. The poem is complex; I'm able to translate about three quarters of it, but some of the words and phrases I have never seen before. I stop Rafa several times, asking what a word means, an expression.

He keeps reading, the two of us straining to see the poem. The sensuality of Neruda's words, coupled with the lilting way Rafa says them, makes my head spin.

I stop him again, leaning over the table to point at a line, our fingers touching over the last word.

Without saying a thing, Rafa turns the page to face me and stands. He slides onto the booth next to me, setting his beer on the table in front of us. "This way, you see better, yes?"

"Sí." I scoot over, my body thrumming with the awareness of his beside me. He's very close. Close enough that we look like one of those annoying couples sitting on the same side of the table on a date.

"Tienes razón, Rafa." I say. "Esta poema es . . . fuerte." *You were right, Rafa. This poem is strong.*

Strong isn't the right word though. This poem can't be described using an adjective, it's weightier than that. It deserves a verb, or a noun at least. It's not strong; it's longing in another language. It's a feeling, a captured moment. A meditation on love and sex and meaning.

We finish translating the poem. I take a sip of my beer. Rafa does the same. I can hear him swallow. I glance at him from the corner of my eye. His eyes are dark, hooded, what I imagine Neruda's eyes looked like when he wrote this poem.

I finger the edge of the page, looking away. "I see why this is your favorite poem. It's beautiful."

"I was very romantic in my teenage years," he scoffs. "When I was sixteen I had a very big crush on the daughter of my parents' friends. She didn't like me very much."

I make a face. "Really? I don't believe it."

"I was awkward still," he says, shrugging. "I thought I would go crazy thinking of her. Neruda knew my mood."

"Do you still think about her?" I meet his eyes.

He grins. "No. She isn't the one I think about."

His gaze lingers on my face one beat, then another.

"What about you?" he asks, carefully. "Is there someone you think about?"

My restless fingers move to the damp label on my beer bottle. I've only known Rafa for, what, a week now? But our friendship—if you can call it that—already feels broken in, comfortable. Easy. I want to tell him everything. I want to know what he thinks.

"No," I say. "There used to be a guy, a little less than a year ago. My story is the same as yours. I liked him. A lot. More than I have ever liked anyone. We would talk for hours, you know? About everything. Our families, our dreams. Stuff I never really told anyone else. I felt like we had something special. The way I felt when I was with him—it was really nice. But then I found out he had a girlfriend, and he didn't like me the way I liked him, so. Yeah. God, I hope I'm not weirding you out, telling you all this."

"I want to hurt this idiota who hurt you," Rafa says. "But no weirding out. I asked, and I will listen to whatever you want to say."

I meet his eyes. He is so sincerely interested it makes my heart flutter.

"I was pretty devastated," I say, looking away. "I mean, he was a total dickweed. Totally not worth it. But it hurt."

"It hurts like hell," Rafa says.

"It does."

"But hopefully it hurts less now?"

I glance up at him. "Yes," I say. And for the first time, I actually mean it.

He smiles at me. "The love that is not returned is the worst. But sometime our day will come, yes? Sometime the person we want will want us too."

I want you, Rafa.

Only I can't have him. I like him, I do. How could I not? It's his smile, his eyes, the things he says and does. It's the beer and the way he read the poem and the way he dances. He's excellent, and I like him.

But I am good at tamping down my feelings. At smothering them until I can convince myself they don't exist. There is too much at risk—my heart, my hard-won sense of what I want—to feel anything for Rafa besides distant, torturous admiration.

The kind of admiration Neruda would approve of, I think.

I open my notebook to a blank page. "Let's get some bullet points down that I can use in my essay. The image of the wind, maybe that's an allusion to the shifting nature of one's feelings . . ."

"En español, Vivian."

CHAPTER TWELVE

Friday
Toledo

All of us—fifty Meryton in Madrid students, Elena, and a few of our professors and student liaisons, Rafa included—catch a bus on Friday morning to Toledo. It's a short ride, a little less than an hour. But with Maddie in the seat beside Rafa, laughing and flirting and cuffing his shoulder like they're old pals, it feels a hell of a lot longer. He's the only one who seems to make her smile these days; up until this morning, she's been pretty down. I overheard a conversation she had with her mom last night, and she could hardly talk, she was sobbing so hard.

I didn't think things could get worse with her family, but they are. I'm happy to see her happy.

I just wish she would be happy with someone besides Rafa.

"Wow," Maddie wheezes, hand on her chest. "I haven't laughed that hard in a while. It feels good. Like, really good. Thanks for that."

"Thank *you* for laughing at my jokes. My friends are always telling me how I am not so funny." Rafa turns to face her. "Why haven't you done more of it? The laughing, I mean."

"It's a long story," she replies, her smile fading as she stares into her lap. "And not a pleasant one. Trust me, you don't want to hear it."

"Hey." Rafa ducks his head, imploring her to look at him. "Hey, Maddie, of course I want to hear it. I am always here to listen for a friend."

She's looking at him now, a funny gleam in her eyes. "Friends? We're friends?" There's a hopeful note in her voice. It makes my stomach clench. It's obvious she sees it too. Rafa's handsomeness. His overwhelming wonderfulness.

"Of course we are," he replies easily. "Now tell me why you haven't been laughing, and then maybe after we laugh some more."

She studies him for a minute. "You sure?"

"I'm sure. I am thinking you really need someone to listen, yes?"

"Yes," she almost breathes. "Yes. That would be nice."

Maddie's gaze flicks to me. I look away, quickly turning back to Al, who's sitting next to me. He offers me some of the digestivo cookies his aunt—Rafa's mom—packed him for lunch, and starts to chat away about his thoughts on Madrileño sleeping habits. ("I've figured it out. They just sleep less than we do. Way less.") My head hurts from listening to two conversations at once: ours and Maddie and Rafa's.

I can smell the woodsy scent of Rafa's aftershave. He's wearing a blue and white checked button-down today, the sleeves rolled up to his elbows. His hair is still a little wet from the shower, curlier than normal. I wonder what he looks like in the shower. Naked—probably very naked. My vision

131

goes a little blurry as I imagine what that nakedness would look like exactly.

"Hello?" Al is saying. "Earth to Vivian."

"Sorry," I say. "Sorry. I didn't have time for coffee this morning. So you think we should adopt the siesta in the States, huh? I'd vote for that."

The bus gets quiet when we round a bend and the sweeping view of Toledo fills the windows. The city is set high on a rocky hill beside a river that glistens turquoise in the morning sun. A square castle, each of its four towers topped with pointy spires that impale a wide-open sky, dominates the city. Medieval walls loop across the hill like pale ribbons.

I glance away from the window and find Rafa looking at me, that funny expression softening his face again. He's wearing sunglasses, but I can still see the outline of his eyes through the lenses.

"What?" I ask, grinning.

"It is fun, seeing your thoughts," he replies.

"You can see my thoughts?"

"You wear them on your sleeve, remember?"

Rafa remembers everything.

I bite my lip. "I do."

"Toledo is beautiful, yes? Wait until you see the El Greco paintings they have here. You will love it."

My heart skips a beat—for Rafa and for El Greco.

"El Greco?" Maddie's head appears over her seat. "He's one of my favorites. I like how dark his work can be."

"Very dark," Rafa says. "Very moody."

"Like Neruda's poems," I say.

It's his turn to grin. "My student is learning."

"Poetry hardly counts."

"Of course it counts. Especially if it's Neruda."

I catch Maddie's gaze again. She's watching me. Watching us.

We divide ourselves into several smaller groups—I'm with Rafa, Mads, Al, Laura, and a couple others—and make our way into the city. The sun bears down on us like a burning weight, radiating off Toledo's ancient stone streets and walls. Walking behind Rafa, I see his shirt is spotted with sweat. The nape of his neck is wet. I want to run my finger along the skin there, taste the salt of his sweat.

I blink. *Stop.* I have to stop. First the nakedness, now the sweat. I'm going to melt if I don't get my mind out of the gutter.

Our professor takes us to the cathedral, a synagogue, a bakery, a silversmith's shop. I follow the group through Toledo's steep, winding streets, sweat dripping into my eyes. All the while Maddie and Rafa are talking, talking, sometimes in English, mostly in Spanish. Rafa is charming as ever, hearing the happy lilt of his voice as he speaks, seeing him look down at Maddie as she does. He's handsome, and he's a good guy, a good listener. I only wish he was listening to me.

I watch them and a familiar knot tightens in my stomach. I'm starting to think this whole situation was a bad idea. I should have told Maddie about my feelings for Rafa, regardless of whether or not I could act on them.

I should have kept it to one beer with Rafa during our tutoring session on Monday. And I should have picked a different Neruda poem, one without a billion explícito allusions to sex.

But it's too late. It's obvious that Rafa helps Maddie forget about her family, for a little while at least. What kind of monster would I be to ruin that? Rafa isn't mine; he's totally fair game.

We duck into yet another church, this one smaller. Our

group lets out a collective sigh of relief as we step into the shadowed cool put off by stone. My legs ache and my dress sticks to my skin. Now Rafa and Maddie are whispering. I look at Maddie, who is smiling like an idiot as Rafa tells her a story in Spanish that is probably both hilarious and wonderfully inappropriate.

"Why don't you just tell him?"

I nearly jump at the sound of Laura's voice. She walks beside me, eyes focused on the couple a few paces in front of us. I may be sweating like a pig, but Laura merely glistens, complementing her tan.

I look at her. She looks back. She knows. I don't know how, but she knows I like Rafa. Maybe she isn't the rich girl fembot I thought she was.

I look away. "Please don't say anything."

"I won't. But you should still tell him you like him. You've been watching him all day."

"I know. I can't though—I can't tell him. Telling him would make it real. It would give him the wrong idea. I don't want to date him, Laura, because I think I would end up liking him. A lot. Too much. And then what? We'd have to break up when I leave. And that would totally suck."

Laura arches a brow. "Really? Having great sex with a hot Madrileño all semester would totally suck?"

"The sex would just be a distraction I don't need."

Her eyes move back to Rafa. "He is very distracting."

"I know," I say. "Lord, do I know."

"So does Maddie. Are you cool with that?"

I swallow, hard.

"Here," Laura says, swiping a thumb underneath my eye. "You had a little mascara smudge there."

"Thanks."

"You know," she says, rubbing her thumb against her forefinger, "whatever's going on between you and Rafa could really be anything. Maybe it's a six-month love affair. Maybe it's a fun little thing where you let him touch your boobs every once a while. Maybe it's the real deal. But we're only in Spain for a few months. Then we get on a plane and go back to real life in Durham. You don't think you'll sit on that plane and not regret taking a chance with señor hotpants over there, no matter how it ends?"

I glance at Rafa. "He does look good in those jeans, doesn't he?"

"My eyeballs are on fire."

I smile. Laura smiles back.

Our professor leads us into a small side chapel. I strain my neck to look up at a monumental El Greco painting set into an alcove above a marble altar. *The Burial of the Count of Orgaz*, the professor explains, depicts members of the church and aristocracy sending a count's soul into the soaring heavens above. It's a triumphant scene, a vibrant one, with angels and clouds and heavenly light. I notice the exquisite detail of the clergy's jeweled robes and can almost feel the silken velvet between my fingers, the glittering facets of the rubies and sapphires.

But there's something dark about the painting. Something sinister in the pinched faces of the nobles, the grey swirls that surround the angels. They wear expressions of seriousness, even agony.

I look away at the sound of Maddie's laughter. She's leaning into Rafa's shoulder, trying to muffle the sound. Rafa is laughing too, already under her spell. The knot in my stomach tightens as I wonder what they're laughing at, if it's the start of an inside joke.

Watching Maddie work her magic on Rafa is nothing short of torture. I look back at the painting. I can certainly relate to those angry, grey-faced angels; I can relate to their agony.

An agony of my own doing.

That Night

"I think I like him, Viv," Maddie says around her toothbrush. "No. I *know* I like him."

I hold my hair back and spit in the sink. It's late and I'm tired. Even so, my stomach clenches at the thought of Rafa and Maddie together.

Get over it, I tell myself. Just because I can't be with him doesn't mean no one else can. And Maddie could definitely use a little fun these days. A little distraction.

"He is cute," I say.

"Cute? He's fucking *hot*, Viv."

"Yeah, you're right. He is," I say, wiping my mouth on my towel.

"I mean, how great was he to listen to all my bullshit on the bus? And he really listened. Like, really. I'm going to go for it. For him, I mean." She meets my eyes in the mirror. I feel like she's asking me for something. Not permission, necessarily. Something else. I can't put my finger on it, but the question—whatever it is—annoys me.

"That's cool," I say, and walk out of the bathroom.

When Maddie climbs into our marital bed, it's my turn to pretend I'm asleep.

CHAPTER THIRTEEN

One Week Later
Madrid

I set my phone on the lip of the sink and turn up the volume. Shakira's latest single fills the bathroom, bouncing off the tiled walls as Maddie and I dance in front of the mirror, swirling our makeup brushes in time to the beat.

We've settled into a nice little routine. Wednesday nights we meet the girls at that tapas place where the same waiter with the wandering eye serves us every time, Thursday nights mean more wine, Fridays are pretty chill, and Saturday is the big night out.

Hence the shimmery purple eye shadow Maddie and I pass back and forth.

"You think it's too much?" I ask, closing my eyes so Maddie can get a look.

"Hell no," she replies. "This isn't Durham, Viv. We gotta step it up a notch. Here, try my eyeliner, it's darker than yours."

I line my top lid, giving myself a nice cat-eye swoop. I

blink, looking at the girl looking back at me in the mirror. I dig it.

"Super guapa," Maddie says, smiling. *Very pretty*. Madrileños love putting "super" (pronounced soup-err) in front of everything. Maddie and I have adopted the habit.

I look down at my jeans. "I think it's too hot for pants though."

"What about that black skirt you got the other day?"

I bite my lip. I don't know what possessed me to buy that headband-sized piece of fabric, but for some reason I had to have it.

A reason that may or may not go by the name Rafa Montoya.

"I don't know if I can get away with wearing it in public," I say. "My vagina might fall out."

Maddie shoots me a look in the mirror. "Have you seen what those chicks outside the discotecas wear? Trust me, you're going to look like a nun next to them. Wear a lower heel if that makes you feel better. There will be no vagina sightings."

Maddie is right. The lower heel—black suede pumps—do the trick. When I return to the bathroom five minutes later, all skirted up, she whistles her approval. Even Stella approves during a commercial break—she watches *Bailando Con Las Estrellas* religiously—she sticks her head in the bathroom and smiles.

"Ooooh, chicas, que guapas con esta ropa!" she says. *How pretty you girls look in those outfits!*

We thank Stella for dinner—leftover paella from lunch, *super* delicious—and scoot out the front door before Chiquitin can harass us.

We meet up with our Wednesday night girls for a quick carafe of sangria, then head toward Plaza Mayor. It's almost midnight, and the square is buzzing, the low roar of the crowd surrounding us. The air is warm but clean, not at all sticky, sweet with the potent smells of wine and whiskey.

I've got a good buzz going on and I'm laughing with my girls, our heels clicking on the cobblestone sidewalk as we make our way to another bar. Katie tells us about an awesome bottle of wine she found at the grocery store for eighty-nine Euro cents. Laura confesses she masturbated four times today while fantasizing about one of the hot fútbol players on the Madrid team going down on her. Apparently she's really into a good man-bun these days.

A guy whistles at us, I tell him to go fuck a fish, and the girls erupt in laughter.

This is what everyone was talking about when they said studying abroad is the best thing ever.

Maddie tears up a little bit when Rachel asks her about her parents. It's a touchier subject than ever, and I feel terrible for Maddie. We take turns giving her hugs and pouring her more wine at a tiny, crowded bar lit solely by neon blue disco balls. It—the wine, not the balls—seems to help.

My heart jumps when I see Al lingering outside the next bar. I quickly scan the crowd around him: lots of Meryton in Madrid kids, but no sign of Rafa. My heart falls. I can't tell if disappointment or relief is to blame for these vascular acrobatics.

I catch Maddie doing the same thing, her eyes searching the faces around us. She's tipsy enough to have forgotten her tears. I hate that we're both looking for the same person.

I hate to think about what will happen if we actually see him.

I drink more beer than I probably should. Even though there's no sign of Rafa, I'm still nervous. It's the kind of nervous you get when you know you're about to see someone you like. The jittery stomach, the thumping pulse. *You don't like him*, I remind myself. *You can't like him, especially now that Maddie does.*

Our pack of Meryton kids moves to another bar, then another, until it's late enough—close to two—to head to the discotecas.

I'm about to get in the back of a *very* long line when Al takes me by the elbow, shaking his head. He types furiously on his phone.

"Vale," he says. "We're in. C'mon."

I follow him to the front of the line. He speaks to the bouncer in fluent Spanish—must be nice to be raised bilingual. The bouncer, crisply dressed in a tailored suit and black tie, checks his list. He makes us wait. I feel like I might throw up I'm so nervous. At last he unclips the velvet rope.

Just like that, we're in the hottest club in Madrid.

I follow Al through the entrance. Already my breastbone throbs in time to the bass. Behind me, Maddie grabs my hand as it's a little crowded in here. I look back and smile and she smiles too then jumps up and down on her toes, excited, a little drunk.

I look up.

There, waiting for us by the entrance to the bar, is Rafa.

The three beers I just downed hit me all at once. My heart explodes, a supernova of relief and fear and desire bursting through me. *He's here.* I should've known he was the one behind our expedited entrance to the club.

He looks painfully handsome, a little dressier than I'm used to seeing him. He wears his usual dark jeans and a button-down, but tonight he's wearing a navy blazer too, emphasizing the breadth of his shoulders and arms. He's so . . . God, he's everything. He's hot. Madrileño. Sexy and charming. Tall.

Looking at him I fall apart. *I want.*

He's leaning against the wall, one hand in his pocket, the

other curled around his phone. His hair sticks up from his head in careless waves. He looks up and our gazes collide, his pale eyes darkening as they move over my body slowly, deliberately; he wants me to know he's looking. From the way his lips move into a wicked half-smile, he's looking, and appreciating too.

I'm glad I wore the skirt.

I'm about to smile back when Maddie pushes past me. I stumble a little on my feet. She launches herself at him, snaking her arms around his neck. He falls back, like he's startled, but he recovers quickly. She accepts the kisses he presses into her cheeks with a wide, flirtatious smile. Her body is plastered against his, she's standing on her tiptoes to get in his face. I can't tell if he's into it or not. Ever the gentleman, he's too polite to show his dismay, if that's what he's even feeling. Maybe he likes it.

I have to give it to Maddie. When she wants something, she goes after it, balls to the wall. She doesn't tuck away her feelings beneath layers of guilt and responsibility and fear. I'm jealous of her ability to face what she's feeling head on, even with all the heartache she's experienced this semester.

I'm jealous she's claimed Rafa as her own tonight. I have no right to be jealous, I know. Rafa can't give me the forever I'm looking for. I did the smart thing, I made my choice.

But the things I feel when Maddie slides her hand down Rafa's arm, grasping his hand—it's like the smart thing doesn't matter. She tilts her head toward the bar and starts pulling him in that direction. Rafa looks over her head at me.

I muster a smile. I wave.

And then I proceed to the other end of the bar, tugging Laura behind me. I need a nuclear-grade Cuba libre, stat.

The DJ is on fire. Multicolored lasers spear the dance floor as we push our way through the crowd. We find a spot toward the back, a knot of Meryton kids already waiting for us—including Rafa and Maddie.

She's shouting something into his ear. He laughs. I wonder if it's that inside joke they probably shared back in Toledo, when Maddie was working her black magic on him. My stomach clenches. I can't watch them. I shouldn't watch them. I should dance with the girls, make this a good night.

I gulp at my drink and start to dance. Our favorite Juanes song comes on, and the girls and I go nuts. Laura, Katie, and Rachel dance like the world is ending, shimmying up on each other, and I join in. They're adorable, laughing, grinding on random dudes as they pass us. I grind too. Why the hell not?

"Hey!" Katie shouts over the music. She points behind me. "What's up with them? That's supposed to be you!"

I turn to see Maddie *all* up in Rafa's business, her butt pressed firmly into his crotch, her fingers tangled in the hair at the nape of his neck as they dance.

I look away, my stomach clenching. *It's killing me*. They are killing me.

I shrug. "I'm glad they're hitting it off."

Katie pins me with a disbelieving look. "Yeah right."

"No, really," I say. "Rafa's fair game for her, so why not?"

"I think you're full of shit," Katie replies. "But whatever."

I grab the nearest guy and start dancing on him, hard. He doesn't seem to mind. He dances back, rolling his hips against mine. I look up to see Rafa watching me, a weird, hard look in his eyes.

He's jealous.

Good. Now he knows how it feels.

Curling into the guy's arms, I dance harder. In a fucked-up way, it feels good to know I'm hurting him. I'm hurting too. I take another long pull of rum and Coke. I keep dancing. This guy can't dance like Rafa. I don't think anyone can, even Justin Timberlake.

Every so often my gaze meets Rafa's. That look in his eyes hardens, darkens. He's angry.

Maddie is practically straddling him, her face tucked into the crook of his neck. It's only a matter of minutes, seconds, even, before they start making out. The thought of Rafa kissing her the way he kissed me makes me feel like dying.

I can't take it anymore. I can't watch it happen.

I duck out of the crowd, my heart pounding. I make my way toward the bar and look around for the bathroom. I need a minute to catch my breath, to clear my head. I don't want to be seen stumbling out of here with mascara streaking down my face.

I finally find the bathrooms at the end of a hallway. They're unisex; I push through the first door that's open, relieved to find it unoccupied. It's one of those bathrooms that has its own sink in the corner. Good; a little cold water might help me calm down.

I reach behind me to close the door, but to my surprise someone pushes back, swinging it open. I stumble farther into the bathroom, *go fuck a fish* on the tip of my tongue.

The words die on my lips. Rafa fills the doorway. The anger radiating from his body is palpable. He looks huge. I reach for the wall behind me.

Oh God, oh God, oh God.

Before I have a chance to say a thing, he's slamming the door shut and stalking toward me. His nostrils flare as he stares me down.

"What the hell was that?" he demands, his voice rough, strained with barely contained rage.

"What was what?" I ask.

He's close now, he keeps coming, relentless, and I have nowhere to go. I fall back against the wall, my chest working as I struggle to breathe. I press my palms to the wall; it's cool to the touch.

He looms over me, so close I can smell his aftershave. Even in his glowering, he looks and smells delicious. I feel trapped.

I feel turned on.

"You know what I'm talking about. Who is he?" Rafa growls.

"The guy I was dancing with? I don't know."

"Is *he* going to give you what you want? Is he going to keep you from getting hurt? I thought you didn't want to start something while you were in Madrid."

I blink. Rafa must be as drunk as I am. There's no way he'd be saying these things, here, in a bathroom at Ático, if he were in his right mind. But just because he's tipsy doesn't mean he's not right.

Still. I have to defend myself. He was just doing the old bump and grind with my best friend, wasn't he?

"That's none of your business," I say. "It was just a little fun. I can dance with whoever I want to. Just like you, Rafa."

He puts his hand on the wall beside my head, leaning into me. My courage wavers, even as the place between my legs throbs with heat. The light in the bathroom is low, but I can see the fine sheen of sweat that glistens on Rafa's skin. *He's killing me*.

"Maddie was the one who danced with *me*," he says. "I did not invite her attention. I was just being polite."

"Just being polite?" I cry. "Are you kidding me? You were practically having sex out there. With my *best friend*."

Rafa moves closer. I'm bunched up against the wall now.

Someone pounds on the door and it creaks open. Rafa flies across the bathroom to slam it shut, shouting something in rapid-fire Spanish as he throws the bolt into the lock. The guy on the other side of the door shouts something back, and Rafa's got an angry reply for him.

He turns to me. "You think I want Maddie?"

I swallow, hard, and look away. It's unfair to call him out for dancing with Maddie, I know. I shut down whatever Rafa and I had before it even began. Just because I can't have him doesn't give me the right to keep him away from someone who can. He doesn't deserve to be treated this way.

I let out a breath, tucking my hair behind my ears. "I'm sorry. It's okay, you know. It's okay if you like her. I told you I couldn't . . . that I didn't . . . God, I'm sorry, I'm making a mess of this . . ."

In one, two strides Rafa is across the bathroom. He plasters his body against my body and takes my face in his hands and presses his hips into mine, a hot, hard, deliberate grind. A cry escapes my lips at all this sudden, searing contact, the onslaught overwhelming. The smoldering heat inside me sparks into huge, heady flames.

"You think I want Maddie?" he repeats.

"It's all right," I breathe. "It's all right if you do."

"It's not all right." He looks at me. Bends his neck.

"Rafa," I plead. "Please."

He angles his head, his breath warm on my mouth, and my eyes flutter shut. He's killing me. He's been killing me ever since I laid eyes on him my first night out in Madrid.

He crushes his lips to mine. In the space of half a heartbeat the kiss is overwhelmingly deep. My knees buckle and I let out a moan as he holds me up with his weight, his mouth moving hungrily, deliciously over mine, drinking me in, making me his. I fall into him, into this kiss I've been waiting for. I don't want it to end.

The kiss isn't hurried, it's not messy, but it's hard and relentless, all our pent-up longing spilling over. Like we're saying with our bodies what we can't say with our words. My hands move up his chest and my arms circle his neck, pulling him closer, closer . . . he can never be close enough. The wall is hard and unyielding against the blades of my shoulders. It will probably bruise me. I don't care. I want to be marked. I want Rafa to mark me.

Our first kiss was a little hesitant, polite. There is nothing polite about this kiss. This kiss is all sensation. All sex. I've wanted to kiss Rafa like this forever. I've wanted to feel the weight of him pressing into me, squeezing the air from my lungs, I've wanted to see how perfectly, exactly, our bodies fit together. I've never felt this wild before. This sure, this scared.

"There," Rafa pants, pulling back. He searches my eyes. "Is that the proof you need? I don't want Maddie. I want you. Maddie is your friend, and so she is a friend of mine. I know she has shit going on with her family, and I'm trying to be there for her, trying to be a good friend. But that is all she is —a friend. Vivian, you are the one I want."

My heart is pounding. That's all I've ever wanted to hear —that I am the one.

I want to smile. I want to cry.

Rafa is leaning in again, taking my bottom lip between his teeth, his mouth moving over my jaw, down the slope of my throat.

"Tell me you don't want me," he says, his teeth nicking at the skin beneath my ear. He's doing it again—reading my thoughts. "Tell me to stop, Vivian."

No way, I think. *Not for all the sangria in Spain.* I never want him to stop. Just this once, I want to feel what it's like to be the star. The *one*. It's so sweet, so poignant. So lovely.

My desire liquefies as Rafa's mouth moves over me. He somehow manages to be both careful and carnivorous at once. We move well together. There is no awkwardness, no sloppiness. Only urgency and need.

The idea that we could be caught, Rafa having me against the wall of a bathroom at a discoteca, only intensifies the desire surging through me. It's lewd, what we're doing, and I love it.

I want more.

His mouth moves to my shoulder. His fingers glide down the skin there, curling around the tiny strap of my tank top. I dig my fingers into his hair, tugging at his curls.

"Tell me to stop," he repeats, his voice a murmur against my skin.

"Don't," I breathe. "Please, Rafa, don't stop."

He slips the strap over my shoulder, pulling it down, down, revealing the half-moon of my breast that curves over my strapless bra.

His fingers slip inside my bra. I suck in a breath when they brush against my nipple, coaxing it to a hard, tight point.

I see stars. My pussy pulses.

And then Rafa ducks his head, using his fingers to prop my breast, swollen with need, above my bra. His mouth finds my nipple and he bites, tears at my skin, soothes with his tongue.

The back of my head hits the wall.

I'm coming apart. I'm in Rafa's arms, exactly where I promised myself I would never be, and I am coming apart, helpless against the onslaught.

CHAPTER FOURTEEN

Stars shoot across the depthless space behind my closed eyes. I arch against Rafa's mouth, sensation spiking from my breast through my core. My hips circle against his, wanting, begging. I can't believe I'm letting him to do this to me, here, now.

I can't believe how much I'm enjoying it.

It's excruciating, the desire I feel for him. I am never, ever going to get over this, but I let it happen anyway. The way I feel right now is worth it.

His hands move down my body, caressing every curve, every inch of skin. His touch is exquisite. Slow. Possessive. His fingers trail over my hips, slipping to cup my behind. One hand slips lower, his fingers toying with the hem of my non-existent skirt.

"I like this skirt," he says. "You look fucking hot tonight. I never got to tell you."

I let out a breathy little laugh. "Thanks. I was hoping you'd notice."

"I always notice you," he murmurs, pressing kisses onto my chest. "Only you."

Rafa's fingers curl around the back of my thigh, high up,

so high up his first finger brushes the lace of my thong. I am so sensitive, so swollen, I almost jump.

He meets my gaze, straightening so that he towers over me.

That finger digs a little deeper from behind, sliding underneath my underwear. His eyes darken when he finds the soft wetness hidden there.

"Fucking hot," he breathes. "Díos, mujer, estás mojada." *God, woman, you're so wet.*

Somewhere in the back of my mind, I'm thinking I should have shaved, I should stop this, now, before we do something we'll both regret. But even though this is lewd, even though it's frank and not at all what I should be doing, it's also lovely. Good. Especially when Rafa whispers dirty Spanish nothings in my ear. Nothings that have, well, nothing to do with economics.

Rafa grasps the back of my thigh, pulling up my leg. Of its own volition my knee bends, and Rafa guides my bent leg onto the edge of the sink. My skin stings a little from the contact with the cool porcelain. My skirt gathers around my waist, literally nonexistent. I'm bare to him, my legs spread wide; the air feels cool against me, even as I throb hotter at the shock, the indecency, of being so exposed.

He doesn't give me time to second guess what's about to happen, to feel embarrassed. He hooks his first finger in the crotch of my thong and in one swift, sure movement, rips them off, the sound of rent fabric filling the space between us.

Oh. My. God.

"I liked those," I pant.

"I didn't," he replies gruffly. "I like you better without them."

He holds me steady with one hand firmly on my ribs, his thumb plucking at my nipple. The other hand moves back up my thigh, his fingers creeping closer, closer, oh, I'm going to burst—

He slides two fingers up the length of my slit, back to front, front to back. Slowly, exploring me, opening me to him. It feels so good it hurts. He's watching me, taking in my reaction, seeing what I like, what I don't. He's so gentle. So sure. My heart swells and so does my pussy.

He gathers moisture on the tip of his fingers and swirls them around my clitoris. Oh, oh, *oh* he's good. I glide my hands up his chest, inside his blazer, holding onto his shoulders for dear life.

"Muéstreme," he whispers in my ear. *Show me*.

He takes my arm by the wrist and brings my hand to where my legs meet. With any other guy I'd be too shy for this. But not with Rafa. I don't know why. Maybe because I trust him; maybe he makes me feel worshipped.

Beautiful.

Whatever the reason, I want to show him. I trap his first finger between mine and I show him what I like. We both look down, watching our hands move over my body.

He is a fast learner.

Our fingers trace circles around the tip of my pussy, lazy at first. I feel the stirrings of a familiar tightening. Yes. Yes.

Our fingers glide in and around each other. It feels so good that for a minute I think I'm going blind. I look at him and he looks too, grinning, and then he's kissing me, long, languid strokes that match our increasing rhythm. I know in this fevered moment Rafa would be a fucking unbelievable lay. I wish it was Rafa between my legs and not our fingers. I wish he was inside me, our bodies sticking and sliding, sweaty, I wish I knew how he moved in the moment.

I want to know how it feels with him. I want him to show me how it feels.

I'm getting close, hurtling toward the edge with unstoppable speed. My legs have started to shake, the muscles pulling, grasping.

I guide one of his fingers inside me.

"Yes," I whisper against his lips. "Just like that."

He bites the corner of my mouth. "You're so little," he says, the finger inside me exploring, tickling. "So perfect."

He's moving inside me and I'm circling my clit, our fingers working in delicious tandem. The tightening spirals, deepens, devastates. I'm close. I'm right there.

Rafa dips his head. I watch as he takes my nipple between his teeth.

I cry out. It's coming. I'm coming.

"I have you," he says, pressing his weight against me, ducking his head to kiss my neck. "Go, Vivian. Go."

His mouth moves back to my mouth, and he kisses me deeply, absorbing my cries as I get closer, closer, I really *am* blind—

I arch against him as a burst of white-hot heat moves through me. The release is violent, my body writhing in response, a surge of sensation ricochets between my legs. I clench around Rafa's finger inside me, a spasm I can't control, and he makes a guttural sound, something between a growl and a grunt of appreciation.

In that moment, a sense of starry-edged clarity comes over me. I want Rafa. I want to feel this way again, and I want it to be with him. I want to hole up in a hotel room for a week with nothing but Rafa and a huge box of condoms for company. This is it. *He* is it. I am the one, and so is he.

The throbbing reaches a crescendo, unbearable, the rush of blood in my ears deafening, and then it subsides, each beat a quieter echo of the one that came before it. I break the kiss, burying my head in Rafa's chest. His button-down is damp with sweat. I can hear his heart, a thick, insistent sound.

The clarity fades as my senses, prickly, unwelcome, flare back to life. Heady certainty is replaced by confusion. The sound of our labored breathing fills the room. I open my eyes. Rafa looks at me in wonder. In awe. I can't believe what just happened either.

I look down and see myself practically spread-eagled around Rafa, our hands tangled between my legs. The salty smell of sex hangs between us. Rafa holds me against him, smoothing the hair away from my face with his free hand. He presses a kiss onto the top of my head.

"You're killing me," I whimper.

He laughs. "That is sort of the point. You know in French an orgasm is called the little death?"

That's not what I meant, I want to say. The way he kissed me in the heat of the moment was nothing to scoff at, sure. I loved every minute of it. But that tender little kiss he just gave me?

Dear Lord. No one's ever kissed me like that before.

"That death was not so little," I say.

"Definitely not little," he says, "from what I felt."

He gently pulls his finger out of me. I draw a sharp breath, wincing.

Rafa's eyes go dark. "Did I hurt you?"

"No," I say. "I'm just going to be a little sore."

"Fuck." He glides his hand, gently, around the back of my thigh. "Was I too rough?"

The note of panic in his voice makes my heart clench.

I meet his gaze. "You were just right. It's been a while, that's all."

"I was not doing the kidding when I said you were little. *Really* little," he says, narrowing his eyes. He guides my leg off the sink, tugging my skirt back into place. I stand, the blood in my leg rushing back to painful life. "Vivian. Are you a virgin?"

I look away. I had no shame about basically fingering myself in front of Rafa in a public restroom. But confessing I'm almost twenty-one and still a virgin? Somehow that's far more mortifying. I have no doubt Rafa has slept with a dozen —maybe even dozens—of women. You can tell just by looking at him that he's one of those guys who lost his virginity at fourteen to his super-hot older neighbor or something. From the way he touched me—confident, just the right amount of push, of give—I know he's no novice. I feel childish, and a little ridiculous, in the face of his obvious sexual prowess.

"It doesn't matter," I say.

"Hey," he says, ducking his head to catch my attention. "Hey. Miráme, Vivian." *Look at me*. "It matters very much. I don't want to hurt you. We can go slow. I cannot keep my hands from you, Vivian. It makes me crazy, how much I want to touch you. But always I will be your gentleman."

I will be your gentleman. It sounds like something Richard Gere would say in an 80s military-themed rom com, doesn't it?

"I want to know you," he continues. "Everything about you, I want to know. I'm not going to judge you. Whether you are virgin or you are not a virgin, it's not going to make me like you any less."

I swallow. He likes me. *Likes*. That fun, fluttery kind of like. The kind of like I'm starting to think I feel for him too.

The kind of like I swore I'd only feel for a guy who would stick around.

A guy who wouldn't inevitably break my heart.

"Why?" I ask, glancing at him from the corner of my eye. "Why do you like me?"

Rafa shrugs. "I just do. I can't stop it."

This blows my mind. For so long I thought I had to work for it—attention, affection. I realize now that I had to

153

work my ass off to get Keith to notice me. Wear the right clothes, be at the right parties. *Like* has never come easy for me.

But this—what Rafa feels for me—it just *happened*. Sure, in a way I made the first move by talking to him. But beyond that, I really didn't do a thing. I certainly wasn't trying the way I try back at Meryton. I've just been myself. My messy, slightly crazy self.

And for some reason, Rafa's really into that chick.

I squeeze my eyes shut. It's finally happening for me. Only it's happening with the wrong guy, and at the wrong time. I want forever, but Rafa can only give me five months—if that. Once those five months are up, I'm staring down the barrel of horrible heartache. A heartache that lasted more than a semester after I stopped hanging out with Keith. I don't think I can go through that again.

And then there's Maddie. She told me point blank she likes Rafa. And like I said before, the girl really needs a win this semester.

Finding out that the guy you like actually likes your best friend is definitely *not* a win.

How am I going to tell her? I can't be sneaking around behind her back like this, especially after I told her in no uncertain terms I didn't want Rafa, that there was nothing between us.

It's obvious now there is something between us. It's big and loud and impossible to ignore.

"Vivian," Rafa says, his voice betraying his concern. "Talk to me."

I open my eyes. He searches them. His face falls. As always, he knows what I'm thinking. He pulls the strap of my tank top back onto my shoulder, shifting my breast into its bra cup.

I open my mouth, ready to explain myself, explain why we

can't happen, when the pounding on the door returns. A guy shouts something; Rafa curses under his breath.

"It's the manager," he says. "We need to go. Now."

Rafa grabs my hand and tugs me out of the bathroom, apologizing to the manager as we pass. He holds me close to his back, protecting me from curious eyes. We move through the bar, past the dance floor. It's so crowded I have to cling to him to keep from getting lost. I am exhausted, suddenly. I've had too much to drink, done too many wonderful, stupid things tonight. I'm ready to go home, get a good night's sleep so I can deal with the fallout tomorrow.

We stumble outside, gulping at the mild morning air like we've been underwater. I dig my phone out of my purse and see Maddie texted me, asking if I'm all right. She and the girls are going to get churros, do I want to join?

Guilt settles like a stone in my stomach. Mads is a wonderful friend.

I am not. I haven't been since I lied to her about my feelings for Rafa.

I text her back, telling her I'm tired and heading home. I want to face her when we're both sober and have the energy to deal with the things I've done.

Rafa keeps moving down the sidewalk, slowing his pace when he glances at my heels.

"Do they hurt?" he asks.

"I mean, I can't feel my pinkie toes. But as far as heels go, they're not too bad. Why?"

"We have a little walk to do. It is much easier, yes, to find a taxi on Gran Via."

Even though it's well past four o'clock in the morning, traffic chokes the six-lane behemoth that is Gran Via. We weave our way through the throngs that clog the sidewalk, dodging fragrant falafel kiosks and drunk, shouty people. It's a total circus.

Rafa hails a cab and holds the door open, sliding into the backseat beside me. My skirt rides up and Rafa catches the driver adjusting the rearview mirror to get a better look. Rafa tugs the tiny headband scrap back into place, casually draping an arm over my bare legs like we've been at this I'm-his-and-he's-mine thing forever.

I'd be lying if I said it doesn't feel good, if I didn't lean in just a little, so that my body curls into the solid curve of his side. We fit so well together. We'd fit even better in bed.

Not that that's ever going to happen.

I give the driver my address in surprisingly coherent Spanish, heading off any suggestion Rafa might make about us going home together. This—whatever this is—can't go any further. We were both dangerously close to losing control tonight. I can't control myself around him. It's all happening so fast. Too fast.

"Se ha mejorando much tú español," he says, turning his head to slay me with that smile of his. *Your Spanish is getting much better.*

Even though I shouldn't, I smile too, and tell him—in Spanish—*thank you, I have a very good teacher.*

I will teach you other things, he says, his eyes flashing with heat. *Whatever you want to know, Vivian, I'll teach you. I want to be the one to teach you.*

I imagine learning him, what his body feels like, its quirks, its corners. What it craves. Where it is most sensitive. How it fits into mine.

I sigh, resting my head on Rafa's shoulder. He curls his hand around my thigh, his thumb tracing an arc just above my knee. The tenderness of the gesture—the familiarity and possession it implies—makes my heart hurt.

I want him to teach me, more than I've ever wanted anything.

Except Maddie's happiness. Her friendship.

Except, maybe, the well-paid corporate future guaranteed by a good GPA and an economics degree.

Or maybe I don't want that at all. I don't know.

As we speed through the nighttime swirl of Madrid, I think about my conversation with Rafa about Goya and Sorolla, our favorite Spanish painters. I think about the art class Rafa lobbied so hard for me to take, the class that has turned out to be my favorite this semester, hands down.

I think about the way Neruda's poem of longing sounded as Rafa read it out loud to me, the happy buzz his nearness— and the ice-cold beer—gave me.

I came to Madrid thinking I knew exactly what I wanted. But now, with the scent of Rafa's aftershave wafting between us as the breeze from the open window teases the hair at my temples, lines of singsongy Neruda floating through my head, I'm not so sure anymore.

Rafa is quiet. He firms his grip on my leg, his way of saying I'm here if you need me, I'm here if you want to talk. But I don't. It is up to us now to decide what does or doesn't happen next.

I dread the moment the ride ends, because it means this instant of suspended bliss—when we can revel in the things we feel without worrying about what to do with them—ends too. I love just *being* with Rafa, it's so nice. Easy.

Which is going to make it hard to pull away. *I have to pull away.* For a handful of very good reasons, my friendship with my bestie chief among them, I have to pull away.

The driver swerves to a stop outside a familiar blue door on Calle de Villanueva. For a heartbeat, neither Rafa nor I move. The coughing hum of the engine fills the silence that swells around us.

He presses his lips to my hair. "Can I see you tomorrow?"

I blink, straightening in my seat. Rafa's arm falls away. I

tug at the hem of my skirt. "That's probably not a good idea," I say. "I'm always getting carried away with you."

"That is what is supposed to happen, yes, when you like a person?"

Reaching for the door handle, I swivel my head and meet his gaze head on. He is gorgeous. I take a breath, let it out.

"Rafa, I—"

He doesn't let me finish. He dips his head and presses his lips to mine. I close my eyes. It's a short kiss, a sweet one, and it leaves me reeling.

"You are always doing the thinking too much," he says. "Tomorrow. I want to see you."

I may or may not intentionally flash Rafa with a little butt cheek as I climb out of the car. I turn back to face him. "Quizás," I say. *Maybe*.

Rafa makes the driver wait at the curb until I'm inside the building. I close the door behind me and fall against it, listening to the sound of the taxi fade as it speeds down the street.

In bed I lie awake, trying to breathe around the fluttering of my feelings.

I can't.

I shouldn't.

But I think I'm falling for Rafa.

CHAPTER FIFTEEN

I wake up with a headache and a sour taste in my mouth. The tacky remnants of my eyeliner and mascara make it impossible to open my left eye. I bet I look like a scary clown gone wrong.

Awesome.

I throw back the sheet and sit on the edge of the bed. I wince at the twinge of pain between my legs. I am sore.

Rafa.

Ohmigod I came in a sink in a club bathroom last night while Rafa fingered me against the wall. I remember totally abandoning myself to the moment, unafraid and unashamed. I also remember the soul crushing orgasm I had in his arms.

My vagina really did fall out of my skirt.

Ohmigod.

The things I felt then—the desire, the confusion, the bliss —bloom inside my chest, elbowing for room, each one demanding to be felt first. My heart is racing, and I struggle to catch my breath. God, my head hurts.

Rafa likes me. And despite the promise I made to myself that I would protect my heart at all costs—despite the fact that he's caught Maddie's eye—I'm pretty sure I like him back.

I glance over my shoulder. Maddie is bundled beneath the thin cotton blanket, silent as a mouse as she snoozes. Her dark hair is tucked neatly behind her ear, and glittery remnants of our eye shadow dot her cheeks. She is so pretty.

She likes the guy who likes me. My best friend and I like the same guy. *Like*.

I have no idea what to do.

Locking myself in the calm, cool quiet of the bathroom, I sit on the edge of the tub and check my phone. It's almost six o'clock—dinner time back home in the States—and for a minute I'm hit by wave of homesickness. Not for Meryton. For *home*. For my mom's Sunday night spaghetti and meatballs —funny how Rafa and I both love our moms' balls of meat— and for our sweet little weenie dog, Lucy, who always sits at my feet because I sneak her bites under the table.

I wonder what my mom would think of Rafa. I bet her eyeballs would pop out of her head. He's gorgeous, for one thing. He's charming for another. And kind, and funny, and Spanish, and he smells like sex and he's a great dancer . . .

Speaking of—I have a text from Justin Timberlake, sent earlier—much earlier—this morning.

Can't sleep. Thinking of u. I know u r scared that u'll get hurt. But don't u c you are hurting now? I can stop ur hurt. Let me teach u to feel good. Quiero ser novios, Vivian.

Butterflies take flight in my chest.

I love how the Spanish language has shortened our unwieldy "boyfriend and girlfriend" into one delicious little nugget of a word—novios. *I want to be boyfriend and girlfriend.* Rafa is telling me he wants to be my boyfriend.

(!!!!!!*!#*$**!@#$*!*#!)

My first thought is a resounding, neon-pink, confetti-strewn YES. Yes, I want to go out with the sweetest, hottest guy I've ever met. Yes, I want him to teach me everything he knows. Yes, sex. Yes, yes, yes to the way he makes me feel.

I'm smiling so hard my lazy eye cracks open. I blink away specks of dried mascara as I hold my phone in my lap. What happened between Rafa and me in the bathroom last night proves I can't run from the things I feel for him.

I don't want to run anymore. I want to see Rafa today and every day after that.

Maybe Rafa is right. Maybe I should stop thinking so much about the future and live, wildly, in the present. Maybe things will work out, and my heart won't lie in a thousand broken pieces on the floor when this semester ends. Maybe Rafa *is* worth the risk, even though my past tells me otherwise.

But then I think wait, *wait* a minute. Wait. A. Minute. What about Maddie? I haven't been honest with her about what's going on with Rafa and me. I told her our relationship was strictly business, which led her to believe it was cool to go after him herself. But now it's obvious I like Rafa and Rafa likes me—only me—and because of that, because I lied, she's going to get hurt.

Like an asshole, I let my friend believe that the guy who was falling for me might be available to fall for her. I set her up for heartbreak. And then, as if that isn't enough, I hooked up with him. *Him*, the guy she's crushing on because I told her he wasn't crushing on me.

In my defense, I never intended for last night's hook up to happen. I think it's fair to say Rafa was the instigator in our bathroom situation.

But I could've stopped it and I didn't. I didn't want to stop it. And that fact—along with the fact that I've been lying to Maddie all along—could very well destroy our friendship.

I can't to lose Maddie as a friend. We've been close for

years now, and she's stuck by my side through thick and thin, through bad guys and good grades and everything in between. She's excellent. She saved me after the Keith thing blew up. I would never let a guy come between us. Chicks before dicks always. Now, more than ever. I want Maddie to be happy. If I gave into the things I felt in Rafa's arms last night, and I said yes to him, and we started dating, I feel like I'd be rubbing it in her face—the fact that Rafa likes me and not her. And I don't think that would make her very happy.

I love her.

But I also really, *really* like Rafa. Like really. I haven't liked a guy—or been liked—this much, this intensely, ever.

I don't know what to do.

I look down at my phone.

Hi, I type.

Rafa replies right away. *Hello Vivian. How r u feeling?*

Hungover.

Me 2, he says. *Want to get a falafel? I know very good place near Plaza del Sol.*

God, he's relentless. I want to see him. But then I also want a little space. Time to think—he's given me a lot to think about.

Going to hang with Maddie tonight, I type. *Maybe tomorrow after tutoring?*

Vale, he replies. *U still have not responded to my question.*

Question?

I asked u 2 b my girlfriend. Waiting not very patiently 4 ur answer.

My thumbs hover over the keypad. *Way to put me on the spot*, I type.

He does not respond.

I will think about it, ok? I type.

Vale, he replies. *U sure u r ok? Want 2 talk?*

I don't know what I want.

But I do know I have to tell Maddie.

"So, hey," I say, glancing over my shoulder at Maddie as I rinse my dinner plate in the sink. "Want to take a quick walk through Retiro? The sunset looks like it's going to be *super* ridic tonight."

Maddie picks at her food. She looks a little green. "Sure. Although I gotta warn you, I don't think I'm going to last very long. I had *way* too much to drink last night. Plus I still have some homework to finish up."

"Same here. I promise to keep it short," I say.

We walk into the park at dusk. I wasn't lying about the sunset; the sky glows pink, the clouds on the horizon lit with the fiery warmth of the day's last light. The air is cool, crisp with the first hint of fall. It would be a gorgeous night if I didn't feel like I was about to vomit.

Maddie and I make for the formal gardens, our footsteps crunching on the gravel path. My heart is pounding. I glance at Maddie. I can't tell what she's thinking. She seems distracted, actually, or maybe she's just zoned out from being so hung over.

I clench and unclench my hands at my sides.

"You're walking too fast," Maddie says.

"Sorry," I say, slowing my stride.

We walk in silence as I work up the courage to tell her. I don't want to upset or disappoint her. But I also don't want to keep things from her either.

I take a deep breath, let it out. My hands are shaking now.

"Maddie," I say. "There's something I need to tell you."

She gloves her hands in the cuffs of her sweatshirt and crosses her arms. She doesn't say anything.

I swallow, hard, willing myself to continue. "Last night, at *Ático*. I was with—"

Maddie lets out a choked sob. My body turns to ice. *Does she already know?* I stop and face her. Her eyes are screwed shut.

"Maddie? Mads, oh my God, are you okay?"

She holds her sleeve up to her eyes. Through the fabric of her sweatshirt I can see her hand is shaking too. Tears roll down her cheeks, gathering specks of glitter as they go.

"I'm sorry, Viv," she says, sniffing. "I'm sorry. I didn't mean to interrupt."

"No," I say. "No, it's okay. What's going on?"

"My parents," she breathes. "I talked to my mom while you were in the shower. It's not good."

My stomach does a backflip. "Oh shit. Here," I say, nodding at a nearby bench. "Let's sit."

Maddie sits heavily on the bench. I sit beside her, my thoughts racing. What in the world do I do now?

She sniffles, wiping her cheek on her shoulder. Her bare legs are covered in goose bumps. "So, turns out my dad went to his first AA meeting today. He's an alcoholic, Viv. My dad is a freaking alcoholic."

That word—*alcoholic*—drops like a dead weight between us.

"Holy shit, Maddie." I suck in a breath. "I don't know what to say. I am so sorry."

She's crying now, really crying, her shoulders shaking in time to her sobs. I hold her against me, feeling my own throat tighten in sympathy. Maddie's family is really falling apart. It's sad, and it's scary.

"That's why my mom left," she says when she can finally

breathe again. "Well, part of the reason. But I guess he's had a problem for a while now."

Maddie tells me about her suspicions, how her dad would fall asleep in his chair at dinner, his chin lolling on his chest. Her brother had to help her mom carry him into the house one night after a party at their neighbor's. "I'm angry at him," she tells me, "but I feel sorry for him too. And feeling sorry for your dad sucks."

The tears keep coming. She talks. I hold her and I listen.

"I love him and I hate him. And I am so glad I am not there right now," she says, scoffing. "I don't know what I would do if I had to see him."

"It would be awful," I say. "But you would deal with it. You're stronger than you think, Mads."

"I don't know if I'm strong enough for this shit," she says. I wipe the mascara from underneath her eyes. "Thanks, Viv. For listening. And for being here. I feel kinda bad, unloading on you like this."

The fact that she feels bad makes me feel even worse.

"Seriously," I say with a grin. "Shut the hell up. I'm your wife, remember? We share a marital bed. It's my job to listen to your shit and put up with you."

Maddie laughs, leaning her head against my shoulder. She lets out a long, low breath. "I love you. You know that, right, Viv?"

My throat is so tight I can't breathe. Would Maddie be saying this if she knew what I did last night with the guy she likes? If she knew I lied to her about the way I felt?

"I love you too, Maddie," I manage.

She takes my hand. "I'm lucky to have you with me this semester. I wouldn't make it without you."

"Thanks," I say.

I am at a loss. Maddie is hurting. The last thing I want to do is cause her more pain.

"I wouldn't make it without you," she repeats, "and I wouldn't make it without Rafa. I really like him, Viv. Like, more than a crush. I thought for sure we were going to hook up last night, but then he, like, just disappeared off the dance floor. I mean, we were pretty drunk, so maybe he got sick or something. But I was really looking forward to finding out if he's a good kisser. They don't make them like that in America."

My breath leaves my body. If there was ever a time to tell Maddie about the bathroom orgasm incident, this would be it. But I'm so afraid. Afraid of hurting her, of losing her as a friend. Afraid of losing Rafa too.

What if she freaks out? She has every right to tell me to go fuck myself. But even if she doesn't—even if she forgives me, and our friendship survives intact—I highly, *highly* doubt she'll be cool with me saying yes to Rafa's novios proposal. As if finding out that her dad is an alcoholic isn't enough—now her best friend wants to date the guy she likes, the guy who chose me over her?

How's that for twisting the knife?

It would be the ultimate insult. The ultimate betrayal. I can't be Rafa's girlfriend without hurting Maddie. I'd be rubbing it in her face, my beautiful, budding romance, while she cries herself to sleep.

I can't do that to her. As much as I want to be Rafa's girlfriend, I can't keep hurting my friend. I just want to be done with this whole love-triangle-in-reverse thing so I can go back to being besties with Maddie.

But first, I need to tell her about what happened last night.

"Eh," Maddie says, wiping her nose on her sleeve. "I'll figure him out. Anyway. You said you had something you needed to tell me?"

My pulse thumps in my ears. Heat floods my face.

The words come fast, stumbling incoherently over each another. "Um. Yeah. Yes, actually. I, um. I hooked up with Rafa last night in the bathroom at Ático. Maddie, I think I'm falling for him. And I feel so, so horrible about—well, about everything. About not telling you the truth. It's all horrible, and I am sorry. So fucking sorry, Maddie."

CHAPTER SIXTEEN

Monday Afternoon

The bell jangles above my head as I step into the café. It's raining cats and dogs—or, as Madrileños say, llueve a mares, *it rains like the seas*—and my sneakers and jeans are soaked through. I shiver at the sudden gust of air conditioning.

Rafa is waiting for me. He looks up at the sound of the bell. He waves from a high table set with two beers and a plate of pastries. He stands, smiles. That kind, killer smile that turns my stomach inside out.

He looks so hopeful. So happy, as always, to see me.

Don't cry, don't cry, don't cry.

I cried all night. I cried twice during class. I cried on the Metro ride over here. I promised myself I wouldn't cry in front of Rafa.

"Como estás?" he asks, warmly. *How are you?* He leans in for his customary *kiss kiss*, but instead of pressing his lips to my cheeks, he cups my jaw in his hand and kisses me on the mouth. By now it's familiar, the feel of his lips on my lips, but the loveliness of it still makes my skin pulse, a rush as I rise to my tiptoes to meet him. His palm is warm against my face. The kiss is soft, a little hungry, possessive.

It's the kind of kiss a guy gives his girl.

I came to tell Rafa that I can't be his girl. I should have known he would make it difficult.

It's impossible to pull away, to not fall into his kiss, into the desire roaring inside me. Why does he have to make me feel so wonderful? So wonderful and so, *so* turned on. I am out-of-my-mind, wildly, madly attracted to this man. One kiss and I could wring out my underwear.

Fuck.

Rafa releases me. I look down at my feet, trying to calm the frantic beating of my heart. The familiar scent of his aftershave wafts off his French blue button-down.

He tips up my chin with his first finger. *Are you all right?* he asks in Spanish.

Has his gaze always been so intense? I feel like he can see everything I'm trying to hide.

I look away, unprepared for the onslaught of his concern. His interest.

Digging in my bag, I say, "Tengo buenas noticias." *I have good news.*

I put the exam on the table. A B+ on my first in-class economics test.

"Your tutoring is working," I say. "In a pretty huge way. Even the professor congratulated me when he handed it back. He said to say hello to you."

Rafa grabs the beers off the table and hands one to me. "You deserve it," he says. "You've been working hard. Felicitaciones." *Congratulations.*

We clank bottles and I take a long, hard pull as I slide into the seat opposite Rafa's. There's a moment of awkward silence as we get settled in our chairs. I want to talk to him, really talk to him, about last night, about what happened with

Maddie, but right now I can't breathe around the lump in my throat.

Later. I'll tell him later, after I've had a beer and I'm a little less verklempt about this. Us.

"I thought we could skip econ today and work on some art history," I say, reaching for my textbook. "You know. To celebrate."

"There's my crazy white girl," Rafa says. "You have adopted Madrid's party spirit I see."

I smile—he's always making me smile—and open the textbook, flinging back chunks of chapters until I land at the correct one.

Rafa swallows a mouthful of beer. "Goya. Vale, he is one of my favorites. Very dark too, like this weather," he says, leaning over the table to get a better look at the pages.

I only need to lean forward too, just a little bit, to kiss him. Watching him cozy up to my textbook, his blue eyes coming alive as he tells me all about Goya's patrons, his style and his technique, all in that lovely, lilting Spanish—God, I want to kiss him. And then I want to take off all his clothes and explore every inch of his skin. And *then* I want to fuck his brains out.

Rafa looks up and catches me checking him out. One side of his mouth kicks up in a saucy, knowing little smirk. "A masterpiece, no?"

I scoff, tucking my tongue into my cheek. "You and the bragging. Really, you're the worst."

"What?" Rafa holds up the textbook, his smirk deepening into a grin. "I was talking about Goya's Majas."

I glance at the two paintings stacked one on top of the other on the page. Both are of the same reclining woman. In the first painting, she wears a gauzy white dress with heavily ornamented black and gold sleeves.

In the second painting, she wears nothing at all.

"Of course you would pick a painting of a nude chick," I say.

Rafa sets the book on the table between us. "I like La Maja Vesitda—the dressed Maja—better, actually. She is—how do you say—bolder. She will make you work harder for it, yes? And it will be so much better. More satisfying."

"But they're the same maja, right? What *is* a maja?"

Rafa meets my eyes across the table. "Today it means a great beauty. A beautiful person. And yes, it is the same woman in both paintings."

I trace my finger over the embroidered—or maybe it's beaded—detail on the first Maja's sleeve. "I love old portraits like these. Getting the clothes right was just as important as capturing the faces."

"In Toledo," he says. "El Greco's *Burial of the Count of Orgaz*. I saw you looking at the clothes in that painting too."

I pull back. "You did?"

Rafa slides the book toward him and closes it.

Finish your beer, he says in Spanish. *I want to show you something.*

We hurry up the Prado Museum's steps. My heart works double time—I love museums, and I haven't had a chance to visit the Prado yet (I blame it on all that econ homework). Of course Rafa would take me to my personal paradise on the day I have to practically dump him.

He holds his umbrella between us so we have to walk close to keep from getting wet. He slips his arm around my waist, guiding me in time to his steps. I try to keep my distance, I do, but it's impossible not to melt into the magnetic pull of his body. I'm overwhelmed by the feel of his hands on me, especially in public like this. It's silly, I know, but I imagine it's his way of claiming me, of telling everyone we pass to back off, bitches, she's mine. I imagine that I am his.

Only, I'm not.

I have to tell him.

But I can't. Not yet. I want to see whatever it is he's so hell-bent on showing me first.

Rafa flashes his student ID, and not only gets us through the semi-private group entrance, but gets us in for free. Our shoes squeak on the wet marble floors as he veers right and I follow him into a series of galleries.

I recognize Goya's work right away. Bucolic country scenes, dark, manic snapshots from the Peninsular War, aristocrats and their broods, the requisite Jesus paintings. I buzz with the desire to stop and examine each one, but Rafa keeps walking. It's late—close to six—which may explain why the galleries are mostly empty.

Rafa and I have Goya to ourselves.

He slows his stride when we reach the last gallery. There, side by side on a long wall, are Goya's Majas. My breath leaves my lungs as I take them in. They're enormous, slightly smaller than life size, encased in baroque gilt frames. They are indescribably more beautiful in person than they are on the page of my textbook.

My skin prickles with goose bumps. I'm a little starstruck, to be honest, like seeing the celebrity you've stalked online in the flesh. I see what I could not see before. The aliveness, the details. The dark seam running up the clothed maja's sleeve, the naked maja's stubby little toes, and her whispery patch of pubic hair.

Without meaning to—it's a reflex, like scrunching your nose when you sneeze—I grab Rafa's hand and give it a squeeze. It's my way of saying *thank you* and *ohmigod I love this* and *you are so wonderful it hurts.* He grins. His palm feels warm and safe against mine.

I drop his hand, remembering myself, remembering Maddie, and move to stand in front of the woman with her clothes on. It seems less dangerous with Rafa next to me.

"It is better, yes, to see the real thing?" Rafa asks. He tucks his hands into the pockets of his jeans and stands beside me, so close his arm touches mine. "For someone like you, who is the lover of the art, it is excellent. Like living inside your favorite movie."

"Yes," I say. "You're right. That is how it feels."

For half a heartbeat I close my eyes, and will the heat and the longing flooding my limbs to slow their roll. This is perfect—Rafa is perfect—it's the perfect end to a really shitty day. I wish it could stay like this, always.

I make mental notes as I pore over every detail of the maja's clothing. Her white gown, the pink sash, her orna-mented sleeves-slash-bolero thing, her little pointy slippers. I could stare for hours, but with Rafa beside me, I'm a little distracted.

At last I turn to the naked maja, taking a few steps to stand in front of her. Rafa follows, only this time he stands half a step behind me. Every time he inhales, his chest brushes my shoulder. He's so close, and he smells so good, I think I've died and gone to heaven.

Looking at the naked maja with Rafa is a lot like dissecting that *super* sexy Neruda poem together. A little awkward. Heated. There's so much nakedness to look at, it makes me crave some nakedness of my own. My nakedness, and Rafa's too.

The things that inspired all this beautiful art—love, angst, God—I can relate to them in way I never have before.

Spain, I'm learning, is a place of the senses. People here don't shy away from nudity, public displays of affection, or sex the way we do in America. This side of our nature is embraced here—as evidenced by this painting of a very naked woman in a very public place.

Rafa leans closer. His breath tickles the baby hairs at the nape of my neck. I am frozen, too scared to lean back, too roused to walk away.

"Thank you," I say. "For bringing me here. I've been meaning to come to the Prado. There's just never a good time, you know?"

"You have to make time," he replies. "Some people, they think art is boring, or stupid. But it matters to you, Vivian, and so it is important that you come to these places."

I look down. It's so quiet in the gallery, I swear I can hear my frantic heartbeat echoing off the walls. Rafa is leaning closer. I can tell because his breath, warm before, is hot now on my bare skin.

"You're killing me," I whisper. "You're always killing me, Rafa."

He presses a kiss onto my shoulder, just where it slopes into neck. "We have been killing so much of the one another lately," he murmurs. He slides a hand up my back to cup my nape, holding me the way he held me that first morning at the Metro station. With intention. Possession. "It is a miracle there is anything left."

I suck a breath through my teeth and goose bumps return in a poignant, vengeful wave. His hair, still a little wet from the rain, brushes my ear. I shiver. My head falls back as he moves up my neck. Oh *God*. I appeal to the coffered ceiling for help. For the courage to tell him to stop. To not maul Rafa right here, right now.

It just feels so damn good, his mouth on my skin. Each lingering kiss, each playful stroke of his tongue, sends spikes of heat through my center.

"Rafa," I breathe. "We need to talk."

"Do we?" he asks, nipping at the hollow beneath my ear. His thumb works small, slow circles at the base of my neck.

I see stars. I blink them back.

"Come home with me," he says. "We have done enough work for today. I want to kill you how I killed you at Ático. Quiero estar contigo." *I want to be with you.*

I don't need to ask how Rafa wants to be with me. He wants to be with me in the same sense I want to be with him. The naked sense. The images flashes through my mind: the delicious weight of Rafa pressing me into his mattress, my hands shaking as I unbutton his shirt, the feel of his naked chest against mine. Me wrapped up in him as the wet, grey afternoon fades to dark around us.

The sweetness of it makes my whole being ache. Rafa is offering me everything I want—the relationship, the romance, the *real*—but I'm going to turn him down. I never want to have another fight like the one I had last night with Maddie. I never want to upset her like that again.

And if I say yes to Rafa—if I become his novia—I know it would upset Maddie.

My eyes smart. I try to pull away, but Rafa holds me tight. We turn our heads to look one another in the eye.

"We need to talk," I repeat.

CHAPTER SEVENTEEN

We stand at the narrow counter at a bar not far from the Prado Museum. It's uncomfortably humid inside the small, bustling space. Rafa and I sip vino tinto de la casa from small glasses, picking at the bowl of potato chips the jolly bartender set between us. Outside it's getting dark; Mads will be wondering where I am.

"If this is about the naked women—the Majas—" he starts.

"It's not," I say. "Well. Not exactly, anyway."

Rafa spears me with a look. "Now *you're* killing *me*, Vivian."

Our arms brush as we reach for our wine at the same time. He covers my hand with his. His palm is warm and dry against the back of my hand. My heart counts an uneven drumbeat inside my chest.

"We can't," I say.

"I want to," he says.

"I want to too. But I can't, Rafa."

"Por qué no?" *Why not?*

I swallow. "Because. Because I'm terrified of falling so

hard for you that it's gonna hurt too badly when I leave. Rafa, we'll have to break up—"

"We don't have to break up."

"Really? You want to do long distance across an ocean? You're in grad school here, and I'm a broke as a joke college student there. It will never work."

"Come on, Vivian, you don't know that."

"It won't work," I say. "Not the way I want it to. I want more. Dinner and a movie, spooning in bed, a shared future. I want forever, Rafa, a guy who's in it for real. And I don't think email or Skype or whatever can be real."

His face tightens. He takes a step toward me, lowering his voice in disbelief. "You don't think what we have is real?"

"I don't know. If it's real now, it won't be after we're apart." I pull my hand away, take a gulp of wine. "I've been hurt by guys like you before—"

"Guys like me?"

I sweep my eyes up the length of his body. "Super guapo guys."

"That's not fair," he says, digging a hand through his hair. "That is so not fucking fair. You told me about this guy who hurt your heart. You said he led you on. I am not doing the leading. I think you know this, Vivian, but you are denying it to yourself because you are scared. I am scared too. But more than the scare I am feeling, I feel—" He winds that same hand through the air, searching for the right word. "Light. That is not the word, but you understand me, yes? You make me feel light. Contento." *Happy*.

I understand him better than I care to admit. Rafa makes me feel the same way. I am more myself with him than I am with anyone else.

"You make me—" My voice wavers. I look away. "You're so freaking excellent, Rafa."

"If you feel that way, why can't you be with me? I am not

understanding. You don't want to get hurt, but you're already hurting, Vivian."

I take another sip of wine. "There's something else."

He meets my eyes. "What?"

"Maddie," I say. "I don't think it's any secret she likes you, Rafa. A lot. And I'm not going to date the guy my best friend likes—especially not when I lied to her, and told her to pursue that guy who was never available in the first place. A guy who liked me."

"A guy who still likes you," Rafa replies. The muscle along his jaw ropes against his smooth, tan skin. "So you will not be with me because you do not want to hurt your friend."

"Yes."

He looks away, running his tongue along the seam of his bottom lip. A lip I would very much like to take between my teeth, if just to end this awful conversation.

"Maddie is a very cool girl," he says at last. "But I don't like her like that. You are the one I want, Vivian. What kind of friend is she if she won't let you be with the guy you want?"

"She didn't say I couldn't be with you," I reply. I sip my wine, praying for liquid courage. "Maddie isn't like that. We had a fight, yes. But she never, like, forbid me to date you or anything. She told me to do what I wanted. She's hurt, and rightfully so. I lied to her about how I felt about you. None of this would have ever happened if I'd been honest with her from the start."

"So be honest with yourself for once," he says. "If you want to be with me, let's be together. Maddie will get over it."

I bite my lip. "I can't, Rafa. I can't do that to Maddie. She's going through some awful stuff this semester. She didn't say I couldn't be with you—this is my decision. I'm the one who made such a fucking mess of this whole thing, and I'm the one who's going to clean it up. If I date you, it'd be like flaunting it in her face—the fact that you picked me over her.

She'd pretend to be cool with it, but I know it would crush our friendship. She needs me, Rafa. She's been there for me, and I want to be there for her."

There it is—the terrible truth. I'm choosing Maddie over Rafa.

His eyes darken with hurt, and for a minute my confidence wavers. When I left the house this morning, I was sure I'd made the right choice. Chicks before dicks, being a good friend, fixing the damage I've done, all that stuff. The fight Maddie and I had in Retiro last night totally sucked. I apologized for lying about my feelings for Rafa, but I promised her they wouldn't go any further. I told her I would talk to Rafa, and that nothing—absolutely nothing—would ever happen with him again. "You're too important to me," I told her, "to ever let a guy get between us. A clean break with Rafa is best for everyone, I think."

It's best for everyone if Rafa and I keep our distance so we can all move on, even if it hurts right now. God, does it *hurt*.

I mean, there's no way Maddie and I can repair our friendship if I'm romantically involved with Rafa. Just imagining her face if she saw the way he touches me, the way he looks at me—she'd be so hurt. And she's hurt enough this semester.

I want to grovel and make things right between Maddie and me ASAP. I know she won't forget my betrayal so easily; still, I have to start somewhere.

But now, looking Rafa in the eye, I recognize this is so much more complicated than that. This isn't black and white, right or wrong. I want them both, Maddie and Rafa, and having to choose between them is the worst thing ever.

I don't know what to do.

So I stick to my guns, because that's what I *should* do.

Isn't it?

"I'm sorry," I say. "I feel like shit about this whole situation. But I've known Maddie for years, and I'm only here for a few more months . . . we can still be friends, I guess, the tutoring thing, and Al . . ."

"*Friends?*" Rafa hisses. He leans forward, eyes widening with disbelief. "The things I did to you on Saturday—those are not things one friend does to another. I do not want anyone else doing them to you, Vivian. I would never have touched you like that if I knew we would not be novios."

Anger ripples beneath the surface of his deadly calm. I can tell he's trying to control it, to not lose his shit in this cute, muggy little bar. I hate myself for putting us in this position. But I had to decide. I can't float in this angsty almost-maybe middle ground forever. It's no man's land, and someone I care about—someone I love—is going to get really hurt.

I chose to take on that hurt myself instead. Considering all the damage I've caused, it's the least I can do.

I finish my wine and slide it across the counter. The bartender takes it with a toothy smile and asks if I'd like another. Lord, would I, but I'm about to burst into tears. I need to get out of here, stat, before I ugly-face cry in front of Rafa and all these nice, hot Madrileños.

"I'm really sorry," I say.

Rafa looks at me. "I am too."

"Please," I say. "Please try to understand."

He sticks his hands in his pockets and nods at the door. "Come on. I'll walk you to the Metro station—you'll get soaked without an umbrella."

Of course Rafa is excellent to the bitter end.

Wednesday Night

Maddie and I sit at the table in silence as we wait for the other girls to arrive. Our usual waiter does his usual sweep past the table, sniffing with annoyance when he sees gorgeous, glowing Laura isn't here yet.

"Poor bastard," Maddie sighs into her wine glass. "He doesn't stand a chance with Laura."

"You think?" I ask. "He's decent looking. And he gives us free wine."

"True," Maddie says. "But I heard a rumor that Laura is dating some super-hot fútbol player."

I pull back. "Like, one of the guys who plays for Madrid? The dudes on TV who make fifty million dollars?"

"Apparently it's the guy with the man bun she loved to masturbate to," Maddie says with a shrug. "No idea how that happened, but I bet he is ri*dic*ulous in bed. The bodies those guys have . . . sheesh."

I bet Rafa is ridiculous in bed. Too bad I'll never know exactly how ridiculous. How delicious and dirty and devoted he would be to making my first time the best time.

Silence settles between us again. It's been . . . awkward between us ever since our fight on Sunday. I apologized a hundred times, Maddie forgave me a hundred more. I thought—I hoped—it was over.

But I know it's not—how could it be, considering that I had an orgasm in a public bathroom with the guy she really likes? Maddie's snapped at me a couple times this week over stupid shit—finishing the last jar of peanut butter, accidentally using her towel—and I've thought resentful things (please see the "I'll never know how ridiculous Rafa is in bed" comment above). I could be imagining it, but the air seems to tighten whenever Maddie and I are together, a painful, tangible stretch that makes me feel sick to my stomach. Even though I did everything I thought I was supposed to do, something isn't right.

Weirdly, I wish I could call Rafa and tell him everything that's going on between Maddie and me. It's only been two days since I saw him last, but I miss him. I know he would make me laugh, make me feel better. He would understand. He'd get it. I didn't realize how close we'd become as friends until we weren't friends anymore.

I check my phone, discreetly, under the table. Nothing. No texts or missed calls from Justin Timberlake. My heart falls, just like it fell this afternoon, this morning, yesterday when I checked to see if he'd tried to contact me. I need to get over it already.

I see Maddie checking her phone too. Is she hoping for a text from Rafa, like me? I feel a stab of jealousy at the thought that they exchanged numbers. It's silly, I know, especially after Rafa assured me in no uncertain terms he isn't interested in her.

Still. It only makes this strange, off-kilter feeling between Maddie and me worse.

Katie is the first to arrive, followed by Rachel and Laura, who stroll through the restaurant arm in arm.

"Hey," Katie says, glancing from Maddie to me and back again. "Everything all right here?"

"Of course!" Maddie and I say in unison, a bit too brightly.

"It's just been a long week," I say.

"Yeah," Maddie says, "I had a big assignment due today and I'm beat."

Katie looks at us a long moment, her gaze lingering on me before she finally turns to her wine. "Whatever y'all say," she murmurs.

Laura holds up her glass. "To my Madrileñas—my Madrid girls. I'm so glad we started this tradition."

"Madrileñas," Maddie says, mulling over the word. "I dig it. Can we call ourselves that from now on?"

"Absolutely," Katie replies. "I'll start this time. *Arriba* . . ."

Giggling like twelve-year-olds, we perform the toast our waiter with the wandering eye taught us. *Arriba, abajo, al centro, al dentrooooo!* The people around us stare, a few of the old men smile. We're smiling too. I feel a surge of affection for these lovely girls I've gotten to know over the past month.

It's a relief, frankly, to be with the other girls. They form a sort of buffer between Maddie and me. We can talk with them, and even with each other, without having to really *talk*.

"I'm finally getting into this red wine thing," Rachel says, waving down our waiter to order her second glass. "I think a red wine drunk is my favorite drunk of all time."

"Ditto," I say. "It's the only drunk I feel in my knees. It's like my bones are laughing. Nothing quite like a red wine buzz."

"So we're getting into vino tinto de la casa," Laura says. "I think we're getting into Madrid too. It's finally starting to feel less terrifying. For me, at least."

Maddie leans back, allowing our waiter to set a couple tapas on the table—gambas (shrimp), some tortilla with potatoes, manchego cheese. "I'm getting into a good routine. It's so nice that things happen at a slower pace here. Life is, like, manageable."

"And fun," Rachel adds. "A walk to school isn't just a walk. You pass a palace, you see a friend, you grab a coffee, you see a cute little restaurant and make plans to have dinner there that night. Living in a big city like Madrid can be exhausting, but there are some definite perks."

I nod, swallowing my cheese. "Like the shopping. It's so damn good. Maddie's practically had to drag me out of every store we've gone into."

"You do love your clothes," she says. The way she says it— I don't know, I guess she's just trying to make conversation, but it rubs me the wrong way.

"You were very patient," I say. "And you helped me pick out some great stuff."

"Yeah," she replies, focusing on her wine glass. "Like that ridiculous little skirt you wore to Ático."

Katie is looking at us again. I drink my wine and do my best to ignore the hurt that churns in my stomach. Hurt that's tinged with anger. I didn't deserve that. Did I?

On the walk home, Maddie loops her arm through Katie's, leaving Laura and me a few steps behind.

"How are things with Mads?" she asks, her voice low as she glances at the girl in question.

"Not great," I say. "Some shit went down this weekend, and now Rafa and I are . . . well. Also not great."

"I'm sorry, Viv. I've been in that situation before, and it totally sucks."

"You have?"

"Don't act so surprised! It's more common than you think —you and your best friend liking the same guy. I mean. You wouldn't be best friends if you didn't like some of the same things."

"How did you handle it?" I ask.

Laura's pretty-girl hair glides over her shoulder as she shrugs. "Time. Honesty. Mostly time, though. It hurts, I know."

"Did your friend ever forgive you?"

"For what?"

"For getting the guy, obviously."

Laura turns her head and grins at me. "I didn't get the guy. She did."

Wait. Laura—gorgeous, gloriously tan Laura—didn't get the guy? I certainly didn't expect that. It kinda blows my mind, actually.

But Laura, I'm learning, is not at all the girl I thought she was when I first met her.

"I heard an interesting rumor about you and a certain man-bunned soccer player," I say. "Is your picture in the Spanish tabloids yet or what?"

Laura bites her lip, looking away.

"Ohmigod," I say. "It's true. You really are hooking up with a man-bunned footballer. Holy shit, Laura"

"It's nothing serious," she says. "Just fun. I saw him at a bar, and I was drunk enough to say hello. Hello turned into a drink, and a drink turned into me waking up naked in his sick apartment the next morning."

It's my turn to grin. "You woke up naked there this morning too, didn't you?"

"Maybe," she says. "And maybe I'm headed over there now to do it again tomorrow."

What I would give to wake up naked with Rafa.

I push the image of us, tangled in his blue sheets (for some reason I picture them being blue), from my thoughts.

It's not meant to be.

I look up at Maddie, laughing at something Katie says.

I *have* to get over Rafa.

CHAPTER EIGHTEEN

Next Monday

I close my notebook with a heavy sigh of relief. Not only am I done with the first draft of an economics essay, I'm also done with my first tutoring session with Rafa since we had our soul-crushing talk at that bar by the Prado Museum last week.

We've traded our beers for huge, shallow mugs of cappuccino. But even with the jolt of caffeine, I feel exhausted—wrung out—after tamping down my decidedly *un*platonic feelings for Rafa for the past hour and a half. It's impossible not to be charmed by him. His smile, his Spanish, his patience with my (slowly) improving language skills.

I watch him tip back his mug, finishing off the dregs of his coffee. I'm entranced by the sinewy working of his throat as he swallows. I swallow too, resisting the urge to sink my teeth into that throat and run the pads of my fingers over the flawless skin there, darkly tanned. After not seeing or speaking to him for a week, my desire for him is as overwhelming as ever. I can't shake it. And trust me, I've tried everything. Cold showers. Economics homework. Hitting on other guys in terrible, halting Spanish.

Nothing has helped me stop thinking about Rafa Montoya. It's like a sickness.

"Como estás?" I ask. *How are you?*

He meets my eyes. It's like a sock to the gut. "Así así," he says. *All right.* "And you?"

I miss you, I want to say. I miss seeing you, and laughing with you, and telling you about my study abroad misadventures. I miss you as a friend. I miss you as more than that.

"The same," I say. "Así así."

"And you and Maddie? Things okay there?"

I shrug. "I guess. I hope. It's a little weird still, but it'll get better."

I really, really hope it gets better.

Rafa settles his mug into the ring inside its saucer. "The drop/add period ended last week. What did you decide about the art class?"

"You'll be happy to know I kept it," I say, brightening at the change in subject. "I absolutely love it. I think it was our impromptu trip to the Prado that really convinced me though. I dropped one of my econ classes so I'd have the time."

He grins, a lopsided one that gives me all the feels. Like, *all* of them. "That does make me very happy. I knew you would love it."

"How did you know?" I ask. "That I would love an art class, I mean. When you and I sat down with Elena, we'd only just met."

Rafa shrugs, his blue eyes boring a hole through whatever resolve I had. "I pay attention, Vivian. Most people, they do not talk about art outside of a bar on a Saturday night. But you did, the very first time we met. I remember very clearly how your face changed, and your eyes, they went—" He flashes his fingers in a burst. "I always think you are beautiful, but you are the most beautiful when you talk about the things you love. And you love art."

I'm squeezing my mug so hard I worry it's going to break. How did this—Rafa knowing me in ways I didn't know myself, me wanting him in ways I didn't know I could want a guy—happen so fast?

"More than I love econ, that's for sure," I scoff. "But thank you. For convincing me to give that class a chance. And for paying attention."

Attention I've craved and never gotten from a guy before.

"Elena asked me to go to Sevilla and Grenada with your program next week," Rafa says quietly. "I wanted to ask you first. I don't want things to be, ehm . . . weird, yes? Between you and Maddie if I am there."

I swallow the last of my cappuccino. My heart races. I want Rafa to come with us next week. Being with him makes any experience—art, a bathroom make-out sesh, even econ—ten times better. I would experience everything with him if I could.

Only I can't.

"Up to you," I say. "It wouldn't bother me, and I'm pretty sure Maddie would be cool with it. I mean, there are fifty of us in the program, so it's not like you'll be hanging out with just us."

"Vale." Rafa turns back to my notebook. "Art history next?"

I grin. "Yes please."

"How was tutoring?" Maddie takes the earbuds out of her ears. She's propped up on the bed against the pillows, her legs bent. A psychology textbook rests on the slope of her thighs, the light from the lamp reflecting off its shiny pages.

I toss my bag on the desk beside our bed, the candy wrappers strewn across its surface crunching under its weight. "All right. Hard not to spend all our time on art history. How was class?"

"Fine. The usual."

Maddie looks me up and down, like she's searching for some clue that I'm lying, that I boned Rafa instead of doing my homework. A used condom dangling from my leg, or some hickeys on my neck. It sets my teeth on edge.

"That's cool," I say. "Did you get my text? The girls are getting together tonight instead of Wednesday, because we'll be on our trip."

Maddie turns back to her book, highlighting some text. "Yeah, I did. I'm not feeling so hot today, so . . . yeah. Plus I have a lot of work to do."

I toe off my sneakers. The silence stretching between us makes me sweat. Is Maddie mad at me?

"Are you okay?" I ask, unable to keep it in any longer.

"Yeah. Just tired," she says. "So how is Rafa?"

She says it nonchalantly, but we both know her question is a loaded one.

"He's good," I say. "My grades are definitely improving, so he's doing something right."

"Good for you," Maddie says.

I look at her for a long moment. Something's up.

"I'm gonna grab a quick shower," I say.

"Okay," she says, and puts the earbuds back in her ears.

My hand shakes as I close the bathroom door behind me. I'm angry. Angry at myself. Angry at Maddie. Angry that I can't be with Rafa. It's not Maddie's fault, I know it isn't—it's my fault—but still I feel resentful toward her.

This was not how I pictured things playing out. For the first time, I wonder how it would be if I told Rafa yes, and we were together now. I know it would hurt Maddie, at least at first. But would she eventually be happy for me? Would *I* be happy with the choice I made?

CHAPTER NINETEEN

Next Tuesday

Maddie wasn't lying when she said she didn't feel well. Her headache turned into a sore throat, the sore throat turned into a fever. The diagnosis: a bad case of the flu.

Which totally sucks, because that means she's going to miss our program's trip to southern Spain. I promise Maddie I'll take plenty of pictures of Sevilla and Grenada, and that yes, of course I'll fill her in on any info we get about the upcoming exam in our experience class.

"Viv," she says as I'm about to head out the door. "Have fun, okay? Really. I mean it. I want you to have a good time on this trip."

"Thanks," I say, giving her hand a good squeeze. "Don't worry, I'll puke in the bushes twice. Once for me and once for you."

"I can't wait until my puke is booze induced," she replies with a weak smile. She looks at me for a long moment. I get the feeling she is trying to tell me something, but as she tries to speak she winces. The hand that was in mine goes to her throat.

"You sure you don't want me to stay with you?" I ask. "You look like you're in pain."

"I told you a million times." She clears her throat, a grating, gasping sound. "No fucking way are you missing this awesome trip because of me. Now go before I infect you with this Ebola disease I have. Go!"

I leave her wrapped up in bed with a month's supply of what we think is Spanish cough medicine and a few deliciously naughty romances I downloaded on my eReader. I feel bad for Maddie—really, the flu is awful—and she's had such a tough semester already.

But as I head for the Metro, I feel like I can breathe a little easier despite the backpack that weighs down my shoulders. I think a break might be a good thing. Maybe after spending a few days apart, we can finally get back to being good friends to one another. Maybe we can forget Rafa, and remember the laughter and the love that made us such good friends in the first place.

Only Rafa isn't so easy to forget.

Especially when I bump into him at the train station, and he hands me a coffee—in a to-go cup—with a grin that could slay all the ladies in the land.

"Cappuccino with one sugar," he says. "That is how you like it, yes?"

"Yes. Wow. Thank you," I say, folding back the plastic lid. "Where in the world did you find a place that sells coffee to go? I've been looking for one for, like, ever, but I haven't had any luck."

Rafa nods to a café across the station, the pale morning sun that streams through the skylights above silvering his hair. "There is a little place inside, just over there. I know how very hard you have been looking."

Stop being so excellent, I silently say as I sip at my coffee. It's just right.

Of course it's just right.

"How is Maddie feeling?" he asks. "El gripe is not of the joke."

"She's all right," I say. "Pretty bummed she's missing this trip. I told her I'd bring her something fun back, like a flamenco dancer."

He glances at my backpack. "I think we can fit one of those in there. You know we are taking a flamenco dancing lesson this afternoon?"

"I didn't," I say. "That sounds kinda fun, actually."

"I was hoping to see your white girl again," he says. "It has been too long."

I take another sip of coffee. Two minutes and already our conversation is going someplace it shouldn't. Just the thought of flamenco dancing with Rafa makes my heart beat a little faster. I want to do everything with him. Most of all press his body against mine under the guise of cultural edification.

"Our train is leaving soon," I say, blinking away the image of him swaying his hips in time to the rousing tune of a guitar. *Think about Maddie, your friendship,* I tell myself. *Think about keeping it in your pants.*

Seville
That Afternoon

We stand in a loose circle around the perimeter of the dance studio. The fans that purr from the windows do little to keep us cool. It may be October, but it's hot as hell; summer's last sigh in Spain.

We're all sticky after this morning's walking tour. Sweat prickles along my scalp as I watch a pair of professional flamenco dancers twirl and clap at the front of the room, their reflections following them in the floor-to-ceiling mirrors. The guitarists in the chairs behind them strum a throaty, thumping acoustic beat, voices trilled in haunting melody.

I've never really seen flamenco before. It's much more sensual than I thought it would be. Angsty, even. Maybe I'm projecting, but it's like watching thwarted lovers dance around one another, daring a touch here, turning away there, faces taut with suppressed longing.

I'm hypnotized. It cuts, their dancing. Cuts close, so close to home. Like Neruda's sexy poem, and Goya's Majas, flamenco grabs my heart and squeezes. It plucks at the strings inside me, making me vibrate with want, with hurt.

The dancers finish with a dramatic flourish. We clap, smiling despite the heat and our aching legs. They tell us it's our turn to learn the dance, to pick a couple, they say, to lead the rest of the class in a traditional flamenco routine.

I turn my head, hoping they won't choose me, and my gaze collides with Rafa's. He's on the other side of the room, his tan skin dewy with sweat, his hands in the pockets of his jeans. The skin at the edges of his eyes crinkles as he smiles at me. I try not to smile back, I do, but I can't help it. His cuteness is contagious.

"Ahhh!" someone is saying. "Estos novios!"

I look up and the flamenco dude is pointing at me and Rafa, a wide, knowing smile on his face. *Yes,* he says in Spanish. *I'm pointing at you two!*

My stomach drops to the floor. I feel the eyes of the entire room turn to Rafa and me. My face flushes with a heat so violent I worry my skin is burning off.

"Um," I say. "No somos novios." *We are not together.*

Whatever you say, the man says in Spanish.

No no no this can't happen. My self-control is hanging by

a thread. The last thing I need is to dirty flamenco dance with Rafa Montoya in front of our entire program.

Rafa strides toward me, the rolled-up sleeve of his white button-down sliding up his arm as he holds out his hand. "Venga, Vivian." *Come, Vee-vee-an.*

Saying no to that smile is like plucking my eyebrows. Painful. Futile. It's gonna hurt, so why do it?

I take his hand and he guides me to the front of the room. Around us, our friends clap, whistle, and call out lewd things that make me blush even harder.

The dancers give us a few instructions, telling the rest of the class to follow along. We count out our steps, clapping out the beat. I sneak glances at Rafa. and of course he's a natural, a smile splitting his face as he moves. Even the female dance instructor is impressed with his dancing. Or maybe she's impressed with his whole perfect person. It's hard to tell.

Vale, she says. *Now let's put it all together with the music. But oh, wait, the costumes, we forgot the costumes!*

Rafa steps forward to stand in front of me. His eyes flash with laughter, the light blue tinged with heat. His smile deepens as his fingers glide down his chest to his shirt. He unbuttons one button, then another.

"Esto es mi disfraz," he says. *This is my costume.*

The room echoes with applause, some laughs. I look away, rolling my lips between my teeth to keep from smiling too hard. He's so damn cute. Hot. Handsome. He is all the things, and he is killing me.

The instructor helps me into a red and white polka dot dress with a flouncy skirt and flowy, lace-edged sleeves. It's a little tight with my clothes underneath, but from the look in Rafa's eyes I guess it fits okay.

The guitars sound behind us, and we begin to move. I can't look at Rafa or I'm sure I'll combust. He grasps my hand, spins me around, his fingers gliding through mine. A shiver darts down my spine. Inside my chest my heart flutters.

I step on his foot and curse. He laughs and so do I. The dress whirls around my ankles as Rafa turns me, and turns me again, clapping his hands while he sways his hips. He dances closer, closer, his body brushing against mine. Warmth spreads through me. I know we're dancing in cheesy costumes in front of fifty people, but I am so, so tempted to grab Rafa by the shorthairs and tongue kiss him like the world is ending.

He trails his fingertips up the length of my bare arm, and in the space of a single heartbeat the dance goes from sweet and fun to fun and hot. The music swirls to a screaming crescendo and then the song ends.

I am on fire.

The class erupts in applause, a few lewd whistles. Rafa smiles at our audience, slipping an arm around my waist easily, like we've been murdering Flamenco together for years. We make a silly little bow. But when he rises and we meet eyes, his are slick with heat, full of something that scares me.

It scares me because I can see he's on fire too. I can feel it, my body arching into the magnetic pull of his. I am aware of the blood moving in the space between my skin and bones, pooling where my legs meet. The way he touches me—even now, pulses of warmth emanate from the place where his palm meets the small of my back—what I wouldn't give for him to touch me like that all over.

Rafa's expression, soft with interest, makes my heart hurt. No one has ever looked at me the way he does, like I'm the only one in the room, in the world, and it makes me feel things I shouldn't.

I'm glad Maddie isn't here to see him looking at me like this.

We're both breathing hard. A a fine sheen of sweat prickles on his forehead. I want to mop it up with my fingertips, taste it with my mouth. I want him, more than I've ever wanted anything.

I want him, and I can't have him.

Elena makes her way to the middle of the studio, quieting everyone before giving us instructions for tomorrow's schedule. We are dismissed and people bolt out the door, eager to get a nap in before heading out later tonight. The girls told me everyone is meeting for dinner at a tapas place across the river in Triana.

I turn away from Rafa, trying to tug the dress back over my head. Somehow I get my head stuck in the collar.

"Shit," I murmur, sweat trickling down my temples.

Through the bright red tunnel of my dress, I see Rafa's scuffed suede boots step toward me. "Here," he says. "Let me help you."

"Thanks," I say. My skin burns where he touches me. I keep waiting for my response to him to cool, to fade.

It's only gotten hotter.

Rafa tugs the dress over my head, grinning, and I let out a sigh of relief.

"Whew." I wipe my brow. I glance at his chest, peeking through the open lapels of his shirt. I swallow. "You should button that back up. You're going to scare the villagers. And by scare, I mean seduce."

He looks down at said buttons. Looks back up, a smirk quirking the corner of his mouth. "I don't think I will."

We step out into the late afternoon, bringing up the rear of our group as we walk the few blocks to our hotel. My heart is still beating hard, my body alive with the knowledge that Rafa is beside me. We are quiet, listening to the voices of our friends ahead. Our hands brush. I close my eyes and allow the warmth I feel to overwhelm me. The sun burns pink through my closed lids.

I feel his hand on my back again, guiding me slightly to the right, and I open my eyes to see him grinning down at me, his sunglasses setting off the fullness of his lips.

"You were about to walk into a pole," he says.

I look over my shoulder at the offending pole. "Yikes," I say. "Thanks for saving me from breaking my face. Also from that dress. God, I'm a mess today."

"De nada," he says. *You're welcome*. "What were you thinking about?"

I turn my head to look at him. *You*. Always, always you.

His smile softens.

His fingers find mine. His touch is achingly gentle as he entwines them. We keep walking. I should pull away. I should have the courage to pull away.

But the joy I feel walking next to Rafa fills me from head to toe. I don't want to feel it. I shouldn't feel it.

But I do. And for the first time, I allow that feeling to swallow me whole.

Maybe it's not doing what I *should* do that requires courage.

Maybe it's doing what I *want* to do that is the courageous thing.

And I want to hold hands with Rafa. I want to take the risk and be with him.

I want to be with the guy who feels like *home*. Thousands of miles from the house I grew up in, I found him. He's with me here, and I have never felt safer or more alive than I do right now.

I thought being with Rafa would break my already fragile heart, that it would ruin my friendship with Maddie. So I told him no, I kept fighting and denying what I felt for him. And it turns out *not* being with Rafa—not being honest about what I want—is just as toxic.

By trying not to betray my friend, I have betrayed myself.

I love her, and I love him, and I am going to figure it out.

But today—tonight—I am going to be with Rafa.

The sun slants between buildings, the heat oppressive on our shoulders. We're trailing farther and farther behind the rest of the group. Our joined hands swing idly between us, and I think of our first night together; all that feeling and excitement that coursed from this place where palm met palm. It's still there, that crushing, effervescent desire. I didn't think it could get any bigger, any better. But it has.

It hits me then—him walking beside me, me walking beside him.

Somewhere along this twisty, sometimes terrible, sometimes amazing path that led us to this moment, I fell in love.

CHAPTER TWENTY

We squeeze into the elevator at the hotel with a bunch of other Meryton in Madrid kids. I hear Laura giggling with Katie somewhere toward the back.

Rafa hides our joined hands between our legs.

We huddle close to let people off at each floor.

At last we reach my floor—four. I move to get off the elevator but Rafa holds me tight. I meet his eyes. I can't read his expression, but I know what he wants.

He wants me to go up to his room. Doubtless as a chaperone he gets his own. The thought of being alone with him is delicious.

I don't move.

We get off on the sixth floor. Rafa hangs a sharp right and pulls me after him. It takes every ounce of my self-control not to pull back. I'm so used to resisting him, to protesting, and it's a hard habit to break. The reasons I resisted his advances are still there. I'm scared out of my mind and I'm so turned on and I can't believe this is happening, I can't believe I'm in love with this gorgeous man who is taking me to his room.

I've been waiting forever for him. For this. It's indescribably lovely, wanting and being wanted in return.

His room is at the end of the hall. I follow him inside.

Rafa turns on his heel to face me. He reaches behind me and palms the door shut, drawing close, oh, he's so close. I fall back against the door, my body throbbing with need. I need him to touch me.

"Vivian," he says, his voice quiet. I suck in a breath as he slides a hand onto my face, his fingers tickling my hair. In this single, exquisite moment, my senses ignite, singeing my fears in an instant. "Enough of this bullshit. I can't stay away from you. I can't be a friend to you. I want to be more than that. I want more than that, Vivian, and I think you do too."

I nod my head. "I do, Rafa. I can't stay away from you either. I've tried, I thought it was the right thing to do—"

"This"—he presses a lingering kiss onto the angle of my jaw—"is the right thing. I know you are scared. Be brave, Vivian. Open up for me. There is no one else. There is only you and me."

He looks me in the eye. His are wild, wet with desire. He's waiting for me to tell him yes, to tell him I want this as badly as he does.

I love you, I think.

"I want you," I say, fingering the buttons on his shirt. "I want you to teach me everything."

He cocks a brow, grin tugging at the edges of his mouth. "Everything?"

"Everything."

"I will go slow—"

"I don't want to go slow," I say.

"You haven't done this before," he says, thumbing my chin so I look up at him.

"But I never told you—"

"I guessed you were a virgin that night at Ático. I was right, wasn't I?"

I pause. "Yes."

"Then we go slow. Trust me, you do not want to just do it —just get it over with. I don't want you to miss a thing."

I bite my lip. "Vale."

Rafa curls a stray lock of hair behind my ear. "I need to go downstairs very quick, yes? I don't have any—"

"Condoms," I say. "You don't carry any around with you?"

His grin deepens, revealing a flash of white teeth. "No. I think it is rude to . . . how do you say? Assume?"

"Yes," I reply. "That's kinda sweet of you."

He looks at me. "I don't have anything—my tests came back negative from my doctor a few weeks ago. But I am not sure if you are using the contraception or not?"

"I'm negative too," I say. "But I haven't, um, you know, been with anyone, in a relationship or whatever, so . . . yeah, I'm not on the pill or anything."

"Even if you were, it is good to be safe." He pecks my cheek. "Give me five minutes. Help yourself to whatever you want—there's some bottled water in the fridge, I think."

"Okay," I say.

Rafa leaves. I step into the room. It's warm, a pair of windows pushed open onto a tiny courtyard. The gauzy drapes bow out in a small, golden-hued breeze. I can hear the muted sounds of the street outside. The buzz of a muffler, people talking.

And then, of course, there's the bed, a delicious-looking affair with fluffy white linens and mounds of downy pillows. I'm tempted to launch myself into its crisp embrace, burying my face in the sheets Rafa and I will dance between in a few short minutes. A whole freaking bed, just for the two of us. Heat spikes through my center. I can't *wait*.

A long, languid stretch of afternoon is all that we have between us, Rafa and me.

That, and our clothes.

I look down at my tank top and skirt. Should I take them off? Or should I wait for Rafa to do it?

I decide to wait. In the meantime, I head to the bathroom with a bottle of water from the fridge. It's strange, seeing his toiletries lined up on the vanity. Razor, shaving cream, floss, a comb. It's like a still life, a scene from everyday Rafa Montoya. I like being part of his everyday. I want to know him, his habits, the way he brushes his teeth.

As his girlfriend, I will.

I'm just about to reach for his aftershave—for a minute I think about stealing it, it smells *so* good—when I hear the door open and close.

I duck my head out of the bathroom. "That was fast."

"I am impatient, knowing you wait for me." Rafa smiles, tossing a plastic bag onto the nightstand. I can see the shape of the box through the bag. The box of condoms I've fantasized about—it's here.

It's happening.

Holy *shit*. I am going to have sex. Here. Today. Now.

With Rafa.

I bite the inside of my cheek, just to make sure this is real.

Rafa reaches for me, pulling me against him in the middle of the room.

"Be with me," he murmurs in my ear. "Be mine, Vivian."

I press my body to his, reveling in the barely contained strength of his thighs, his flat belly, the rounded muscles in his chest. He's more than a head taller than I am. He's huge and he's strong and he is offering it all to me.

"Be mine," I say.

There it is again, that devastating quirk of his lips. *I've been yours since the night we met*, he says in Spanish.

203

He takes my face in his hands. I grasp his wrists; his pulse beats an uneven tattoo against the skin between my thumb and forefinger.

"Estoy lista," I say. *I'm ready*.

He smiles. I smile. A smile he captures with his lips, ducking his head as his mouth moves languorously over mine. I meet him stroke for stroke, kissing, kissing, has there ever in the history of the world been a more perfect kiss?

I've been waiting for this kiss. Behind my closed lids I revel in the velvety darkness, velvety like the slick inside of Rafa's mouth. He takes my bottom lip between his teeth, working slowly, patiently, just the right amount of tenderness, of bite. I drink him in, his scent, his erotic patience.

He guides my head this way, that way, telling me where to go to deepen the kiss. Tiny explosions of light ignite in my chest, shooting stars of sensation that tickle my sides and land, smoldering, low in my belly.

My fingers work at the few remaining buttons on his shirt that are still actually buttoned. I slide one through its hole, then another, my fingers trailing over the taut skin of his chest, the whirls of dark hair peeking through the *V* of his shirt.

He kisses me harder. His lips demand more, always more, overwhelming in their need. I'm breathless from the effort of trying to keep up.

I could kiss Rafa all. Freaking. Day. For the rest of my life.

But there is sex to be had, nakedness to be explored.

I begin to back Rafa toward the bed, nudging his hips with mine. I can feel his hard-on through his jeans. I reach for his waistband—

"Todavía no," he says, grabbing my wrist. *Not yet*. "We go slow, remember?"

"We've gone slow all semester," I pant against his lips.

"And we go slow today," he says, capturing my reply in a kiss.

The backs of Rafa's legs hit the bed. I pull away, looking down to tug the shirttails out of his jeans. My clit twitches at the sight of his happy trail, the veins that stand out against the planed muscles of his groin.

Rafa rolls his shoulders back and I slide my hands up his torso to help him out of his shirt. His skin is hot to the touch. There is so much of him, too much to explore in one afternoon. I stare at his naked chest, my eyes flicking from his belly to his shoulders to his enormous arms, rippled with muscle.

Arms that swallow me as he wraps them around me, his hands sliding down to cup my ass. He presses me, gently, against the bulge in his pants.

"Not fair," I say, looking up at him.

He grins, catching his tongue between his teeth. "I know."

He presses a little harder. The breath catches in my throat. His dick is angled so that it presses right between my legs, just shy of the place that is the center of all this wild sensation.

I press a little harder, rising to my tiptoes. My vision blurs. This is going to feel so damn good.

I place my palm on the center of his chest and push him onto the bed. He laughs, his body sinking into the crisp white duvet as I climb on top of him, straddling his hips. I sink onto his dick, his jeans and my flimsy thong the only barrier between us. Heat spikes through my center. I grind my hips, slowly, against his, biting my lip. The zipper of his fly hits me *right* there, equal parts pleasure and pain.

His eyes darken, nostrils flaring as his palms ride up my bare thighs. I gather the hem of my tank top and yank it over my head, tossing it off the bed. I'm wearing a plain strapless bra, nude colored, no peek-a-boo lace or anything fun like that. Rafa doesn't seem to mind as he moves one hand up my torso, running his first finger inside the top of my bra. He catches my nipple, uses it to angle my breast out of the bra. He swipes the pad of his thumb across my nipple, once, twice, three times. I gasp, rearing into his touch.

He reaches around to unhook my bra. It glides down my torso, landing with a small sigh on the bed. My breasts are hard with desire, my nipples puckering beneath Rafa's gaze.

"God, Vivian," he says, swallowing. He takes my breast in his palm, gives it a possessive squeeze. "You're so beautiful."

I lean over him, my nipples brushing against his chest. I kiss my way up his throat, the salty tang of his sweat on my lips, the woodsy scent of his aftershave filling my head. He draws his fingers down the slope of my bare back, dipping into the waistband of my skirt as I press my mouth to his.

It feels so good, him pressed between my legs, the fingers of one hand plucking at my nipple, the fingers of the other toying with the lace edge of my thong. I'm so turned on I could scream.

Rafa's tugging on my skirt, but with me straddling him he can't get it off. He turns his body, bringing mine down onto the bed. He's on top of me now, our legs tangled. He loops an arm around my waist and lifts me farther up on the bed, pressing kisses into my belly as he hooks his fingers into my skirt and thong and pulls them off. I bend my legs to help him, and he slides them down my calves, tossing them aside.

I am naked as the day as I was born, the duvet cool against the backs of my thighs.

When I used to hook up with Keith, my nakedness would embarrass me. I'd try to cover up, I'd try to slide under the covers so he wouldn't make fun of whatever he saw. I guess I didn't really like myself when I was with him.

But with Rafa, it feels good to be naked. I'm unafraid. Unafraid of what he thinks—I know what he thinks, he thinks I'm beautiful—unashamed of my body and all the marvelous things it can do and feel.

I close my eyes as Rafa covers my body with his. The weight of him, pressing me into the duvet, making me just the littlest bit breathless, is lovely. We are skin to skin, our naked arms gliding against one another. He balances his elbows on either side of my head, a grin on his lips as he dips his head to kiss me, a kiss that he trails down the slope of my throat. He covers me, overwhelms me, and I love, I *love* it.

The breeze from the windows, warm, moves over us, a long, lingering caress. The sun sears my skin, catching a shoulder, a leg. Rafa's teeth nick my collarbone as he moves over me, shifting his weight in subtle, delicious ways. Our skin slides and sticks, too much, never enough. He makes his way down my chest, catching a nipple in his mouth, biting, soothing, stoking, moving to my belly. He is thorough, heart-breakingly thorough, and when he looks up, his smile full of light and happiness, I have to look away. There is so much going on inside me I'm scared I'm going to cry.

He plants a kiss on the edge of my hip and my eyes fly open. He's going to go down on me. I haven't—I'm not ready —oh, *eff* me—

"No, no, Rafa—" I say.

"Yes," he says, meeting my eyes. "You are perfect. Let me love you."

My heart twists inside my chest. *Love*.

I dig my hand into his hair and give it a small tug. He is so handsome. Boyishly, devastatingly handsome.

And he wants to love me.

"Vale," I breathe.

He lifts my hips and palms my ass and gives it a squeeze, turning his head between my legs to trail kisses up the inside of my thigh. My pussy smarts, pulses, and his hands are on both my thighs then, hooking my legs over his shoulders as he licks the tendon connecting my leg to my groin. I squeeze my eyes shut against the painful intensity of my desire.

"Look at me," he says. "Vivian, look at me."

I inhale a trembling breath. I do as he tells me.

And then his eyes and mouth are on me. I'm so wet his lips glide easily over me; he lets out a groan of approval that reverberates through my folds.

I feel the first stirrings of an orgasm.

Watching him kiss me there, his head ducking in time to his movements, heightens the already blinding sensation of his mouth on my pussy. His tongue feels warm and light against me, swirling around my clit—just where I told him I liked it.

He remembers. He always remembers.

His pale eyes are slick, latched onto mine. I fist the sheets in my hands, holding on for dear life as his mouth and lips and tongue move more ardently now. He juts the tip of his tongue inside me and I gasp, my hips beginning to dance against his mouth, wanting, needing.

"Rafa," I pant. "I can't—I'm close—"

The feeling between my legs spirals tighter. The muscles in my thighs and calves contract, my back arching off the bed as I beg for more. He gives it to me, his hands kneading my ass, his tongue burrowing into the tip of my pussy, teasing my clitoris with small bites.

It's infinitely erotic, watching him love me like this. I've never felt so free with a guy before. Free to get a little dirty, to show my pleasure and take it too.

Maybe that freedom explains why I'm coming so quickly. I try to hold back, but I'm lost in the sensation of his attention and his affection. I've never been loved like this, adored like this.

His tongue circles me again, and again, and again, and I'm

there, I'm right on the edge, I'm climbing higher, tighter, *yes*—

The orgasm hits me with white-hot force. It's got hands and teeth, and it won't let me go. Pounding throbs of poignant sensation move through me, one momentous wave after the next, leaving me reeling. It hurts. It's the best thing ever. I cry out, the space behind my closed eyes a blessed blank as I give my body up to Rafa.

CHAPTER TWENTY-ONE

He's climbing back over me, pulling me into his arms as I try to catch my breath. He kisses the tip of my nose, my forehead, my lips, and I burrow into the warmth of his body, allowing him to hold me, allowing myself to be held. I feel vulnerable, aroused, alarmed.

"It's just you and me," he murmurs. "Estoy aquí, Vivian, estoy aquí." *I'm here, I'm here.*

I'm so glad he's here.

I've had plenty of great orgasms before (mostly alone, with the help of a "back massager" I picked up at the mall). But they've never been quite like this. This is a whole new kind of orgasm. One that blows the others out of the water.

One that I feel in my body and in my heart.

A heart that works double time as I inhale the scent of Rafa's bare skin. I slide my hands around his torso to rest in the gully of his lower back. His skin is smooth, thick, tantalizingly damp with sweat. I feel the pull of his muscle, strident and strong, beneath my palms. He's so much bigger than I am, so much more powerful, his tenderness that much sweeter.

Rafa pulls back, nuzzles his nose against mine. He meets my gaze. Up close I can see the specks of green and yellow that shade his blue eyes.

"Okay?" he asks, tucking my hair behind my ear.

"Better than okay," I manage. "Much, much better than okay."

One side of his mouth quirks into a grin. "I do not mean to brag. But do you always come so fast?"

I scoff, tracing small circles into his back. "No. I think I may like you a little bit."

"A little bit?"

I press a kiss onto his mouth. "A lot more than a little bit."

"Good." He kisses me back. "I like you a lot more than a little bit too."

I slide my hands around the waistband of his jeans. This time he doesn't stop me as I unbutton them, unzip the fly. I kiss him as I work, long, lazy strokes of mouth and tongue. We kiss really well, naturals at kissing one another.

Outside the open windows, the afternoon is fading to dusk. The oranges are now dusky pink, the blue sky mellowing to violet. The air is still warm, the breeze a cooling sigh. Once you've experienced a sunset in Spain, nothing else compares.

Especially if you're experiencing that sunset in bed, naked, with the Madrileño of your dreams.

I slip a hand inside the front of Rafa's jeans.

"You're a boxer guy," I say.

"Did you expect tightie whities?" he murmurs against my lips.

"I don't know what I expected," I say. "But I like them."

This little detail about Rafa would charm my pants off if I still had any on. I love knowing these things about him. I can never know enough. I want to know everything. To be a part of everything that makes him Rafa.

I feel his cock through the thin fabric of his boxers. He's rock hard, easily filling my hand. He's not too small, not too big, just right. I wiggle two fingers through the fall in the front of his boxers. I brush the head of his dick and swirl the wet pre-cum with my fingertips. Rafa's body tenses against mine. He gently bucks his hips, urging the tip of his dick into my hand. I swipe a thumb across it.

He sucks a breath through his teeth, wincing.

"If you want to stop," he says, "you need to tell me this now, Vivian. If we go any further—I don't think I will be able to stop. You feel so good."

He pulls back and looks me in the eye. "Are you sure?"

"I'm sure."

His eyes search mine. "I'm sure too."

I don't know what he means by that, but then he's wiggling out of his jeans, his boxers, and I'm helping him, my hands greedy to know what he feels like, what he wants, what he likes.

We lie side by side, completely naked, looking at each other. I take his dick in my hand and squeeze. Rafa's eyes darken. I can only imagine how he'll feel inside me. How good it's going to be. How well we will fit together. Already I feel a familiar tightening between my legs stirring back to life. The head of his cock presses against my lower belly. I bite my lip. I can't *wait*.

All this skin is making me dizzy. His belly, his hips, the way his parts fit together—he's beautiful, tan skin pulled taut over perfect muscle and sinew. I look, and keep looking, until I hear laughter rumbling in Rafa's chest.

"Sorry," I say. "You're just, um. I don't know. Ridiculously hot?"

I lift my face. He's grinning, his eyes soft with something I haven't seen before.

He thumbs my nipple, plucking it between his thumb and forefinger. "You're ridiculously hot."

The beat between my legs deepens.

"Can we stop taking it slow?" I whisper. "I'm ready, Rafa."

"Sí," he says, reaching behind him. "But first, one more very important lesson."

He digs the box out of its plastic bag and rips it open, retrieving a foil packet. My stomach flips. I've seen condoms before, plenty of times—student health, sex ed, in the bathroom Maddie and I shared last—but I've never actually had the pleasure of using one.

Rafa rises to his knees, tearing open the packet with his teeth. His dick juts obscenely—tauntingly—from the veined slope of his groin.

"Oh my God," I say, transfixed. "You're ridiculous."

He goes still. "Do I scare you?"

"Not at all. The opposite, actually. I kinda want to eat you alive right now."

"Later." Rafa holds up the clear disc of the condom. "First, I teach you how to put on a condom." He smirks. "I am your tutor, after all."

I bite my lip, taking the condom from him. "Then tutor me."

Covering my fingers with his, he guides the condom onto the tip of his cock. "Pinch the tip," he says. "Yes, exactly, just like that. Now roll it down . . . ah, fuck, Vivian, you're killing me."

"Am I doing it right?" I ask, sliding the condom farther onto him.

He winces. "Like all of your lessons, you do it very much right. *Too* right."

When I'm done, I lean forward and kiss the tip of his cock. Rafa looks down at me, his face a mask of barely controlled need.

"I want this to feel good for you," he says, using a hand to guide my legs apart. "I need to get you ready. Tell me if I'm hurting you, vale?" That same hand moves to my clit, meddling in the wetness there before sliding lower, lower. He slips one finger inside me and I'm so soft with arousal it goes easily, slowly, sinking deep.

"Vale," I breathe. I want him inside me so badly I can hardly see straight.

Another finger slips inside me. I feel a pinching stretch, the pleasure edged with a charge of pain. Nothing bad, just full.

Rafa swallows. "You're perfect, Vivian. So fucking perfect."

He begins to thrust his fingers, a small movement, while he uses his thumb to play with my clit. I rise to his touch, my heart hammering in my ears. I'm excited.

I'm nervous.

I close my eyes. "That's okay. That feels good."

He slides his fingers out of me, moving them up and around my clit, making me cry out again, louder this time. I know the window is open, I know the nice people out on the street can probably hear us, but I don't care. I want to lose myself to this, to Rafa.

Rafa settles himself between my legs, splaying them wider. He rests his weight on one elbow. Anticipation surges through me at the feel of his cock against me, probing, eager. Just a little lower and he could push inside me and finally deflower this twenty-year-old virgin.

He reaches down, gliding the latex tip of his penis up and down my pussy, up and down, stoking my need to new, unbearable heights. He presses himself against my clitoris, and I arch against him. It feels so good it hurts.

"Please," I say. "Oh, God, Rafa, please."

His mouth finds mine and he kisses me, hard, a long,

ardent kiss that has me moaning into his mouth. This—all of this—his passion, his body's response to mine, his tenderness, the anticipation of what we're about to do—it's overwhelming. Tears well in my eyes. I close them, I don't want to ruin this moment by crying. I've cried enough this semester.

And I'm not going to be *that* girl who cries during sex.

Rafa guides himself into the cleft of my pussy. The pressure is there right away. I feel myself opening to him, stretching. His belly slides against mine as he bucks his hips, gently, sinking the tiniest bit into me.

My body tenses. This is definitely uncomfortable. He feels huge, too huge to possibly fit inside me.

Rafa's mouth moves over my jaw, biting at my earlobe.

You're mine, he whispers in Spanish, his breath warm in my ear, *I've wanted you all this time, and now you're finally mine*.

Falling in love with Rafa, I realize, has been a slow unraveling of all my fears, my doubts, my hang-ups. He's opened me, he's given me the courage to be who I *am*, given me the courage to abandon thoughts of who I *should* be. He is safety and he is home and he is sex. He is everything I ever wanted.

I am so, so in love with him.

I am in full bloom.

I relax. His lips are on my neck as he settles his full weight on me, both elbows on either side of my head. He surrounds me, his body, his scent, loving me as well and as intentionally as I ever dreamed of being loved.

He tucks my hair behind my ear with fingers that tremble.

Are you okay? he asks.

I'm okay.

I glide my hands down his sides as he works his way farther inside me. It takes some effort, at first, not to pull back. It stings and makes me wonder why people say sex feels so amazeballs, because this is definitely less than pleasant.

The farther he goes, the more it hurts. My fingers dig into

the skin between Rafa's ribs as he presses his lips to mine, and I lose myself in his kiss. He pushes farther, always farther, farther when I didn't think there could be any more room. If he wasn't holding me captive with his weight, his kiss, I would be scrambling for the headboard.

"Un poco más," Rafa whispers. *Just a little bit more*.

He cocks his hips, pulling back the slightest bit, and then with a solid thrust he surges inside me, sinking to the hilt. My eyes fly open at a flash of searing pain. My breath catches in my throat. Rafa is looking at me, the skin around his eyes tense. The light from the window gilds the pointed licks of his dark hair.

"Still okay?" he asks.

I nod. I'm afraid if I try to speak I'll end up crying.

He is still for some moments, allowing me to stretch, to adjust to the feel of him inside me. He draws his mouth up and down my throat, biting my lips, kissing my closed eyelids. Inside my chest my heart swells as the pain between my legs dims.

Rafa begins to move, slowly at first, baby thrusts. Beneath my palms I feel the muscles rippling beneath the skin as he swivels his hips, small circles that hit me in just the right place. I can tell he's holding back and has a lot more to give, a lot of strength left to lend his thrusts, but he's careful, always so careful with me.

He moves over me, kissing me, teasing me. He pulls out, dives back in, pulls out again. I start to move too, when it stops hurting and starts feeling good.

Really good.

I draw my knees up, deepening each thrust. We sweat and stick and suck, his body making small slapping noises each time it meets mine.

"Open your eyes, Vivian," he says. "I know you like the watching. Look."

He lifts his hips, allowing me to see where our bodies are joined. His dick, glistening with my arousal, slides in and out of me, in and out, the veins in his groin throbbing against his skin. Heat pulses between my legs as I watch him move.

It's lewd.

It's awesome.

"Touch yourself," he says. "You're close—I feel it."

I reach down and do as I'm told. I gasp. My clit is stretched around the great mass of Rafa's dick, soft and swollen and ready to burst. I glide my fingers over it, the memory of pain evaporating as pleasure rises in its place.

Pleasure unlike anything I have ever felt before. Pleasure that spirals deep inside me. Pleasure I can't hold back.

Rafa is gliding smooth, strong strokes in and out of me now, his body gorgeous as it moves over me. His butt is perfection. Like, true, he-should-be-a-butt-double perfection.

I keep touching myself, and Rafa keeps moving, and now I understand, now I am open, now I am ready.

I come hard, a blinding orgasm that has me shouting Rafa's name. He cries out at the same moment. I feel myself clenching around him as he thrusts one last time, the two of us lost to the manic rush inside and between our bodies. It's eviscerating, experiencing this with him. I feel full, so damn full, full of love and satiation, full of fear and longing and contentment.

I close my eyes.

Rafa presses a sweet, lingering kiss onto my lips. He's on top of me, crushing me in the best possible way. My heart is racing.

"Vivian," he whispers. He touches his forehead to mine.

"Is it always this good?" I breathe.

"No," he says. "No, Vivian, it's never this good. Especially not the first time."

He pulls out of me, gently, but I still wince. I'm already

sore. He reaches down for the condom.

"Shit," he says, feathering his fingers over my raw flesh. "You're bleeding. Do you hurt?"

I look down. "I mean, it hurts a little—"

"I don't want it to hurt at all," he says, meeting my eyes.

Something about the softness in his eyes—how easily, how lovingly he is touching me—I don't know what it is, exactly, that makes me burst into tears, but I do.

Damn it.

"Vivian—"

"Don't worry," I say. "They are happy tears. I think."

Through a film of tears, I see Rafa smiling, the handsome lines around his mouth deepening as he shifts his weight to the other elbow and wipes away my tears with his thumb.

"Sorry. I'm sorry—I didn't want to be the girl who cried, you know?"

"It's okay," he says. "It's all right. I love the girl you are. Whether she cries or not. I love everything about you."

The tears come in earnest then. *I love the girl you are. I love everything about you.*

"I"—he kisses my cheek—"love"—he kisses the other cheek, my nose—"you"—and finally my mouth. "Te amo, Vivian. I know it has not been a very long time between us, but it happened for me so fast. I knew. Right away, I knew. I waited so long to find someone as brilliant and passionate as you are. D'you really think I'd let an ocean keep us apart?"

Tears roll down my temples, soaking my hair as I smile up at Rafa and he smiles down at me and the intensity of our connection, of the overwhelming sweetness of this moment, hits me full force.

"I love you too, Rafa," I whisper.

"So is that a yes? Will you finally be my girlfriend?"

"Yes," I laugh. "Por supuesto." *Of course.*

And just like that, I am no longer a virgin, and Rafa and I

are novios.

There is no going back now.

I am in bloom.

Later that night

I wake up slowly, my eyes heavy with sleep. It's dark outside; the windows are still open, the curtains still dancing in the breeze. I listen to the clack of high heels against the pavement beneath our window and smell the slightest trace of cigarette smoke. Someone laughs. People are heading out for a night in Seville.

I glance at the clock beside the bed. Nine twenty-nine. We fell asleep sometime around seven, exhausted from a day spent on our feet and an afternoon spent . . . well, you know.

That was one hell of a nap.

The room is warm. Or maybe it's the body wrapped around mine, the burn of his skin on my skin, that is to blame for the fine sheen of sweat that covers me from head to toe.

I'm the naked little spoon to Rafa's naked big spoon. I can feel the beating of his heart through my back. His legs, long, powerful legs, are tangled in mine, his penis nestled just above my butt.

A penis that moves, suddenly, tickling my skin.

"Buenas noches," Rafa murmurs sleepily in my ear, trailing a long, lazy kiss down the slope of my throat. His breath is warm on my skin. "How are you feeling?"

"Good. Wonderful," I say. A shiver darts down my spine and lands in a pool of slick, sticky warmth between my legs. "Turned on."

My pussy pulses and stings a little, but I don't care. In the space of a single heartbeat I'm soft and wet and ready.

We're supposed to meet our friends for dinner.

I don't think that's going to happen.

"A condom," I say, reaching back to dig my hand into the hair at the nape of Rafa's neck. It's wet with sweat. "Put on a condom. Now."

"Vivian." He slides a hand up my belly and cups my breast, softly working the nipple between his thumb and forefinger. Ah, *God,* that feels delicious. "You bled before. Aren't you sore?"

"I don't care," I pant. "It's not that bad. I want to. Please."

Rafa reaches between my legs and slides his middle finger between my folds. He lets out a guttural sound. "Always so wet. This doesn't hurt?"

"No," I lie, rolling my hips against his hand. "Please, Rafa."

"You sure?"

"How many times"—I gasp when his finger finds my clit —"do I have to tell you? Yes. A million times yes."

He pulls his finger gently from my pussy. A minute later I hear a familiar tear as his knuckles brush the small of my back and he rolls the condom onto his dick.

I press my ass against him. "Can we try it this way? On our side?"

Rafa is already there, lifting my leg, using his other hand to find my pussy and hold it open so he can guide himself inside me from behind. I bite my lip at the pinch of pain when he first enters me. I'm going to be sore tomorrow. *Really* sore. But as he slides into me the pain is subsumed, bit by bit, by desire. This feels so good. *Rafa* feels so good.

Sex, my friends, feels so fucking good.

It's a little different, doing it from behind. I feel fuller. The angle is more direct. Rafa guides my top leg over his, opening me to him. He reaches around again and his fingers are on the tip of my pussy and I feel like I'm going to come— again and again and again.

He moans as he pumps into me for the first time. He goes so deep—I feel so safe in the warm cradle of his body—I whimper. He kisses my neck. I pull his hair.

Te amo, he breathes. *Dios mío, Vivian, te amo.*

He's holding me against him, our bodies working in time to each other, my legs starting to shake from the force of my impending orgasm. He thrusts deeper, harder, slow, thorough strokes, biting my shoulder, and I'm muffling my cries in the mussed sheets. It hurts.

It feels so, so good. Sweet.

Early the next morning

My eyes flutter open, flutter shut.

The blackness behind my closed lids is complete. It must be early, very early, in the morning.

Something warm is moving over my breast, warm and familiar. The woodsy scent of aftershave tickles my nostrils. A weight, a delicious, shapely weight, settles itself over me, parting my thighs.

I moan, a small, quiet sound, at the sudden pressure between my legs as he enters me.

"Rafa," I whisper, my hips rising to meet his thrust.

I'm still half asleep, aware only of the tightening low in my belly, the rasping sounds of our labored breathing between us.

He tangles his fingers in mine above my head. There's that warmth again on my breast, a stab of pleasurable pain as he takes my nipple in his teeth.

I come and he comes and when we are done he pulls the covers up over our heads and curls me into the shapely nook of his torso.

CHAPTER TWENTY-TWO

Later that Morning

Rafa holds a Styrofoam cup in one hand and two ibuprofen pills in the other. I perk up instantly at the smell of strong, fragrant coffee.

"Buenos días, Vivian," he says. His voice is still rough with sleep.

"Buenos días, Rafa," I say, shyly.

I sit up in bed, remembering I'm naked only when the sheet falls from my shoulders and reveals my bare breasts.

"Oh—" I say, pulling the sheet back up.

Rafa grins, the lines around his mouth carved handsomely into day-old stubble. He sits on the edge of the bed and with his first finger tugs the sheet down.

"I have to say good morning to them too," he murmurs, pressing a kiss onto my mouth. Before I know what he's doing he ducks his head and kisses one breast, then the other.

I'm beginning to think being in love with Rafa means living in a constant state of arousal.

"Not fair," I breathe, running a hand through his hair.

This motion—me running my fingers through his bed-head waves— it's playful and possessive and I love that I get to do it. To my *boyfriend*, no less. My super guapo, totally amazing-in-bed boyfriend.

"How are you feeling?" he says softly, raising his face to me.

"Really great," I say. "Tired. But great. And you?"

He thinks a moment before he responds. "Happy. I'm happy, Vivian, to be with you. I hope I make you happy too."

"You do." I grin. "Doesn't hurt that you're a solid lay."

He laughs. "Here," he says, passing me the coffee and the ibuprofen. "There is a little café downstairs I found. We have a long day ahead—thought you could use some help."

"Thanks," I say, curling my hands around the coffee. "What's the ibuprofen for?"

His cheeks turn pink as he offers me a shy smile. "It will help you with the soreness, yes? Last night, I get carried away. We should have done one time only, but I could not keep my hands from you." His gaze falls to my chest, and his blue eyes darken. "You're beautiful, Vivian."

I bite my lip. "You're face-meltingly hot. Like, it's ridiculous how hot you are."

"I am actually very hot in this moment," he says, cupping my breast. He thumbs the nipple to a hard point. "I need a shower. I think you should come with me."

"We're actually pretty awesome at coming together," I say, breathless.

Rafa tears me from the bed. He backs me, laughing, into the bathroom, his hands on my face as he kisses me.

While Rafa finishes up in the bathroom, I check my phone. I have a text from Maddie. She's feeling better, she says, and can finally breathe through one of her nostrils. Chiquitin is staying at the vet for a couple days to get his balls removed, so that's nice. *I miss you woman*, she says.

Truth be told, I miss her too. So much has happened in the past twenty-four hours, and if this were any other guy, in any other city, I'd be sneaking a phone call to Maddie, telling her everything, listening intently to her thoughts, her always on-point analysis. I miss being able to talk to her like the vagina soul sisters we used to be.

The soul sisters I hope we still are after I explain everything to her.

I miss you, I type back. *Glad ur feeling better. Cant wait 2 snuggle in bed with u when I get home.*

Later that morning
  Real Alcázar, Seville

Our tour group shuffles dutifully through the Moorish royal palace. It's hot as hell, and we're all hungover. Rafa and I are hungover from a night spent smushing instead of sleeping. Everyone else is hungover from drinking and dancing until the wee hours (Katie drunk texted me this morning at six thirty).

Which is a shame, because the Alcázar is a really spectacular place. Once upon a time it was home to the Moorish princes of Al Andalus, or Muslim Spain, and the Arabic influence shows. Pointed arches, delicately carved into a series of rainbow-like indentations, are covered in colorful mosaic; endless geometric designs are chiseled into every wall, every panel, every gilded ceiling. The gentle gurgle of the fountains in the courtyard echoes throughout the empty, cavernous rooms.

As I stroll along the open-air loggia bordering the court-yard, resisting the urge to jump the rope and dive headfirst into those inviting fountains that glitter and wink under a fiery sun, I imagine what life was like in the palace. Who lived here, what they ate, who they loved.

Who they boned in the airy royal chambers.

I glance up and catch Rafa looking at me. He's at the head of our group, "aiding" one of our professors with her rambling discourse about Moorish architecture and the medieval period. Instead he's looking at me, really *looking*, the kind of look that even after all this time, all we've been through and done to each other, still makes my stomach flip. As always he is rakishly handsome in his button-down—I helped him pick out a light blue one this morning, a perfect foil to his eyes—and slightly messy hair. When I meet his gaze, he offers me a gorgeous, lopsided grin that fills me with tingly, squidgy delight. I don't know if I'll ever get over how handsome he is.

If I'll ever get past the fact that he belongs to me. That we belong to each other.

Laura, wavering on her feet beside me, elbows me in the ribs. "Where did you two lovebirds disappear to last night?" she murmurs.

My face flushes with heat. I fight back a smile.

"Oh," she says. "*Oh*. You *did* it, didn't you?"

I'm really starting to love this girl.

"Yes," I say proudly. "We did indeed."

She cuffs me on the shoulder, a look of happy disbelief on her face. "Fucking *finally*. The angst was killing me. Like, I was literally going to strangle you if you didn't let Rafa swipe that V-card. How was it? Sometimes it's a little awkward at first."

I meet Rafa's eyes across the loggia. He puts his hands in his pockets.

"It was awesome," I say. "I don't want to sound like I'm bragging—"

"Great sex is definitely something to brag about."

"Are *you* having great sex?" I ask. "What's up with the man-bunned footballer?"

Laura sighs, runs a hand through her long, lustrous curls—unperturbed, of course, by the hundred-degree heat. "The sex is freaking unbelievable, Viv. It has been since the beginning. And that was great, because it was all about sex—he was just supposed to be a one-night stand, you know? I'm not a cleat-chaser or anything . . ."

"What," I grin. "Did he fall in love with you?"

She sighs again. "No. I don't think so."

"*Chicas, chicas!*" Elena snaps her fingers at us, her way of telling us to shut the hell up. Which sucks, because I'm dying to find out what this delicious little tidbit of Laura's means. She's always so confident, so funny, so assured in everything she does. Even a super famous footballer couldn't catch her off guard.

Could he?

My ears perk up when our professor mentions the Alcázar gardens are temporarily closed because *Tournament of Kings*, a popular—and awesomely boobalicious—fantasy series is filming there for its upcoming third season. I'm not a rabid *TOK* fan, but I did watch a few seasons with the stoner guys down the hall my sophomore year. It's got a medieval bodice ripper-meets-*Lord of the Rings* kind of vibe.

The professor conveniently points down the hall, now roped off, that leads to the gardens.

Laura and I look at each other.

And then, loitering toward the back of our group, we duck underneath the rope and scurry down the hall. We cruise past a guard typing furiously on his cell phone and dart past a knot of people arguing over their clipboards.

We spill out onto a covered porch several floors up that looks out over the huge green expanse of the gardens. It is a beehive of activity with people dotting the landscape like so many ants. A camera guy navigates his way around a boxwood maze as an actress, an intricate wig of black hair sitting on her head like an oversized bird of prey, practices her lines beneath a palm tree while a makeup artist pokes at her face with a brush.

But what really catches my attention are the racks and racks of costumes, swarming with people, directly below us. My heart begins to pound as I watch a woman adjust the sleeve of a guy in a dirty peasant costume, pulling a needle from between her teeth to sew it into place. Another woman is poring over the detail on an ornate velvet tunic on a rack, the thread of its golden embroidery glinting in the sun. It reminds me of the embroidery on the sleeves of Goya's Maja Vestida. Still another is fitting a *very* handsome actor in tight leather pants with a worn, waxy finish that does wonders for said actor's ass. In a far corner, a wiry woman digs through a chest of costume jewelry, looping bejeweled necklaces around her neck as she finds them, jewels that are as ridiculously large as those sewn into the clergy's vestments in El Greco's *The Burial of Count Orgaz*. It's obvious the costumes are historically inspired—a mix of medieval, Tudor, and even Japanese court dress.

Laura is saying we should go, they're going to notice we're gone, but I stand rooted to the spot, transfixed by the costumers (Is that what they're called? Costume designers, maybe?) as they work their magic below. One of them laughs at something the dirty peasant says, another apologizes for lacing a corset so tight, a guy with a clipboard sits cross-legged on the ground and sketches an Elizabethan-style dress complete with a wasp-waisted bodice and voluminous sleeves. Someone is shouting for an iron.

Goose bumps break out on my arms and legs. The air is thick with a buzzy, rushed sort of excitement, everyone is working furiously, their faces narrowed in concentration. Like they know their work is important, and interesting, and they are proud of it. Proud to be a part of such a gorgeous, massive hit of a show. The action and the art and the artists—it's such a thrill to watch it; I can't imagine the joy of being an actual part of it. The joy of designing and making and fitting costumes, of being outside on a sunny day in the freaking Alcázar in the middle of Spain, the joy of *that being your job*. Sure as hell looks a lot more fun than being chained to a desk at an investment bank for eighty hours a week. What do you even *do* at an investment bank?

You don't sew super tight leather pants onto super-hot actors, that's for sure. And you don't get to create achingly beautiful costumes from another era, inspired by Goya and El Greco.

It hits me then, a realization so sudden, so frightening in its clarity, it makes my heart clench. *I want to do that. I want to make costumes for a living. I want to work on set.*

I. Want. That. Job.

I have no idea what that job is even called, or how you get it, or what it pays. I bet it pays very little, at least at first, no signing bonus or sexy salary to be had here. No bragging rights or six-figure bank accounts.

I would have to change my major to art history and take some theater classes. I'm a junior, so I'd have to throw myself headlong into studying the history of design, techniques, the industry.

I'd have to start over. There is no set path for becoming a costume designer, the way there's a path with definite steps for doctors, lawyers, and investment bankers. A *costume designer*. I can already see my friends' expressions of "What the hell is that?" and "Is that even a real career?"

It's terrifying.

It's liberating too. The thought of spending my days with art and theater and history professors—forget econ, hallelujah—of someday doing something so cool and inspiring for a living, makes my entire being thrum with excitement.

I don't know how to sew, and I don't know anything about fabric or fashion.

I only know it's what I want to do, and that it will lead me down a long road that could potentially lead nowhere—or lead to a fabulous job on a set like *Tournament of Kings*.

I realize now that I was looking at my major—and my future—all wrong. Seeing the costume designers and the beautiful costumes they create has made my plans come into focus. Suddenly, the blurred lines and ambiguity of my passions and my interests are coaxed into sharp, certain shape.

Now I just need the courage to follow those passions and not get mired in what I *should* study, what my future *should* look like. To not think of art history as a "guilty pleasure" but as a meaningful and pretty sweet way of tapping into my creative side.

I'm in a daze as Laura leads me back to the group. Luckily no one realized we were gone. No one except Rafa, whose eyes gleam knowingly as he takes my hand in his, discreetly, when the tour is over.

"Very sneaky," he says. "Did you see the set?"

"I did," I say. "It was amazing."

He squeezes my hand. I squeeze back.

CHAPTER TWENTY-THREE

A few days later
Return to Madrid

The taxi zooms from the train station through Madrid, the breeze blaring through the open windows. For the hundredth time I swipe my hair out of my eyes; it refuses to stay tucked behind my ears. It's much cooler here than it was in Seville. The first hint of fall—otoño in Spanish—hangs crisply in the air.

"I think you should do it," Rafa says. "It is who you are, Vivian."

I look down. His hand, ridges of vein and sinew standing in relief against his smooth, tanned skin, is on my thigh. Even his fingers are handsome: blunt edged, masculine, the nails clean half-moons. There's an ease to the way he touches me, like he knows my body, wants my body, and isn't afraid to show it.

"I don't know," I reply. "I mean. Am I signing up to be poor and underemployed for the rest of my life? It's gotta be a hard way to make a living, being a costume designer."

Rafa brushes his thumb along the inside of my thigh. "Not if you're very good at it. And you would be very good, Vivian."

"You're just saying that because I'm sleeping with you," I say, glancing at him with a grin.

Rafa wags his brows. "I am no expert in the arts, but perhaps I might inspire you in other ways, yes?"

"Yes," I say. "Definitely, definitely yes."

"Just think about it," Rafa says. "I know it is maybe too early to talk of a thing like this, but if you change your major to the art history, the department at San Pedro is one of the best in all of Spain. You could stay in Madrid for another semester, take more classes . . ."

My heart hiccups. "And be with you?"

"*Sí.*" He smiles. "And be with me. One semester is not nearly enough for us, I don't think."

Two months ago, I wouldn't have considered spending a whole year in Spain for one hundred million dollars. I wasn't sure if I would make it one semester, much less two.

But now? Now I can't imagine going back to Meryton come January. The thought of going back to my old life—a life without Rafa, without the sultry Spanish sun—is kinda depressing.

Rafa feels more like home now than Meryton ever did.

And while I'm sure the art history and theater departments at Meryton are top notch, nothing beats being able to actually *see* the art you're studying—whether it's a painting by Goya or a play by Lorca. If I want to pursue this crazy dream of becoming a costume designer—if I change my major, my career path, everything—it really does make sense to study another semester in Spain.

Maybe I won't have to give Rafa up at the end of this semester after all.

"Think about it," Rafa says. "There is still very much time."

"I will." I look out the window. It's so intense, all happening at once. The dramatic shift in my plans for a major, for my career, my future.

And, lest we forget, the dramatic and sexually stimulating shift in my love life. The irony isn't lost on me; I went from being homesick to deliciously, hopelessly lovesick in the space of several weeks.

And I wouldn't have it any other way.

The taxi pulls up to the blue door on Calle de Villanueva. My stomach hurts. I'm excited to see Maddie, but I'm also terrified. I have to tell her everything I haven't already told her—how I had every intention of cutting things off with Rafa, of staying away from him, but I'm in love with him and couldn't. I tried to think of ways to begin the conversation on the train ride from Seville to Madrid, but nothing stuck.

I have no idea what I'm going to say. Here I am, stranded, strangled by the knowledge of what I have to do and my complete lack of courage to do it.

Rafa climbs out of the taxi and helps me get my bags out of the trunk.

"You sure you don't want me to stay for moral support?" he asks, looking up at my building. "We can talk to Maddie together."

"No." I hoist one strap of my backpack onto my shoulder. "Thank you, Rafa, I really do appreciate it, but I need to have this conversation with Mads one on one. I need to explain myself."

Rafa pecks my cheek. "You were just trying to do the right thing, Vivian. Don't forget that. You did not hurt her on the purpose."

"On purpose," I say, grinning up at him. "So now that

you're my boyfriend, does that mean I get to see you tomorrow?"

"Tomorrow? I thought I see you tonight. My parents want to meet you—my mom is making her albóndigas."

I pull back, surprised. "Your parents know about me?"

"They are sick of hearing me talk about you. All the time, they say, you talk of this chica Vivian. When are we meeting her?"

I never thought I'd be so lucky to be asked to meet the parents. My heart flutters inside my chest, making me forget, for a moment, the bomb I'm about to drop on my best friend.

I look at Rafa from the corner of my eye. He's a little sunburned, and there are small thumbprints of shadow beneath his blue eyes. We haven't exactly slept the past few nights. Even after we were both too sore to do the penis-into-vagina thing, we couldn't keep our hands off each other. So we resorted to endless hours of endlessly enjoyable oral.

"You're killing me, Vivian," he says, a grin playing at the edges of his mouth.

I throw my arms around his neck and pull him down for a long, lingering tongue kiss that has the taxi driver groaning behind us.

"I will come get you," he says, helping me shrug into my backpack. "My parents have a car I borrow. Around seven, okay?"

"Okay."

Rafa bends his neck and covers my mouth with his. His tongue opens me, coaxes me to fall into him, into his kiss. Already my body is coming alive, my pulse deepening with every stroke, every nibble and caress.

I'm starting to kiss him back in earnest when I hear the door to my building open. My heart constricts, stops working altogether.

Oh.

Shit.

I turn my head and see Maddie standing in the doorway. She's looking down at her phone, but when she looks up she stops short, her eyes widening as the realization hits her. Her gaze flits over our bodies, my arms around Rafa's neck, his hips digging into my hips, the casual way he holds my waist. This is exactly how I *didn't* want Maddie to find out about Rafa and me.

In the space of two seconds she's seen all she needs to. Her face tenses the way it does when she's about to cry. Her eyes are hooded with hurt, hurt that slices through my chest and leaves me breathless.

"Maddie—" I say.

"Hey guys." Her voice is thin, dull from being congested. "I gotta—I was going to—medicine, I need more medicine— I'll, um, see you later."

She turns abruptly and takes off at a clip, her sandals clacking against the sidewalk as she struggles to keep her bag on her shoulder.

"Maddie!" I say. "Wait! Please!"

But she ignores me and keeps walking.

I turn back to Rafa. "I'll see you tonight."

And then I take off after Maddie, my backpack bobbing in time to my frantic steps. "Wait, Maddie, Jesus!"

It takes me a minute to catch up to her. My backpack dings someone as I pass. "Lo siento!" I call out. *I'm sorry.* I don't slow down. Despite the flu, Maddie is walking fast, darting in and out of the foot traffic that fills the sidewalk.

I'm out of breath by the time I fall into step beside her.

"Can we talk?" I pant.

"I don't know," she says. "Are you going to tell me the truth this time? Or are you going to keep feeding me that bullshit about you and Rafa being 'just friends'? Again, Vivian —you lied to me *again*."

"I'm sorry, Maddie, really. This is all my fault—I fucked up, I take full responsibility—Jesus, Mads, can you stop for a minute?"

"We're here," she says, looking up at the illuminated neon green cross that designates a farmacia. "I have to get more medicine."

I follow her inside. I can smell her coconut shampoo. It makes my heart dip. Oh, Maddie, I want to say. I am so, so sorry.

"Please," I pant as we make our way down the tampon aisle. "Please, Maddie, at least let me explain myself."

"I think what I just saw sums it up pretty nicely, Viv. You and Rafa are together. I get it. Congratulations."

We turn the corner and head down another aisle. "I don't think you get it," I say. "I haven't told you—"

"Haven't told me what?" she spits, scanning boxes of medicine. "That you're a pathological liar? You remember, don't you, the fight we had after you hooked up with Rafa at Ático? You told me you lied about your feelings for him, but you said you were going to break it off. I told you, point blank, you didn't have to do that, but you said it wouldn't happen again. You said it was best for everyone if you and Rafa were just friends."

I swallow.

"I'm guessing it happened again in Seville," she says. "You lied to me this whole fucking time, Viv. That's not what friends do. They don't lie and sneak around behind each other's backs, especially when it comes to guys."

Maddie's voice is loud and shrill. People look at us as they pass by. I hate to argue here, in a small but public space, and I hate that Maddie won't even look at me, but I'll take what I can get. She's the offended party; she gets to decide the terms.

"I never meant to hurt anyone," I say, ducking around her to try and get her attention. "You're right, Maddie, I lied, and that was wrong. I knew you were going through a lot of shit, you know, with your family and your dad and everything, and I wanted you to have the best semester possible despite all that. I wanted you to have Rafa, I did, if he was going to be the distraction you needed. I swear to you, I would've never —I didn't mean—I would've never done what I did if I knew how it was going to play out."

Maddie grabs an orange box off the shelf.

"Here," I say, grabbing another. "This is the kind I got before, if that's what you're looking for."

"Oh," she says. She swaps her box for mine. "Thanks."

"You're welcome," I say. "How are you feeling, by the way?"

"Better. Pretty tired. But better."

Maddie turns and heads for the register. I follow a few steps behind.

"Do you understand where I'm coming from?" I ask.

"No, Vivian, I don't understand why someone would tell her best friend she didn't like a guy, only to hook up with that guy knowing her friend liked him too. And then you swore it was over—you said that you were breaking it off with Rafa after what happened at the club—but *clearly* you were lying about that too. And then you had to kiss him, right in front of my face?" Her hand shakes as she digs her debit card out of her wallet and hands it to the cashier. "That's a real dick move."

My throat constricts. She's right, but it's more compli-cated than that, and I'm getting frustrated that I can't explain myself any better. My neck tightens beneath the weight of my backpack.

"That first night, when I met Rafa," I say, looking away as she keys her pin number into the pad, "I only flirted with him because I thought I'd never see him again. I didn't want to start another thing—another relationship—that would end after the semester was over—"

"But you did anyway, even though you lied to me and everyone else about it."

"Maddie, I lied to *myself* about it," I reply. My voice shakes. Saying the truth out loud—recognizing it in front of Maddie—is like getting the wind knocked out of me. It makes everything hurt.

She finally looks at me. "And now, all of the sudden, you're gonna stop lying? You think poof, just like that I can be honest and everything will be perfect?"

"I don't think everything will be perfect," I say. "I know it won't be. I fucked up, Mads. But that doesn't mean I can't try. I have to start somewhere. And because you're my best friend, I want to start with you."

I trail Maddie out of the farmacia, my pulse thumping in my ears. Maddie's slowed her pace, which I take as a good sign. I fall into stride beside her, the plastic bag rustling between us.

"I'm sorry, Maddie," I say, softly. "I guess not telling you about how I felt about Rafa was my way of denying I had any feelings at all. I didn't want to feel them, not after everything that happened with Keith. I didn't think a guy like Rafa would even like me back. I didn't want to get hurt again. I didn't want to hurt you, especially with all the shit going down with your family. So I denied everything, thinking it would go away."

"No offense, Viv, but for such a smart girl, that was really a dumbass thing to do."

"I know," I say, scoffing. "If there's one thing I've learned this semester, it's that I'm really, really good at denial.

Denying who I am and what I want. It's so fucked up, I know, and I feel awful all this shit had to go down for me to recognize it. I denied the fact that I am definitely not made out to be an econ major, despite the fact that I hate studying it and I'm *so* not good at it. And then I denied that I had feelings for Rafa. I really did think it would go away—what I felt. I wanted it to go away so you could have him. But my idiot plan *really* backfired. Like, really. I tried to keep things platonic between Rafa and me, I did break it off. But then I realized in Seville that my feelings for him weren't going anywhere. I couldn't fight them anymore, Maddie. I didn't want to fight them."

I adjust my backpack; my shoulders are screaming. "I understand this whole mess could've been avoided if I had just been honest from the beginning. I hope—I hope—you will forgive me. I'm learning from my mistakes, Maddie. I'm trying to be honest with you."

Maddie stops in front of our door. She turns to look at me, her eyes brimming with tears.

"What about you?" she asks.

"What about me?"

"Are you going to be honest with yourself for once about what you want?"

I roll my lips between my teeth. "I am. I want to be with Rafa. And I want to be best friends with you. You're the two loves of my life, and I can't live without either of you."

Maddie looks at me for a long moment. She wipes her nose on her sleeve. A car zooms up the street beside us, trailing the scent of diesel in its wake. I squint against the afternoon sun. It is paler now, more warm than hot.

Abruptly she turns and pushes through the door. It gapes open, and Maddie's footsteps echo across the empty foyer. I duck inside, closing the door behind me. I'm starting to panic. I knew Maddie would be pissed. I was prepared for her anger, her biting rebuttal.

But I was not prepared for the possibility that she would not forgive me. That our years-long friendship would not withstand the blow I dealt it.

I climb the stairs slowly, tears spilling down my face.

CHAPTER TWENTY-FOUR

Maddie must be in the bathroom, because when I shuffle into our bedroom it is empty. Used tissues litter the desk beside the bed. The sheets curl invitingly around Maddie's side of the bed, pillows propped against the wall. The window is open, a small breeze moving through the room.

With a moan of relief, I set my backpack on the floor. For a minute I stand there, tears blurring my vision, not quite sure what to do next, where to go. Does this mean Maddie and I are over? What do I say to her now? My pulse beats a hollow rhythm inside my chest.

Who am I now that Rafa is my boyfriend and Maddie is not my BFF anymore?

I look up at a familiar tinkling noise. Chiquitin is chasing Maddie down the hall, her flip-flop dangling from his jaws.

"Quick!" I say, darting for the door.

She makes a run for it. I close the door as soon as she hurtles into our room, slamming it shut in Chiquitin's face. He barks once, twice, scratching at the door, and that's when we hear Stella hissing at him, calling out her usual apologies as she drags him back to the kitchen.

Maddie is breathing hard. "Thanks," she says, leaning against the desk for support.

"No problem," I say.

"That dog," she wheezes, "is such a dick."

"Yeah," I say. "Almost as big a dick as I am."

Maddie smiles at that. "We're talking some pretty big dicks."

"Porn-sized dicks."

"Schlongs."

"Meat swords."

"Salamis."

"Saber-sized cum slingers," I say with a smile. "Too far?"

Maddie laughs. "Never too far with me, Viv."

And then, covering her face in her hands, she bursts into tears. Her shoulders rise and fall in time to her sobs.

"Fuck," she says, looking up. "I didn't want to cry."

I grab a tissue and wipe my eyes. "Neither did I. But I guess we don't have much choice."

"Viv." She sits on the edge of the bed, hands clasped in her lap. "I miss you. I feel like we haven't been us in forever. You know, Vivian and Maddie. Wife and wife."

I sit beside her, our legs touching. "I miss us, Maddie. I miss the way it used to be between us. I miss telling you everything. And I miss you telling me everything."

"I miss that too," Maddie says, sniffling. I pass her a tissue. "You know what's really fucked up, Viv? I knew you liked Rafa. From the beginning, I knew you had a crush on him. Despite your denial superpowers, you really can't hide what you're feeling."

"I know," I say, thinking of all the times Rafa told me I wear my heart on my sleeve, how he can always read what I'm thinking or feeling.

"I wanted to believe what you were telling me—you know, that you didn't like him, that you wanted something more than what he could give you, something that would last. But deep down, I knew it was all bullshit. I knew you were scared. And like a saber-sized cum slinger, I went after him anyway." She looks down at her hands. "What you did really hurt, Viv. The things you told me—the lies—those hurt. But what hurt the most were the things you *didn't* tell me. Like, you couldn't trust me. I thought we were good friends."

"We are," I say, looping an arm around her waist. "And like a good friend is supposed to, you called me out on my bullshit. You did the hard thing, and I appreciate that."

Maddie tucks her head into the crook between my neck and shoulder. "It's okay to want something and say so, Viv. It's okay to be upset. It's okay to be mad, as long as you tell me what's going on. Yeah, it sucks that we liked the same guy, but if you had told me you liked him in the first place, I wouldn't have touched him with a ten-foot pole."

"I know," I say, toeing off my shoes. They hit the floor with two *plunks*. "I should have told you, and I'm sorry. I promise I'll work on it. I'm working on it now. I was just so worried about you—I *am* worried about you—"

"I appreciate your concern. Really, I do. But that concern shouldn't get in the way of what you feel for a really hot, really awesome guy who's really into you. Look," she says with a sigh. "I know you just want me to be happy, Viv. And I want you to be happy too. When you're happy, I'm happy. If Rafa makes you happy, I want you to be with Rafa. Seriously. That's what I was trying to tell you when you were leaving for Seville. I was just too chicken shit to come out with it then. I was also bummed that you've found a guy who is *home* to you, and I haven't. I'm so homesick, but the home I know doesn't really exist anymore . . . ugh. I just feel so lost right now, and you—you found Rafa. Rafa found you."

"Dude, if I can find a hot Madrileño, you can too."

"I doubt it," Maddie scoffs. "But like I was saying. I want

242

you to be happy, Viv, and Rafa makes you happy. So be with him. He's all yours, amiga."

A new wave of tears hits me. Tears of relief, of exhaustion, of love for this wonderful, fucked-up, gorgeous, selfless girl I call my best friend.

"Thank you," I croak. "Thank you, Maddie, for understanding. And for being my friend."

"We've both been shitty friends this semester," she replies. "Sorry about all my passive-aggressive bullshit. You know, the little comments and stuff. That was pretty gross of me. Nothing excuses that, not even my idiot parents' divorce, or the fact that I'll probably die without ever touching hot Madrileño penis. Let's start over, okay?"

"Okay." I sigh, exhaling the weight of months' worth of worry. Inside my chest a lightness is taking shape. Maybe things actually are going to work out.

Maybe this semester abroad thing really is of the best experiences of my life. Not to say it hasn't been hard. These lessons I'm learning are painful and more than a little embarrassing. But if I hadn't learned to let go of the girl I *should* be, I would've never had the courage to be the girl I *am*. And that chick's got a pretty sweet semester ahead, filled with hot foreign dudes, art history classes, and amazing friends.

Maddie lifts her head and pecks me on the cheek. "You said the L word, Vivian."

"Lesbian?"

"No, idiot. Love! 'You and Rafa are the two *loves* of my life'— remember that?"

My cheeks burn.

"Tell me everything," Maddie says. "And I mean *everything*. When you knew, when he said it back—because I know he said it back—how big his penis is. Tell me, tell me, tell me!"

I tell her everything. Well, except the size of Rafa's penis. That's our delicious secret, one I think best kept between us.

She listens intently, nodding here, providing the perfect expletive there, laughing giddily when I tell her about our first bone/our first *te amo*. It feels so good to talk to her like this again. To feel her happiness for my happiness swelling around me like a giant panda bear hug.

"I will love him," she says, "if—and only if—he loves you well. And from what you're telling me, I think he will, Viv. I really do."

Next Wednesday
  The Usual Madrileña Spot

"Sorry," Laura says breathlessly, sliding into the seat beside mine. "Went a little longer than expected."

Katie cocks a brow. "What did? The sex with the footballer?"

"Yes." Laura unwinds the scarf from around her neck. "What did I miss?"

"Hold up," Rachel says. The bar is loud, and she leans forward so we can all hear. "We need details. All the details. Are you guys, like, together now, or is it still just a hookup?"

Laura bites back a smile; the apples of her cheeks are bright pink, from the cold or from the sex, it's hard to say. I know that sparkle in her eyes, though, that windswept look of bewildered satiation. She's just been boned, and boned well.

"We're not together, per se," Laura says. "But it's more than a hookup."

"So what is it?" I ask.

She shrugs. "I don't know, honestly. He says I'm his 'good luck charm'— when I go to his games, he plays really well, I guess—and I say he's fucking great in bed. So," she shrugs again. "Who knows?"

"Well," Maddie says, looking at me with a smile. "*I* know a certain lady who knows a thing or two about hot Spaniards who are great in bed."

All eyes turn to me.

"Ohmigod," Rachel says.

"You did it," Katie breathes.

"Welcome to womanhood!" Laura exclaims.

"We're so proud of you." Maddie holds up her glass. "A toast to Vivian and Rafa. Lovers, let them love! Arriba . . ."

"Abajo," we reply.

"Al centro . . ."

"Al dentro!"

The wine is almost as delicious as the company. The Madrileñas and I drink, we laugh about awkward sex noises, we discuss why we think everyone in Spain is so skinny (the walking, the smoking, and the big lunches but small dinners). Glancing at Maddie, she's as happy as I've seen her yet since we arrived in Madrid. Laura is filling us in on the Madrid footballers' super-hot WAGs (wives and girlfriends) and Rachel is laughing so hard she is silently sobbing as she mops up a glass of spilled wine with her shirt and I am drunk and happy and filled with a gratitude so huge I think I'm going to burst—and on a Wednesday night, no less.

It took a couple months for us to find our bearings. But I think all of us would agree that studying abroad really is the best thing ever.

CHAPTER TWENTY-FIVE

Saturday

My hand fits easily into the calloused warmth of Rafa's. He's smiling, a smile I know lights up his eyes even though he's wearing his Wayfarer sunglasses. I know because that's always how he smiles at me, the shapely lines around his mouth etched in genuine pleasure. Whether he's having a shit day or the best day ever, he is always, always happy to see me.

Almost as happy as I am to see him.

He kisses my mouth, a quick peck, then turns to Maddie for the Madrileño kiss-kiss on both cheeks. She grins.

"If you break her heart, I will fucking kill you," she says.

He nods. "Understood."

"Good," she says. "Thanks for inviting me along to be your third wheel today."

"Please," he replies. "A friend of Vivian's is a friend of mine. I hope to get together more often, yes?"

"Yes," she says. "Preferably with balls of meat involved. Hunting down Madrid's best albóndigas might be a fun group activity for the three of us."

"I'm game," Rafa says.

"Me too," I say. I smile. Seeing the two of them talk balls makes my heart contract with joy. I have a *boyfriend*. He is *foreign* and he is *hot* and he loves me *well*.

And now he is laughing with my best friend. I don't know what I did to deserve all these really good things. I don't know how I got so lucky that it all worked out in my favor. But it's nice, for once, to not have to fight. Fight my feelings, my desire, the things I want that make me who I am. It could be the nice weather, but I'm at home in my skin for the first time in what feels like forever.

It's actually chilly today. Fall has finally arrived in Madrid halfway through October. The light is golden and clean, the air refreshing, just on the edge of cold. After months of sweltering, sticky heat, this feels nothing short of glorious. Maddie and I were almost giddy digging our coats out of our long-neglected suitcases.

A breeze whips our hair in our faces as we walk through our neighborhood. The trees, rustling above our heads, have started to thin and change color; orange and red and spotted yellow leaves crunch beneath our feet. The smell of roasting chestnuts wafts from a nearby cart.

All of Madrid is out enjoying the weather. We weave in and out of the crowd, Maddie making fun of Rafa and me for taking out fellow pedestrians, as we refuse to unclasp hands.

Rafa leads us through an unassuming gate into a garden, behind which sits a yellow mansion with arched windows. My stomach does a backflip. Halfway through the semester, and we've finally made it to the one place Rafa said I absolutely had to go.

The Sorolla Museum.

I squeeze Rafa's hand. He turns his head, folding his sunglasses into his pocket, and grins. "I told you I take you here," he says. "It is my favorite museum and my favorite artist. I am excited to know what you think."

It's a much different experience than visiting the major museums in Madrid. The Prado, the Thyssen, the Reina Sofía are all fabulous in their own ways, huge institutions that are among the best in the world.

But the Sorolla Museum is much smaller. Much more intimate. Which makes sense, because the Impressionist artist —Joaquín Sorolla—actually lived here while he painted the masterpieces that now hang on the walls of his salon, his living room, the place where he slept.

I can feel Rafa's eyes on me as I move through the rooms, craning my neck to peer at each painting. I understand why Sorolla is Rafa's favorite painter; he's got pretty amazing taste. There is something so quintessentially Spanish about Sorolla's work. Yes, he depicts scenes from around Spain— Moorish courtyards, famous landmarks—but what really catches my eye is his use of light and movement. He captures the light in Madrid so beautifully, that sense of anticipation, of promise.

Most of all, I'm captivated by his beach scenes. There's a massive canvas that depicts two Gilded-era women, dressed in white, strolling along the surf. Looking at the painting, I imagine the way the sheer gossamer veil attached to one woman's straw hat would slip through my fingers, sticky with salt from the sea air. I imagine tucking my fingers beneath the other woman's sleeve. Perhaps it's satin; I can almost feel the sensuous glide of it against my fingertips.

I look at Rafa. Rafa looks at me.

There's a rush at my temples that stirs the sinews in my torso. I know, now I *know*, that I am an art major. That I want to delve deep into the world of clothes, of costume design, of material history.

What I thought I wanted wasn't at all suited to who I am. Looking at Rafa looking at me, I know that *this*—this, the art, and him—is what I want. *This* is what makes me happy.

"I love it," I breathe.

"I love you," he says.

I cross my arms over my chest to keep my heart from bursting. "Did you ever think, that first night, we would actually end up here at the museum together? I mean, I know we talked about coming here, but we also talked about yacking and Justin Timberlake, so . . ."

His blue eyes soften. "I did think. I thought about it very much. I would have taken you here the next day if you wanted. In fact—" He digs into his coat pocket, pulling out his cell phone. "That's what I texted you about, the day after we met. You know, the text you never got? Here, let me find it."

He scrolls through his phone before handing it to me. My heart pops around in my chest as I read the text.

Hola white girl. This is JT. How r u feeling? I hope u do not think I am the stalker 4 calling & texting u but I had the most fun in a very long time with u. Hope u did 2. I would love 2 c you again very soon. The Sorolla Museo I told you of is open today until 3. Maybe we go together if u would like?

I reread it once, twice, the smile on my face growing bigger each time until it hurts. It's the best day-after-introductory-text in the history of the digital age.

"My English was a little rusty then," Rafa says, rubbing a palm across the nape of his neck. He is blushing, and it is adorable. "But you understand the thing I was trying to say, yes?"

I hook my finger into the *V* of his shirt that peeks through his coat and pull him toward me. "I do," I say, inhaling the woodsy smell of his skin. "And I'm sorry I didn't say yes to your invitation the first time. Thanks for giving me a second chance."

"Nada," he says, a shortened version of *you're welcome*. "It took me only two hours to write that text. Al had to help me.

I was very nervous." He looks around the room. "So what do you think? Have I convinced you that art is your passion and you should change your major?"

"Yes," I say, blinking. "I think so."

He cracks a smile that could blind all humanity with its beauty. "Does that mean you'll be staying with me another semester?"

I kiss him, a soft, lingering press of lips. "Por supuesto."

"Excelente," he murmurs. "That gives you more time to learn the language. And other things. You know, your news is so exciting you're kind of giving me a hard-on."

I brush my hand against his crotch. "Am I?"

He pulls me against him, palming my butt. "Yes—"

"You two," Maddie says, strolling up behind us. "Stop humping each other in public. It's five o'clock, which means it's time for a drink. And maybe the start of our albóndigas adventure?"

Rafa smiles down at me. "Sure," he says.

"Sure," I say, smiling back.

"Later," Rafa whispers in my ear as we head for the exit. "I have the apartment to myself this weekend—my parents are in Barcelona, and Al went with some of his fraternity brothers to Amsterdam. Want to come over?"

Vino tinto de la casa and albóndigas with my bestie, followed by a sleepless night of unbelievable sex with my novio?

"Hell. *Yes*," I reply.

The three of us head back out into the afternoon in search of our balls of meat.

EPILOGUE

November

It's so nice out today, I say.

Rafa traces his fingertips in a whirling pattern across my back. Even through the nubby wool of my sweater, I feel his touch as if he were working his magic on my bare skin. A delicious little shiver moves up my spine.

Fall in Madrid is my favorite season, he replies. *But Christmas is pretty great, too. I can't wait for you to see all the lights and decorations they put up across the city. It's beautiful.*

I'm lying on my stomach on Rafa's picnic blanket, the sounds of Retiro filling the quiet space between us. The trees rustle above our heads, a crisp counterpoint to the heat beginning to spread through my body.

I turn my head on the pretzel of my arms. Squinting against the bright autumn sun, I meet Rafa's eyes.

I'm so happy I could go fuck a fish, I say.

Rafa grins, the lines around his mouth deepening with pleasure. *That makes absolutely no sense.*

I know, I say, grinning back. *But it's true. I didn't think I could ever be this happy.*

I'm glad you gave me a chance, Vivian, he says. *I'm so glad you see that it was worth it.*

His fingers move to my neck, working small, poignant circles on my skin. A familiar desire spikes through me.

It was totally *worth it*, I gasp. *God, Rafa, that feels good—*

"Buenos días, Vivian."

I start at the sound of his voice, my body jolting awake. I open my eyes, the edges of my vision still blurry from sleep. I'm on my belly, arms tucked beneath the pillow; his fingers still work those circles on the nape of my neck.

The room takes shape around me. Tall ceilings, pale walls, the fluffy expanse of a bed. Last night comes back in a rush: our dinner date at that cute little *tapas* place in Salamanca; the bottle of wine we split, Rafa's wandering hands on the cab ride home; the quick and dirty sex we had in the foyer of his parents' apartment (don't worry, they're gone for another weekend) because we were too horny to wait one.-more.second.

"Buenos días," I say, grinning up at him. He's mine.

And he's naked.

"Did you have good dreams?" he asks, smoothing back the hair from my face.

I blink. I *was* having good dreams—*in Spanish*.

"Holy shit," I say, turning over. I sit up, the sheet sliding down my naked body. This time I don't try to cover up; instead I giggle as Rafa dips his head and says good morning to my left breast.

"What?" he murmurs, moving to the right.

My giggles turn breathless. "I think," I say, "I dreamed in Spanish. Like, the whole dream, everything. Not a word of English."

Rafa grins from his perch between my boobs. "See? I told you it would happen! Congrats, Vivian. Less than three months in Spain and already you're fluent."

I dig my hand into his bed-mussed curls. "I had a really great tutor."

I begin to pull him up for a kiss when he stops me. "Wait. I have some news."

Rafa waves an envelope between us, the frayed flap hanging open. Even in the dim morning light, I can make out the red and gold Meryton University letterhead.

My stomach clenches. "You heard back already?"

"Just this morning," he says. He meets my eyes. "Vivian, I got the job."

It takes me a minute to process what those four words mean. *Rafa got the job.* He's going to teach undergrad classes at Meryton's school of journalism in the fall.

Which means he'll be coming back to the States with me this summer, when my year-long study abroad adventure comes to an end.

We're going to be together for another year.

I throw my arms around him in the tightest bear hug I can muster, whispering my congratulations in his ear as I tug him down on top of me. I nip his earlobe. He kisses my neck. In the space of half a heartbeat I'm ready again, I am ready for him, as if having sex all night wasn't enough. I want more.

And Rafa can give me more. In fact, he's going to give me a *year*. With any luck it will be more than that; after I graduate, I'll be free to move wherever I want, to *do* whatever—and whomever—I want.

This forever thing that I've dreamed about for so long— the romance I wanted but thought I couldn't get—maybe it can actually happen with Rafa. It *is* happening, right here, right now, my heart so full inside my chest I can hardly breathe around it.

I'm so happy I could go fuck a fish, I say, breathlessly, in Spanish.

Rafa grins against my mouth as he settles on top of me,

circling his hips to nudge my legs apart. *How about you fuck me instead?*

Real Rafa is far wittier than dream Rafa. Who knew?

Vale, I say, and surrender.

We don't have to worry about condoms anymore; we were both screened at Rafa's doctor not long after our Seville trip, and I got on the pill ASAP.

He slips inside me with a small moan, tugging the sheets over our heads.

They're blue, his sheets, just like I imagined they would be.

Later that night

"I hope you don't mind," Rafa says, sipping at his Cuba libre. "But I invited my uncle, Javier, to join us. For one drink only, he says the weather is very good tomorrow so he wants to fly."

"Fly?" Maddie says. "Is he, like, a pilot or something?"

Rafa nods. "He has his own plane, too. Little plane, but it is still very fun. He is just back from a long trip for business, and he hasn't been able to fly for many months. I am excited for you chicas to meet him. He asked me and Vivian to fly with him, but we've got tickets to the fútbol match tomorrow. Maybe Maddie can go with Javier?"

"That wouldn't be awkward at all," she replies, "being on a tiny little plane with your uncle who I've never met."

"You're going to like Javier. He is not like other uncles."

Maddie shrugs.

It's midnight—pretty early by Madrid standards—and Ático, our favorite discoteca, is just beginning to get crowded.

Maddie meets my eyes over her gintonic and grins.

"I like this little Saturday night tradition," she says. "You guys take care of your third wheel, and I appreciate that."

I reach across the table and swipe away a bit of lime from her lip. "Wouldn't be Saturday night without you," I say. "We started that tradition freshman year, remember? Just because we're in Spain—"

"And just because you sleep over at your super hot Spanish boyfriend's apartment," Maddie adds.

"Right. Just because things are a little different doesn't mean the tradition has to change."

"So wait," Rafa says. "I guess I'm the third wheel, then, aren't I? I should be thanking *you*"—here he looks at Maddie—"for letting me crash *your* Saturday night with Vivian."

Drink at her lips, Maddie is no doubt about to make a witty yet profanity-laden reply when her gaze catches on something over my head. She goes still, eyes wide.

"Are you okay?" I ask, glancing over my shoulder.

And then it's my turn to go still.

There is a *very* handsome—and very scruffy—Madrileño standing behind me, his light brown eyes almost amber in the bar's sultry red lights. He's built, broad about the shoulders and chest, like a football player; his beard looks just careless enough to be supremely, intimidatingly sexy.

"Tío!" Rafa launches out of his seat and pulls the man into a bro hug, the two of them trading barbs in Spanish as they embrace. I see the resemblance right away; the handsome slopes of their faces, the muscular roll of their shoulders and arms; even their voices, the way they speak, sounds similar.

Javier can't be more than twenty-five. If that.

I meet Maddie's eyes. She's thinking it, too: *holy shit,* this *dude is Rafa's uncle?*

Rafa turns to me. "Vivian, I'd like you to meet Javier."

"Ah! So this is the Vivian I have been hearing so much

about. It is wonderful to finally meet you." He presses kisses into my cheeks while I stare, and stare, and keep staring.

"Wow," I say. "Just. Um, wow. I gotta be honest, Javier, you are not at all what I was expecting."

"Javier is more like a cousin to me," Rafa explains. "It is a joke, yes?, that I call him uncle, really, because we are almost the same age. My grandfather, he married again when he was very old to a younger woman. They had a small family. Javier is part of that family."

I furrow my brow. "How much younger are you than Rafa's—"

"Father?" Javier says. "I am twenty-four now, so that is, what, Rafael, twenty-two years between me and my brother?"

"Wow," I say.

"*Wow*," Maddie says behind me, standing.

Javier's molten eyes move from me to Maddie. I could be imagining it—I probably am imagining it, because Javier has singed my brain with his hotness—but I think I see a spark of interest in his gaze as he looks at her, and she looks back.

"Javier, this is Maddie Lucas, my best friend," I say.

"Maddie." Javier leans across the table and, bringing a hand to her arm, kisses her cheeks. "Encantado."

Maddie offers him a flirty grin. "*Very* nice meet you, Javier."

He nods at her empty glass. "Might I get you another drink, Maddie? What is that, a G and T?"

"Yes," she says. "It's a gin and tonic. Another would be great—thank you very much."

"Vale,*"* Uncle Javier says with a smile.

I lock eyes with Rafa. He's fighting a grin.

This could be interesting...

Thank you so much for reading LESSONS IN LOVE! Check out the next book in the Study Abroad series, LESSONS IN GRAVITY. This is Maddie and Javier's sexy rockstar romance. Flip the page for a juicy excerpt!

LESSONS IN GRAVITY EXCERPT

Javier

One side of Maddie's mouth kicks up as I take her hand and pull her to her feet. A saucy, knowing smirk, confident and full of promise. I want to kiss that smirk off her face, ravage her mouth with mine.

I want her. *Now*.

I hold her close behind me as I stalk toward Ático's back entrance. I know a few of the bouncers here, and they let me in on this well-kept secret; on nights like this, when a swift exit is necessary, the back door is a godsend.

Just outside the bar, we pass the table where Maddie and I met. I narrow my eyes at a rumpled leather jacket that's shoved onto a nearby ledge. I never forget my bomber—I've had that thing since I was eighteen, for God's sake, a graduation present from my parents—but I guess I was distracted by Maddie's eyes, or maybe it was her legs, or her ass, or her fearless interest in *my* ass.

This girl is fearless. And I fucking love her for it.

I grab the jacket, but I don't put it on.

I tug Maddie closer to me, the front of her body plastered against the back of mine. I feel the rounded softness of her breasts pressing into my shoulder blades, her long, lean thighs plastered against my backside.

Desire, dark and impatient, coils at the base of my skull, between my legs. I walk faster, holding Maddie's hand firmly in my own. She doesn't ask me to slow down; she doesn't stumble; she keeps pace with me, her breaths coming fast and hot against the nape of my neck.

I grit my teeth, praying there's no traffic on the way to my flat. I'm going to explode if I don't get Maddie in my bed, naked, in the next five minutes.

I can't wait to see her—all of her—naked. I imagine the way her tan legs would slope into hips and soft belly. The fullness of her breasts, the hardened points of her nipples.

And that pussy. I can't wait to see it, feel it, taste it.

You'd think I hadn't been laid in a decade for how badly I want it.

I burst through the door. I feel like I'm about to burst out of my jeans, too.

It's freezing outside, but I hardly notice. The alley is dark and quiet; my ears still ring from hours spent dancing too close to the DJ booth. In the sliver of sky visible between two buildings, stars pulse silver against a black velvet sky. I inhale the faint smell of churros, fresh from the fryer. A nearby streetlamp provides the only light—dim, soft.

Madrid after midnight. I've really missed this place.

I'm about to make for the street—*please, please let there be a taxi*—when Maddie gives my hand a solid tug, pulling me around to face her.

Her eyes gleam in the darkness, a dirty little smile playing at the corners of her mouth. She takes a step back, pulling me after her; she takes another, and another, slowly, her hips swaying, heels sounding a decisive beat against the pavement.

We're three steps from a brick wall when it dawns on me.

She wants to fuck here. Now.

She wants to fuck against this wall.

My pulse leaps.

"Maddie," I say, squeezing her hand. "I have a bed. A really nice bed. A *warm* bed."

She takes another step back, our hands still intertwined between us.

"What if I'm bored with bed?" she says. "I've been in lots of beds."

I pull her to me, curling my body around hers as I attempt to move her away from the wall. My mouth hovers over her mouth. As I talk my lips brush against hers.

"But you haven't been in my bed." I glide my tongue along her bottom lip. She tastes like lime, lime and sugar and heat. "I'll do things to you those others guys haven't done, I promise you."

"You know what those guys haven't done?" She stands on her tip toes, pressing her lips to my ear. She curls a hand around my neck and glides her fingers through my hair. "Me, against this wall."

I don't need to ask her if she's sure, if this is what she really wants. She knows what she wants and isn't afraid to go after it. And now it's what I want, too, more than I've wanted anything in a long time.

Using the bulk of my body, I turn her so that her back is once again to the wall. She lets out a small hum of approval as her mouth moves from my ear to my jaw, nicking the stubble there with her teeth. We begin to move backward, small, slow steps.

I clutch my jacket in both hands and pull it over her shoulders, tugging the leather into place. She's a tall girl— definitely not petite—but still my jacket swallows her from her shoulders to the tops of her legs.

Good.

"Wait," she says. "Wait. Why are you putting clothes on me? Aren't you supposed to be taking them off?"

"Because." I take her chin in my hand and thumb her lip. "I don't want you to get hurt. The bricks will tear the skin off your back if...if it gets a little rough."

Maddie bites down on the pad of my thumb. "Is it going to get rough?"

I grin. "Only if you want it to."

"Show me what you got, hombre."

I don't hesitate.

I lean forward, pressing my hips to hers, pushing her backward with one large, forceful step. She draws a sharp breath when her back meets with the wall, eyes flashing with wicked, searing heat. She rolls her hips against mine, her hands trailing ribbons of tingly heat as they move up my torso.

"Show me," she breathes. "Show me everything."

I pull my thumb across her lips, a possessive, almost lewd caress, erasing the last traces of her lip gloss. The soft slickness of her mouth against the calloused pad of my thumb is incredibly, frustratingly erotic. She's so hot, so soft. So feminine.

I slide my hand onto her face, burying the tips of my fingers in her hair, and pull her to me. Her skin is silken, and so are her lips.

There is no preamble, no tentative exploration. I duck my head and kiss her hard. I kiss her hungrily. I kiss her deeply, and she kisses me back like she means it. Like she wants more, more, always more. Our bodies move against one another, into one another. She is so goddamn sexy.

I glide my other hand up the length of her leg. Goosebumps break out on her skin, and I curse—it comes out in Spanish—against the insistent press of Maddie's lips, her tongue.

"What?" she pants.

"You're cold."

She curls her fingers into the front waistband of my jeans, her first finger toying with the button.

"Then warm me up."

"I'm trying. You sure you don't want to go back to my place? It'd be a hell of a lot more comfortable." I curse again when, through the thick denim, her curious finger finds the hypersensitive tip of my dick. "Maddie. Maddie, I also don't have a condom with me."

She reaches down into her bag—it's a tiny thing, the strap slung across her chest—and holds up a foil packet between her first two fingers.

Carefully, her eyes never leaving mine, she tears open the condom with her teeth.

Like what you read? Get **LESSONS IN GRAVITY** today wherever books are sold!

Thank you for reading LESSONS IN LOVE—I hope you laughed, you cried, you got turned on by the sassy bits.

Book #2 in the Study Abroad series—LESSONS IN GRAVITY, Maddie's story—is also now available wherever books are sold!

I'd love to stay in touch—here are a few ways to reach me:

- **Check out Jessica Peterson's City Girls, my reader group on Facebook**
- Follow my not-so-glamorous life as a romance author on Instagram @JessicaPAuthor
- Follow me on Goodreads
- Follow me on Bookbub
- Like my Facebook Author Page
- Drop me a line at jessicapauthor@jessicapeterson.com

DEAR READER

Thank you very much for taking a chance on a new author. There is so much really, really great stuff out there in Romancelandia, and it's no small thing that out of the thousands of books you could've bought, you bought mine. I hope you enjoyed it. Thank you.

I wrote LESSONS IN LOVE on a steady diet of Justin Bieber (sorry not sorry, but *Purpose* is probably my fave album of 2015) and memories from my own study abroad adventures.

I graduated college almost ten years ago, but Vivian's struggle to follow her heart and her interests at twenty years old still resonates with me. In some ways, Viv is the most autobiographical character I've ever written. I, too, was acutely aware of my competitive classmates' accomplishments and ambitions. I, too, succumbed to the pressure of keeping up with them.

Unlike Vivian, I didn't pursue my passion—writing—until I was twenty-five or so (and only very recently did I pursue it fearlessly). But there *was* a time in college when I felt most connected to my romantic, writerly self—and that was when I studied abroad in Spain. It was one of the most magical moments of my life, which is part of the reason why I wrote a "Study Abroad" New Adult series. (The other part is that I love to read New Adult!)

If you have the chance to study or travel abroad, don't hesitate. Do it. Do it for a summer, a semester, a long week-end. As Vivian Bingley found out, it will change your life in ways you can't imagine.

Sorry for the rambling note—I'll stop now. But thank you, thank you, thank you again for picking up LESSONS IN LOVE. And if you have three minutes to spare, listen to the Bieb's "Where Are Ü Now" while rereading the club bath-room/vagina fallout scene (I listened to it on repeat while writing that sassy bit). You're welcome.

Besitos,
Jessica

ALSO BY JESSICA PETERSON

ABOUT THE AUTHOR

Jessica Peterson writes romance with heat, humor, and heart. Heroes with hot accents are her specialty. When she's not writing, she can be found bellying up to a bar in the south's best restaurants with her husband Ben, reading books with her adorable daughter Gracie, or snuggling up with her 70-pound lap dog, Martha.

A Carolina girl at heart, she fantasizes about splitting her time between Charleston and Asheville, but currently lives in Charlotte, NC. You can check out her books at www.jessicapeterson.com.